indecent
acts

indecent acts

by
Nick Brooks

**FREIGHT
BOOKS**

First published April 2014

Freight Books
49-53 Virginia Street
Glasgow, G1 1TS
www.freightbooks.co.uk

A CIP catalogue reference for this book is available from the British Library

ISBN 978-1-908754-45-5
eISBN 978-1-908754-46-2

Typeset by Freight in Garamond
Printed and bound by Bell and Bain, Glasgow

the publisher acknowledges investment from
Creative Scotland toward the publication of this book

Nick Brooks was born and still lives in Glasgow. He achieved an Honours Degree in English from Glasgow University, where he also graduated from the MLitt in Creative Writing. He has had a number of occupations, including musician, cartoonist and stained glass window maker. Nick's first novel was *My Name is Denise Forrester,* published in 2005 and his second, *The Good Death,* was published in 2006, both by Weidenfeld and Nicolson. He has been studying for a PhD at the University of the West of Scotland. *Indecent Acts* is his third novel.

Bud says who is that over the road who is waven. I cant make them out. Wear i say. There bud tells me. By the bus stop by the health centre. Comen over the road. I can not even make out who he is talken about theres to many people over there. Oh bud says she is comen over here do you know her. I cant see i tell him is it a woman i reconise a womans voice. Grace she calls grace what are you doen here. Do you know her bud says and i say yes lets wait up. Bud pulls me along by the hand and i slip on my holiday shoe my espadrill and we have to stop. I have to find my espadrill it is lyen some wear on the ground. I can not even make it out though. I can not even see it anywear. Bud i say can you see my holiday shoe my espadrill i say but now he has let go my hand and i can see him goen away leaven me. Well that is okay. I am okay here out side of the shoppen centre. My shoe will be about near by some wear.

Grace is that you the womans voice says and i look about for her.

Grace it is you i thought so. What are you doen here.

Hello annette i say. I am sorry i should of come to the group.

No no annette says. Your meant to be sunnen yourselve on the beach. Your meant to be in the canary isles.

I look at annette and i just say is bud there. Can you see him annette.

Who is bud annette says.

His nibs i say he has got red hair and a walken stick. He was with me. He looks like he has caught the sunburn but he just sits to close to the fire. Annette is not even sayen any thing so she must be just staren at me. She is out of breath and panten. She gets out her inhaler and pants on it to. She puts a hand on my shoulder to steady her selve.

That is your man is it grace. This bud caracter.

Yes its true i say. Can you see him about for me.

Annette says there he is over by the shops he looks a bit older than you grace.

He is two year younger than my selve i tell her. What can i say annette. He has had a hard life.

Is that right annette says and shrugs he dosent look to happy.

No he isent i tell annette. He isent very happy hes in a rotten mood so he is. I begin to tell annette about the trip to the air port and all that and she just shakes her head and says o thats teribel grace. Thats just a shame. What a teribel thing to happen.

I shrug. Some would think it was funny i say.

No grace. It isent funny its teribel. Can you not get any of your money back.

Maybe i could of got some but they were already thinken i was stupid. They would of laughed at me.

No they would not grace dont say that. They would of helped. Thats what they are payed for.

Maybe. They were already goen to charge extra for senden the bags back from the canary isles. When i showed them my ticket i said my eyes are not so good i can not read the ticket so well. They said did i not hear the flight called. I said not un less it was to canary isles and i dident hear that called yet. Then they told me the plane for port adventurer the canary isles had left 40 minutes ago. I thought the ticket sayed canary isles but it dident it said port adventurer. Port adventurer was called not canary isles. They put my lugidge on board but not me.

O grace annette says. Poor you. Could this bud caracter not of helped.

Annette wants to laugh to but she wont. Annette isent like some people. Even if she wants to she wont.

Did this bud not know to speak to some one annette says.

No i tell her. Bud left me at the door to the departure lounge. He was already headen back home. It was just me goen.

Oh grace you should of asked some one to help you silly. You should of got someone you know to go with you.

I am still feelen about on the ground with my foot for my shoe. That foot of mine is already soaked. I have just come back from the air port and have got only espadrills on. It is a thursday afternoon in drumchapel in febuary the meanest month. Or that could be january. Or maybe an other month it dosent matter. I am meant to be in the canary isles with my sister but instead i am here at hecla square in the rain and with the wrong shoes to boot.

Can you see my shoe annette i say. It slipped of my foot.

Here it is grace she says. She bends down and reaches for my ankle. She puts the shoe on it.

There you go sinder ella annette says. You shall go to the ball.

Then she says shes sorry she dident mean it she was just joken.

Thats all right i say. No harm done. I can go to the ball an other time.

Me and annette just stand there for a while talken about what will happen to the lugidge. Wear will it go. We talk about will marie be able to pick up the lugidge or will it come straight back it selve.

To tell the truth im not in the mood to think about it annette i tell her. I have to phone marie and tell her im not comen and i dont know how she will take that.

She is goen to be upset not to see you annette says. You havent seen her in how long has it been.

Years i say. To tell the truth i dont know how long. Not since the years after our father died any way.

Does that mean you will come to the group this afternoon or to nights one instead grace. Seen as you wont be away on holiday. We missed you the other week.

I will have to think about that one annette. Is it all right maybe next week if you dont mind. Annette nods okay. Next week maybe.

Take your time grace she says. Theres no rush. I just want you to think about it she says. Theres the group as usual this after noon if you change your mind. Up at saint benedicts.

I nod. I will think about it annette.

It will cheer you up to be with every one in the same boat as your selve grace.

Annette is close and i can smell the perfume shes got on but i dont know the name of it. It will be a dear one if its annette. She has expen sive tastes she told me. I dont ask annette what kind it is though. It would only put me in a bad mood knowen.

Okay annette says. Maybe see you this after noon or next week. Do you need a hand just now.

No i tell her. Bud is about he will be in the bookies. I will be fine to get there. Okay grace just say the word. So sorry again about the trip.

Thats okay annette.

Okay see you then.

See you annette.

Then she is away and i can breath easy again. Just you take

it easy gracie i say to my selve. Just have a think about all these shenanigans. You are okay here at the centre for now. Just take your time and consentrate on what is in front of you.

So i am tryen to con sentrate on what is in front of me but it is so grey out that there is only more grey in front of me. Every thing is so dull and dingy and the sky is huggen so close to the ground that it is hard to make much out. I would like to just shout bud come and get me but i know that is not any solushion. I have to get about my selve.

I stand there and wait for bud for a minute but there are too many folk wanten by and i am in the way as usual so i squeeze my way into the bookies. Really i am hopen to find him but maybe his pal will be there bobby if bud isent. In side the screens are all lit up even though i cant make out whats on to well i will know what race hes bet on be cause of the swearen. If bud has put a bet on i will know straight away be cause he will start to swear like a trooper. Oh for effs sake he will say effen jesus christ in heaven you are one nag thats about ready for the glue factory. He always says that about the glue factory then laughs like hes goen to burst. He never does though he always stops when no body else laughs and then gets angry.

I know its him be cause he will be moanen away as usual and the other punters will have moved away a bit. Bud bothers people its his way. Even though he bothers people you can not get him to keep his voice down it is just embarasen some times. Folk have to move away and you start to feel like you are taken up room that belongs to them. That is garun teed to make bud even worse be cause he is in no way stupit he is actually quite smart if folk would give him a chance. But it will set him of no doubt about it. Is that right bud will say think its funny do you. Think this is all a big effen joke do you. Well. Its not. It is no joke you effen so and sos. No way. You shower of effen sees what are you all staren at. Im no dafty. Bud spence is no dafty. Come on over here he will say Come on over here and ill pull that effen beard of your face. You thats right you. Im talken to you i will burst your face you effen see.

I swear to god he has sayed that. He told a man he would pull the beard of his face. That poor man was only standen. Bud is non violent in prinsipal though he has still got a temper on him. He says he would never join the army just be cause hes not worken. I think just as well what army would have him hes way to old he would be on a penshin now. Bud says the young crew are mad to join up dont they know theres a war on. I know he means vincent my son he is tryen to get a rise out of me to make me angry. O please to god dont let my son vincent join up.

Please.

Im only kidden doll he will say.

Buds moods are too much even for me some times. Bud says its his jinjir hair. When ever he loses it he will say after that he cant help it its jenetic so it is. He is red headed and thats why he some times loses it big time.

It isent true though. I am tellen you. I have seen some impashient elder lay people up at costigan house and he would in no way be out of place in there. I person ally think he is a skitzoid. If he drinks it will inter fear with his medicine and his medicine interferes with every thing. That is why he selve medicates bud says. He selve medicatid in the past any way. Not now.

It worries me for sean if that is the case. He is comen up for an impersonable age and he should have an older person who he can look up to. My son his uncle vincent is getten to be a young man now and to tell you the truth i can not tell the difirins between that and a disturbed person.

Just then some one puts a hand on my shoulder not his pal bobby thank god. Bud. He says that you there doll you okay are you.

It was only annette you dident have to run of i tell him. I make it sound like a row but im glad hes here. I always know he isent far but it is dis consterten to have him run of. He gives my hand a squeeze and i ask him if hes betten.

He makes a noise a snorten. Not today he tells me. I just came in to wait for you. Skint. What did that woman want.

Just to say hello.

She was the one who came to the door before wasent she.

Yes but it wasent like you think.

What was it then.

Not like you think. Shes my friend.

Bud makes that snorten again and i ask what is he thinken.

No thing he says and we leave it at that.

Still there is some thing nice about the bookies. It is quite for one thing. Only the noise of the horses and the comintiry. Bud only bets small sums of what we can afford. 2 or 3 pound at a time. Some times he is just in here be cause he only has two days work a week just now. His bad leg makes it difficult. I am about the same with costigan house. I am tryen not to think about our situashion as usual. Instead i just end up thinken about the suit cases goen round and round the carousel with no body to pick them up and marie my sister standen waiten for me all on her own.

Bud i say why dont you tell me what horses are runnen. That would cheer us both up wouldent it.

Some times i like to hear the names of the geegees. Bud calls them that. The geegees.

If you say so bud says.

Go on.

Well bud says theres my sweet lament and iron heart comrade and the one i like in this race now is called daisybuggin.

I like that i tell him. Daisybuggin. Are there any more good ones i ask him. He is leanen on the counter with the light behind him and for a minute i can see what a lanky big so and so bud is. He must have two feet on me. When i have my glasses with me i dont worry so much about a persons size. I can see their face better. But then some times it hits you. They are huge. Even bud is huge in here today.

Plus he can tell you all about horses and odds and the form and chelten ham and that. Bud is big on all that stuff. He is a some body at the bookies. Even though he hardly ever wins much and never makes big bets. For a minute or two it makes me feel good to think about all the mad stuff he knows about horse racen. Not for too long though be cause we have to go to the call box and that will take some worken out callen marie in canary isles. That will be a total night mare even for bud. I am damned if i will ask vincent my son for help though. It is on my own head so be it. Bud sayed that to me when i got back to the house from the airport.

Grace you are just some girl is what he says to me. You did what.

I put my glasses in my suitcase and checked it on board of the plane.

I couldent help it i say to bud. I put my glasses in my suitcase and my case has gone to the canary isles.

Why had i taken them of he asked me. Why had i put them to gether in the same bag. If you will do daft things like that it is on your own head.

It was a nice big bright de parchir lownge in there i told him. I wanted to wear the sun glasses you got me for the trip in stead. I was goen to put them away in my case again before getten on board the plane then i had put the case through any way. I could see well enough in the de parchir lounge. I am so sorry bud ive ruined your week.

You are one hand full of a lassie bud says. I should never of left you on your own you are such an effen stupid so and so some times.

Tell me some thing i dont know.

I just did dident i. I already told you he says. I am so sick of it he tells me.

So am i. So that makes us even i say.

Bud keeps readen the names of the horses to me. It is cosy in the bookies it is still dreich as any thing out side. I feel like i could sit here all day but you cant smoke. Not that i want to do that i quit along time ago but bud is difirint. He will go through a pouch of cutters choice every other day easy. That brand has no great big lumps of timber in it he says. He says he is disdain full of other tobacos. That is an other thing that will set him of he can never get any cutters choice around here. It is always scarce.

Even stevens he says. That ones on good form of late. Also one called fridita and one called a la mode. Theres one youd like in the next race.

Whats it called then. If i like the name im going to place a bet on it.

Yeller kid.

Yellow kid i ask him and he says no yeller kid thats what it says here.

Yeller kid it is then. What do i do now i ask.

Ill show you bud says its easy peasy and i say easy peasy sounds luckier than this yeller kid.

Ha ha he says. Very good.

Ha ha i say back. I ament just a pretty face you know. Now show me how its done.

We spend a few pounds on small bets and win not a sosidge but it is okay. I am used to not winnen any way. Bud of course loses it when our favourite daisybuggin comes in no wear again. Effen heck bud says although he uses much worse words than that.

Effen sees and the like. He goes of on one again and i say come on bud lets get that call out of the way i can see he will be too angry to dial in a minute. Come on bud lets call my sister marie on canary isles then we can take it easy. We can go home and get the tea on. I am hopen menshoun of dinner will get him out of his mood it some times does. Now that he has swore of selve medicaten he has taken more of an interest in his belly. He has even put on a wee bit of wait and has began to worry about it. He has never been fat his whole life he will say. Never. He has always been skinny and lanky. He could eat what he liked and not put on any wait. When he was a boy he used to eat every thing he always says. Every effen thing that was put in front of him he ate it. It is an achiefe ment of sorts i supose.

Lets go and call marie bud i say. It will be getten dark out we should head home soon.

Might as well bud says. We are haven no luck with these nags. How much are we down grace.

It is all right bud i say. It dosent matter. We just wont do it every day that is all.

Okay doll. Lets go to the phone box.

I can hear bud clatter his walken stick down and i take his arm and we go out of the bookies. Well. It is just as dreich as it was when we came out today except now it is pitch black too. All that i can see now is big blotches of orange street lights and car head lights and then the white light up stairs and down stairs of a double decker bus stoppen at the bus stop. Some people get on and of and i can tell that there are still plenty of folk about this side of the road. It is that long since i have had to go about with out my glasses im not used to this.

Are you all right there doll bud says every thing okay.

I am okay bud. Just dont wander of with out me this time.

Aye well i just dont care for that woman he says.

Annette is fine i tell him. If it wasent for her i would not even be worken two days a week.

Bud says no thing be cause he knows i am tellen the truth. We have about four days work between us a week and it is always hard. It is never sertin. Bud is not even suposed to be doen any thing hes suposed to be on the sick.

Bud leads me towards the phone booth on hecla avenue and i take the call money out of my purse the spare one. My other one is on the canary isles plane to port adventurer.

Did you tell this annette bud asks me.

About what i say.

About the air port. About not knowen you were goen to port adventurer.

I shake my head.

Effs sake bud says.

Well. She isent daft you know bud. There is no point tryen to fool her.

Bud opens the door to the booth. There is some one in side already usen the phone and bud says can the man hurry up please the wife is needen to use it. I dont bother to say any thing. I ament his wife and he effen well knows it.

This happy clappy woman will be round at our door again grace you effen dumplen. What do you think will happen then.

Now it is my turn to get annoyed. Nobody will come to the door bud. Annette isent like that shes our friend. She helped me keep my job at costigan house she wants me to come to her thursday group as well. She would not of ofered other wise. Dont be so paranoid i tell him.

Bud says oh for effs sake he isent paranoid hes just looken at the effen facts in the case. How many times in the past have we had the soshal at our door be cause of this sort of a person he asks me. How many times.

It is a few i have to admit. I am about to answer him when the person gets out of the phone box. Bud squeezes me in and i stare at the dial. I can hardly even see it. You do it bud i say to him. Your better than me i say. I will only make a mistake. He is breathen pretty heavy like he does when he is worked up or selve medicaten. Go on bud i say. Pretty please. You know i will only make a hash of it like always. I hand the piece of paper vincent my son wrote the inter nashounal diallen code and maries number on to him. I can not really even make out what the numbers say so it would of been no use me even tryen. Bud is effen and blinden.

Except that then he begins to dial the code for the canary isles to port adventurer. He has to try a few times and each time he hangs up and he effs and bees and sees some more. He is like a walken swear dick shounary that man so he is.

Well theres a lassie talken spanish at me so i must be getten some wear he says.

Whats she sayen bud.

How the eff do i know its in effen spanish.

Are you sure its spanish. You could of dialled the wrong country. Effs sake can you shut up a minute of course its spanish.

I am getten a bit edgy now let me speak to her let me speak i tell him and i pull at his arm anxshous that the woman wont reconise his voice and hang up. I can not face maken this inter nashounal call to day and that is the truth of it.

Bud puts the recever in my hand and i say marie is that you its your sister grace but the voice just keeps talken in that langwidge. Hello i say. Hello marie.

Its an answeren machine bud says but by then i have realised.

I leave a mesidge after the tone because it will be the same as a scottish english tone. I can never think of what to say to those machines so i just tell her i will call back or she can call me on her nephew vincents mobile if he is about.

Well to tell the truth i am sort of glad marie is not in. I ament very good at excuses and she is bound to be annoyed about the wasted flight she loaned.

Bud leads me out of the call box and we walk back over to the orange and yellow light of the shoppen centre. For some reason i dont know why it is always less scary in the dark than in daytime. At least if i have bud with me. There is no way i would come down here on my own at night even with my glasses on though. I dont like the hangers about the drinkers.

Are we going straight up the house bud asks me. Or are we getten any shoppen done first.

Lets just go back to the house i say. Vincent will be getten fed up keepen an eye on sean plus my feet are freezen cold in these espadrills.

Bud just mutters effen some thing about effen chips and vin agar and we go to cross over the road again.

We get in through the door home again and straight away sean comes up wanten a cuddle. He is sounden as though he has been greeten. Then he is off again like a maddy. No thing bothers sean for too long it is all water of a ducks back to him. How was he i ask vincent and he says some thing effen nuisance he growls. Like always. I think that means his nephew was fine but i cant make out his expresshoun so im not sure. I am away out now he says and slings on his jacket. Him and bud give each other a wide berth. In fact they dont even speak any more at the moment. They just grunt. Wear are you away to vincent weve got chips i say. Do you not want any.

Bud is hoveren about in the kitchenette with sean. He is picken him up and slingen him backwards over his shoulder and is laughen. It gives me a mad feelen in my stomuck to see a blurry sean flyen up and down like that i worry bud will let him drop but he never does he is safe even if he dosent look it. The pokes of chips are all rapped up together on the work top and you can smell them from the hall. I know vincent he will definitely be smellen them too.

Vincent i say.

What he says.

Chips i say. From the shop.

Vincent dosent say any thing but he comes in to the kitchenette after me. I know him the smell of the chips and the vin agar have reeled him in. He is not a great talker these days mind you was he ever i have to ask my selve. No.

Bud and vincent say no thing to each other but its like you can feel them pacen. There is a big wall of space between them. Even sean can feel it. I can tell be cause he is suddenly all quite when before he was laughen his head of.

Did any one call for me i ask vincent.

Effs sake he says its my mobile. Get your own.

I knew he would be like this about it but he has got a point. It is his phone. Even though i got him it for his christmas it was still a present. He is right to be fed up with me usen it. I should get one for my selve. Bud even says he will show me how to use it.

Effs sake vincent huffs.

I have given up tellen him of for his langwidge be cause its just to ask for bother. I cant say if hes been picken it up from bud or if he gets it of his pals but they are all talken like that these days.

Vincent i say im waiten for marie to ring. Has she left any message.

He says no. He is acten like a fart would be too much trouble although i know for a fact that this is not the case. He can fart with the best of them. The best is bud of course. Well. At the very least they have got that in common.

Bud says hows the job hunten goen.

Vincent just grunts again.

Not found any thing yet bud says.

There is eff all round here unless your polish man vincent says.

Sean looks up at them both with big brown eyes and curly brown hair. I can see his face upturned in the kitchen light. He is eaten a chip that bud gave him as long as his head. I can make out him mashen it up his mouth openen and closen. It is so mad if you think about it.

Bud unwraps the chips and says weve got two special fish suppers and a special sosidge supper and a bag of special magic chips. Is that not right sean.

Sean laughs but it is a cagey one. He is obviously not sure about buds special magic.

What are you wanten vincent i say. We dident know if youd be wanten any thing so we got the sosidge just in case.

Aw bit of fish would be magic man vincent says. He has forgot to stay in a huff for now. Well that is okay there are two fillets in each bag so we have got plenty and plenty chips too.

Sosidge sean laughs.

Aw look bud says you have dropped your magic chip sean. There it is on the floor. No dont eat it. It is goen to be manky now. Here have a bit of sosidge wee man.

I say why dont we all sit at the table well the counter and eat. No body is much taken with this idea of mine although there isent any thing wrong with it that i can tell. Vincent says he will grab his and take of he has to see his pal so and so who ive never heard of before now. Bud says can we not have a seat in the liven room my leg is pure murder so it is. Only sean wants to sit here at the counter and that is mainly be cause he likes the high stool even though it isent safe for him hes inclined to fall of it frequently. He jigs about on it and then slides of back wards. Bud is always usually there to catch him though. The wee maddy does it deliberate. Of course my eyes bein what they are i ament any use to catch him. I am old for a grand mother round here it would seem. He would get kilt if he was left alone with you bud says. Of course its tiresome him and vincent thinken its a game. Even sean thinks its a game but it is no joke. They arent the one whos his grandmother. That is my job to worry about.

I hear vincent shout seeya then close the door behind him. He will be away half the night no doubt. I dont like to think what he might get up to but hes young theres no point in tryen to find out. They will never tell you the truth anyway why would they. I never did at their age.

When he was a boy well smaller than he is now vincent went of wanderen for a whole day until night and i can never get that day out of my head. He went up to the garscadden woods with his sister francis and they got lost. They were tryen to get lost deliberate and well they pretty much sucseeded. They dident come home for dinner like usual i had to go round all their pals houses and i got a lift of bobby in the street. It was a hot day june or july maybe. They were just playen they said when we caught up with them. They were comen down out of the woods with some older weans who run of. Bobby clouted the pair of them vincent and francis for worryen me and then i clouted them too. What were you up to i sayed but it was just to have some thing to get the fright of it out of me. What do you think you are playen at. Your tea is cold now there is no thing else.

I dident want to let bobby run us back. I dragged them up the road in front of me shouten. You should of let me know wear you were goen i told them. Your not to play in the woods francis you knew that. Vincent you knew that. He was greeten but francis kept still and quite as always. Maybe thats wear vincent gets it from.

We walked and walked and then i know i dont know wear we were even though it was right through the middel of drumchapel. Which way is it francis i asked which way is it vincent but they wouldent tell. They wouldent say any thing to me. They were leaden me round and round on a wild goose chase. I remember them gigglen. What are you gigglen for i sayed to them. It is not funny. I have been worried sick. Your mother has been worried sick.

Eventually bobby drives up in his car again. Eh you sure you dont want a lift gracie. Your away the wrong road. Have you not got your specs.

I wouldent get in though. I wanted them francis and vincent to take me back i wanted them to realise what they had done.

The kids are away on a head gracie. Get in. Come on get in the car. Come on gracie they will be all right now. You showed them.

So i did. I showed them.

I got in the car with bobby. Why havent you got your glasses on gracie bobby says. You need to start wearen them. This is not a good situashion getten lost in your own neighbour hood.

Bobby i sayed. Just take me home.

I want to lift sean up on the big stool but he might fall. Bud is away to put the telly on. He will play neil youngs powder finger on the guitar or ole dan tucker trad arr on the banjo and his food will get cold. He isent a great eater even though he thinks he is. He will only pick at his food and then forget about it. Probably he will roll up a joint for after when the kettle is on. Like i say he is of the heavy medicashion for now. But he has been of before and gone back on again. He does not even need any encouradgement from any one least of all yours truly.

Bud is good on the banjo but better on the guitar. I can hear him pick it up and play with it then put it down again.

Rememberen his dinner i would think.

I have a look in the fridge for some juice for sean and there are cans in it.

Whose are these cans i shout bud. Whose are they.

What bud shouts back. There not mine he says.

I take a can out and hold it up close to my eyes and try to see what it says but i dont reconise that word.

I show it to sean. What does this say sean. Whats this your grans got.

Moo juice he says laughen moo cow juice. But hes only copyen bud be cause he is at that stage.

So theres only one thing to do i open the can and take a sniff. It is definitely cider it is very appley smellen and i know bud will not drink that. It is vincents drink and i am mad hes put them in the fridge he knows better besides of him underage still. I pour the can down the sink but i leave the others. I want to keep on vincents good side. Plus now i will have to listen to buds i told you sos.

I take sean by the hand and lead him through to the telly room. I have got his poke of chips and sosidge but no fish be cause of the bones. Sure enough the telly is on just a big diferent coloured blur with a lot of shouten and yellen and cheeren. Some game show or other. Bud is sayen will you look at these effen eejits what are they up to.

Grace what are they up to.

I dont know i tell bud ive no idea at all what there up to. Youll have to tell me what there up to. Good i think. He has forgot about the cans debacle already. I sit sean down next to the coffee table and put his chips in front of him. Then i plump down in the arm chair too.

Your not eaten your chips grace bud says. They will get cold.

I can get some in a minute i say.

The gods honest truth is that i want my slippers.

Can you see them bud i ask.

He says hell look for them in a minute when he has finished rollen this wee number. He knows fine hes not to smoke it in here but sean is too wee to care just now. Mind you i said that about francis. Vincent as well.

Sean honey i say. Sean can you see grans slippers.

He turns round and says some thing.

Grans slippers can you see them. There in here some wear.

Sean giggles and burbles and eats chips or maybe sosidge how would i know.

I guess i will have to find my own slippers.

It is a mad thing about this house that when you put some thing down it just dis appears never to be seen again. I am always the one putten things down in places wear they go so that i will know thats wear they have been put. It is totally logical. So how come i am the only one that ever seems to lose any thing i ask you. Why is that. Well. You know the answer to that one gracie. It is be cause you are blind as a bat. You can put things wear they go as much as you like they will still not be wear you put them be cause you cant see them even when theyre right in front of you. So why dont you put your glasses on grace. Why dont you wear them silly. Well maybe be cause then i would be abel to see all this mess about me. It would be plane as the nose on my face.

Besides my glasses are in port adventurer goen round and round the carousel with the lugidge. Its best not to think about canary isles and marie. It will only put me in a mood be cause i have got to go and dig out an old pear the ones with the taped arm.

Lets put this telly rubbish of will we wee man bud says. He has the lights on dim but thats okay. I like it dim at home at night. I pick at my chips but have not got any appetite really. Sean is gigglen at buds antics. Silly wee man he calls him. Silly wee man and leans over to put the telly of. There is a big purpley blue ghost in my eyes from the light goen out.

Silly wee man sean says laughen.

Is the body away out bud says. That is his new name for vincent. Vincent has worked laboren now and again and is a big lad. He has mussels all over him. Some times his pals call him the body and bud laughs at that. He is jealous i think. His own body is in some state. He dosent have any mussels at all but just roles of podge on his belly.

He picks up the guitar and plays a few notes then starts tunen it. I hate tunen. Nobody who can play guitar is listenen to a word you say either when they play but even more when there tunen. The sound of the notes benden like that would drive you mad as well. It is never right for them bud especially. Flat he will say. Flat. Flat. Flat. Flat. Sharp now would you believe. Now flat again. Sharp. Effen sharp or flat on this effen lump of wood. If you have said any thing to him at all duren this time he wont take in any of it not one word. Did you hear what i just said you can ask him. What he will say.

Flat bud says. Flat. Flat. Flat. Sharp. Sharp. Flat. Jesus effen christ this thing is ready for the bucket. Or some new strings anyway. Life less so they are.

I think they sound okay i tell him. We could of got some if we dident bet today.

Bud is okay about it though. Its not your fault doll he says. There just old strings. I can boil them in the mean time.

Bud some times does this with old strings. They can last a bit longer that way for some reason.

Flat sean says. He is bangen his hand on the coffee table top. Flatflat he says all one word. Bud starts playen a tune neil youngs powder finger like i told you. Lookout momma theres a white sail comen up the river and after that i cant remember the words.

Our song he says isent that right wee man. Mummy and daddys special song. I ament so sure about that though. I like blondie sunday girl.

You shoudent say mummy and daddy around him it isent true i say.

I know i know bud says. Sorry. I dident mean it he says.

Its not fair to mix him up.

Aye well he is just a wee lad bud says. Hes not goen to remember it is he.

Its not worth argewn about i say. Play us a tune.

Okay. What do you want to here.

What will we get bud to play i say to sean. He laughs and burbles.

Two littel boys sean. Lets get bud to play two littel boys. I sing two littel boys had two littel toys each had a wooden horse i wave my hands from side to side. Bud joins in singen and picken on the guitar then sean too. Then we are all singen me and bud and sean.

~

Not now bud i say please dont. I ament feelen right. Its been a long day. Gracie doll he says and curls next to me. Whenever your ready he says. I pull the duvet up over my selve. Bud says he is too effen hot in here he will have to put a leg out side the covers or he will expire. It is nice in the dark. I cant see any thing at all except some sorts of colour. Blotches of orange and sparks of others too. It is never totally dark. Not really in my experience. Still this is my favourite kind of dark. Lyen in bed about to sleep dark. Bud next to me dark. It is nice how nice he can be here. I dont even mean just wanten some you know what. I cant say here. Not even that. It is like the real bud comes out in the dark alone like this to gether. He is gentle. Well. That is an exageration he isent gentle he is rougher than any thing but he is difirent anyway. Softer.

I keep thinken about marie waiten at port adventurer i say. I feel teribel leaven her there like that.

Couldent be helped could it doll. She will be all right you know. She lives there. She wont get lost.

I know i say. It is only me that gets lost.

Listen doll face you did your best. I should of made sure you knew that the flight was to port adventurer. I should have told you to listen for that. I just forget you need a hand some times that is the problem.

We should try again tomorrow i say to bud.

Try what he says.

Callen marie i tell him.

Okay he says. We can do that.

Lights out i say even though they are already.

Lights out he says and turns over on his side. As usual he fankles about with the covers for about ten minutes. Then he goes for the pillows. Lie at peace i tell him but he will take a good ten more minutes to settle down. He is like a dog at times the way they circle there bed before lyen down. Well he is a bit like that with his leg out of the cover and his duvet tucked between his knees and his pillows all bunched up at an angle under his cheek. It is his routine i know that but it is still a pain. Why can he not lie there still and just sleep. It is not fair of me to be a judge of him since i often lie awake for ages myself but at least i can keep still in the prosess. He must have been weaned to early of the bottle or some thing he hasent adjusted to sleepen like a grown up person a man for good ness sake. He has not finished his routine yet though. He will want his pat.

Rub my back please.

Bud im tryen to sleep.

Just for a minute grace. It will help me to nod of.

I turn on my side and begin to rub his back his shoulders and then in the middel wear he is so tense all the time that is wear his anger settles i reckon. It is all twisted into the mussels of his middel back under the neck.

What are those mussels called bud i ask him.

Which ones he says.

The ones im rubben.

They are dorsals i think. Or they might be laterals.

They are so tense as usual i say.

Hmm he says then says that hes got another mussel that is even more tense and could do with a massage as well. I should of seen it comen i say and then i realise i have done it again.

You havent seen it comen in too effen long he says.

I give him a smack on the arm but not hard.

Then we are both quite for a while. It is just me rubben his back and his breath whistlen about in his lungs from smoken to much of cutters choice. I have told him he should quit the rollups but he wont listen he says what else is there to do all day but roll fags and practice his banjo. It is a worry though. I have told him. When he is lyen a sleep next to me on his back you can hear him weeze with all the smoken he does. Yes he sleeps on his back he will say i am talken rubbish but he does. He thrashes about in the night and in the end he settles on his back and snores. I often have to get up and go of and sleep in seans room next to him. It is a relief to get away from the way bud twists about in his sleep but the noise is worse or just as bad. Sean will sleep through it all no matter what. I wander what he is dreamen about or if he is too wee to dream yet. I dont know if you have to be a special age like five or six to start. Probably not. You just dont remember when you are so small.

Bud rolls over against me again and sighs. I cant sleep he says. Im all on edge.

I know i say. Neither can i.

It is done now gracie theres no point in thinken about it.

I know i cant help it though i tell him. Im so stupid some times. Marie will kill me.

Bud laughs. Well she would if she could get any wear near you he says. But i think your goen to be safe for now.

I laugh too. Can i come under your wing i ask him.

He lifts his arm up and i rest my head on his shoulder. He puts his hand on my waste it is so warm my hands are cold and my feet too. Those espadrills.

Comfy he says.

Yes.

Your glasses will likely be on there way back here now gracie he says. They will be jetten out over the bay of biscay or some wear. Think of the sights they will have seen for you.

The inside of a suit case i say. That is not much to write home about is it.

I dont know bud says. Suit cases can be full of dead interesten things.

I reach over his belly and lay my palm on it. It is so warm i can not believe the heat of it.

You still want to do it dont you i say.

What he says like he dosent know.

You know what i mean. I can feel it there you know. Its liften up the covers.

Bud laughs. He wants me to do it but he will not say be cause its been a long time. He is scared i think.

I dont want to now bud i say. I am sorry.

He sighs. When then grace.

I dont know bud i cant tell you that. I am sorry.

Bud is quite. So am i.

Then he lifts his arm a way and turns on his side away from me. He has to go through his whole routine all over again from the start but he is less noisy about it. After a while he is quite and after even longer i hear him begin to snore and his lungs whistle. I am still awake here though. I am still here in the darkness with all these thoughts runnen around mad in my head. Like wear is vincent and what is he doen right now. Has he been mugged on his way home or is he safe. I try to think him safe and sound. I try to think him back home under this roof which is not the best one in the world but it is ours and the counsils. For a while i think about bobby in the car and francis and vincent tryen to lose me there own mother.

I lie there awake and bud shifts about in his sleep. He some times shouts out to and lashes about with his arms. Eff he shouts. Effen see. Those are the most common utterances he will generally make. Whack his hand comes over and hits me in the mouth.

Bud i say and jump up tuggen the duvet away from him. Watch what your doen.

Bud sits up a few seconds wear are you goen he says. Grace. Gracie wear are you goen.

He dosent know what he is doen he is sound a sleep awake. I can feel the heat of him he is roasten hot wear i am always cold. My feet are always frozin. He sits there a minute like he has heard a sound out side a noise. There it is i can here a siren. It is some wear far of then its gone.

That you francis he says.

Its me grace i say. Lie down and go back to sleep.

Bud listens a bit not here with me.

Lie down bud.

Grace he says i thought you were francis there.

I know i say its okay.

Then he starts to snore.

I lie there a while and breath in the dark in and out and in and out. Then i put on my slippers and dressen gown and go through to seans room wear it is safe.

~

Vincent my son dosent come back til early in the mornen that night so i can not really get rested with sleepen. I have to keep waken up some how and listen for him comen in. I am to light a sleeper to miss those door hinges haven a stretch i would of heard him if he had opened the door and slept properly from then. It is always the way with vincent these days. He sleeps half the day and then is out half the night wear i dont like to think. Well. By the time he does come in i have to start thinken about getten up any way so that is the end of sleep for me. Plus it isent so comfy a whole night in with sean who hogs the bed even though he is only the size of a stout loaf. He is way to small for the bed he should still be in a cot but bud got this singil from his pal bobby whose boy ross has feet comen out of the end of it. He was sixteen year old ross and it was well time he fitted a bed bud says.

Some times bud will play gitar and sing about it to make us laugh me and sean. Vincent just glowers away in his bed room.

Bobby got a boy six foot tall sleeps in the kitchen with his feet in the hall bud says like in ramblen jack eliots song. Eaten hog eyes just loves ice cream especially with gravey. Bud can do east texas talken blues like no body on earth not even ramblen jack eliot. It is some thing else to hear him no doubt about it. Any way bud says sean will grow in to the bed it is an invest ment a free one at that. I agreed at the time. Except sean kept on fallen out on to the floor and waken us all up with his lumpy headed greeten. Some free investment that i sayed. We should have invested in a crash helmet to go with the bed.

Vincent my son and bud had a good laugh to gether at first one of the rare occasions. We can get a leash for the wee man bud sayed at the time. We can put a safety belt on him and stop him goen wanderen over the presipis in the night. Totally man my son vincent sayed. We can just pure strap him in and that.

I said that wasent funny and sean just looked at us all con fused be cause he knew we were all talken about him.

This mornen i am pure done in though. I get up and feel for my glasses automatic then remember they are of on holiday. I rub the sleep from my eyes but it is no use. My eyes will be full of sleep until my glasses come back. It is on times like these i think contacts would be a great thing except my eyes can not take them. I did try them out years ago but i couldent get used to putten them in and taken them out again. It was bad enough putten them in but getten them out again was worse. Plus they were sore in the middel. The hard ness of the lenses the optishian said and that i would get used to it. Well i dont think i ever want to get used to doen that i will stick with my specs i told him. I dont care how thick you have to make them. I will just gogol at the world like always.

And it will gogol back the optician told me. Are you sure that is what you want grace.

Well i sayed to him no one likes to be gogoled at in the street but it is not new for me.

He just looked at me funny and said okay then. We will stick with the milk bottlers for now will we. He was tryen to be funny i think. I find my glasses and put them on the leg is a bit wobbly and the tape makes me look as if i have got dis abilitys. And it is true i do. I can not see a dashed thing. They are goen to have to do for now though so i try to put that thought out of my head.

I get up out of seans bed quite so he wont wake. He is maken littel noises littel huffs of air and the warm smell of him gives me a mad feelen like i could eat him all up. I sort his cover for him and stroke his curls which are francises my daughter. The same colour and feel. Of course he is some of his father too but i havent any idea which of him i try not to think of that man.

I go over to the door and creep away but not be four i stand on a toy of some kind which hurts like eff. I keep quite and just suck in air through my teeth and hop on out into the hall wear vincents door is closed snoren comen from inside and his music still playen quite. I take a look in but the room stinks so bad i come straight back out again. It is a brewery in there. Well he must have friends with money be cause he never got any of me and he has not worked much in the year since he left school.

Gracie buds voice says and his hand on my shoulder makes me jump. He wraps his arms round me he has a duvet over him naked under neath. He hugs close and says gracie come through and lie down with me a while.

He scratches his stubble into my neck and shoulder.

I dont have time bud I say. I have to get ready and go to costigan house.

Why he asks me. They think your away. They wont have any work for you.

I know he is right. But if i cant be on holiday in canary isles they might as well know i can work if they need me. I tell this to bud who is swayen me in a sort of dance. He is in an awful good mood this mornen.

Borrow vincents mobile and call them bud says. You dont have to go down there. Spend the day with me and sean. We can go over and watch the counsel men builden the swing park. Its a nice day out. Nicer anyway.

I say no bud. I want to go in. if you are there in person its harder for them to turn you away. Besides things are always happenen at costigan house that you dont expect.

He pulls me back in to him. Oh aye he says. They oldies are a wild lot so they are.

Bud i say. Let me get ready. I want to go.

Bud sighs.

Bud. Please.

He lets me out from the duvet. Okay but on one condishion. What is that bud i ask him.

If theres no thing doen you come back and meet me and sean after play school and we all do some thing to gether. We can try marie again.

I will think about that bud i say. I know he is tryen to bribe me but marie wont be in duren the day anyway. She will be out worken.

Bud sighs again. It isent worth the bus fare gracie.

Maybe not i tell him. But i want to at least try. You go back to bed now for a while. Its early.

Okay grace he says. But theres one other condishion.

Uh huh.

Make us a cuppa will you. Theres a good girl. He grins and ruffles my head the same way he does with sean then dives back in through the bedroom door. Well. If there is one thing garan teed to annoy me haven my head ruffled must for certain be it. What can i say i have never much enjoyed haven my head ruffled even by bud. He effen well knows it to.

After i get sean up and fed and he is okay to go to play school with bud i decide to head of for costigan house. Those to are content to sit and munch together bud quite and sean gurglen in his way. They are good company for each other i think which is a worry but one for an other time. Well i say when they have forgotten all about me i will be of now. Bud says he will take me down to the bus stop but i tell him no its okay. I can manage by my selve. Bud goes to get up and i say no sit down i will see myselve out. Just try to be civil to vincent when he gets up i say without much hope.

Naturally bud says.

Then i give sean a peck and rub buds hair. Sean looks up at me with francises eyes his mother my daughter. Bud looks at me too. I know he would like more but i dont seem to have it in me to give him any this mornen i dont know why. Thinken of francis i would think is what. It has been a long time a year but it is still raw with in me. I see bud then i see francis then i see bud it goes round in a circle. I am always round in circles these days it would seem.

Now when you go out that door gracie brace your selve i tell my selve. It will be hard work today without your proper glasses. If there is any work to be done that is. Even if there isent it will be hard work just getten about. You will have to have your wits about you not like yesterday at the air port. You should of been of to port adventurer on canary isles with your sister marie soaken up the sun and sangria instead of in dreich drumchapel soaken up the rain. You will have to try marie again and she will not be happy about your absens.

You should do it now grace. While vincents phone is about.

I go back to his nibs room bud i say given him a shake hes of to sleep once again. Bud give me a hand with the phone. I need to call marie.

Bud rolls over and says bring it here then.

I go out in to the hall along to vincents room and knock on his door. Nervis ness makes me shakey as vincent will hate this. He will not stand for his privacy to be compromised in any way these days. Only a year or to ago i could of walked in on him he might even have been getten changed or some thing but he wouldent of minded. Now he is the body his friends call him he has gone that private way. I even used to joke with him but he wouldent take it. O come on vincent i used to say it isent even any thing your mum hasent seen before is it.

Mum he would say and get embarised.

Francis was difrent. She would never undress in your company even when she was just small. She would run of some wear private to change her clothes to put on her pidgamas. She would even bath her selve from a very early age so long as no one looked at her. Her grand father me and maries used to say she would sail away in that bath. Francis can not even re member her grand father now. Only my selve and marie re member him. Roy the boats he used to be called be cause of his surname it was barker which he sayed is boat in spanish. Gracie boats he used to call me some times his grace of ships. Marie is the only one to call me that now the only person who knows she could call me that. If she wanted. Well. We are not that often in touch me and marie. Not in a long time.

Vincent i say its me. Knock knock i say your mums at the door. Open says me.

I hate my voice for this tryen to pretend i am care free not bothered the response i will for sure get from my son. There is just no sound from his room what ever. I open the door a bit to go in and the smell o my god. The smell of the drink is teribel. I push the door open further there is some thing on the floor maken it stick. Dirty washen. O Vincent i say pushen in this place is teribel.

There over on the corner on his single bed is vincent. He is not responden.

Well it isent any of my bisness i say but you shouldent be drinken like that your not of age and that is when he turns over sudden and sits up and shouts right in my face get out.

I get such a fright i just stand there frozen.

Get out of my room he shouts again.

I just want to borrow your phone to contact my sister marie i tell him shaken. She will wander wear ive got to.

He lies back down just as sudden as he got up. He says nothen and i wait.

Vincent your mother is talken to you. My hands are shaken so is my voice.

Buds voice be hind me in the door way.

Bud i say. Please.

Vincent is quite. Bud is quite. I am quite. All of us waiten.

Vincent picks his phone up from the floor a jumble of dirty clothes and holds it out then flops back down.

Tell him to get out my room he says.

You can effen tell me your selve bud says.

Get out vincent says leave me alone this is my room.

No i say its my room vincent my room and the counsils.

Well the phones mines he says.

I will give it back to you in a minute thats all i want it for.

Bud dials the numbers in our room and there is that voice again he says. The effen Spanish woman talken to him the answer phone. There is no marie she will maybe email vincent bud says. Great i say now i will never get in touch with her. I feel like i am about to cry i say to bud plus i have to go back down to costigan house today without my proper glasses. Weve wasted enough money as it is and it wasent even ours to waste.

I am shakey over the way vincent speaks to me these days but i dont tell bud. He will only want a confrontashion with him and that will not do any of us any good least of all bud.

What do you mean we bud says. Youv wasted my break.

Bobby is expectin me to go of and beg for a shift at that effen bee of a colledge to morrow getten stares from they youngsters just out of school. O here comes that mad old guy with the gammy leg holden. What a numpty. He must be cracked in the heed to do that effen job for a weans pay so he must. How can he even work with a busted leg.

I know bud i dident mean that.

Well.

I just ignore him. Of course it was me who missed the flight to port adventurer canary isles to see my sister marie who i havent seen for so many years. Of course it was i know that. You are always doen things like this i tell my selve. Arent you gracie. Well. That isent quite true no one has invited me on a holiday abroad be four with them payen. It is true i havent ever even been out of the country except once with marie not long after our father died. When i met francises father.

When you slept sitten up in the hotel lobby grace. Remember that.

Sitten up in the lobby after you spent all your money driven in a taxi from one hotel to another looken for a room. In the middel of the night your first night.

Til they took pity of you in what was the name of the place.

The hotel san some thing.

A marbil floor in the lobby so the heels of your espadrills slip on them quite quite only a squeak comen from them. The air condishounen cool in the night and the taxi man driven first to the front door the marbil lobby.

You had hardly any money grace.

How were you goen to pay grace

That man asked you and you dident know any of his langwidge but you knew that was what he was asken you dident you grace. You could of understood his meanen in any langwidge couldent you.

Yes.

So you told him to drive a bit further usen your own tongue.

I get out on to the landen and it seems like to much straight away. A big square of sun light has fallen down through the window and landed on the floor and is to bright for me to see through. Every thing else is in the shadow of this big square. Go on gracie just walk through it it will be ok you know fine that the stare well is straight ahead and the lift to the left a bit. Keep goen thats it. Keep on goen grace you are in your own turf here no thing can happen to you. Then i here the lift door ping and the doors open some people getten out. I dont know them though i can hardly make them out they are one of the new families i think. They sound as though they are young which makes me nervis. At least they are speaken in english though which makes it less awkward. Some of the new families dont speak english so well and it gets embarasen not knowen what to say.

Are you okay there need a hand some one says a boy i think. O that would be not bad i think a hand some one a boy. I put one foot in front of an other and hope that the lift is there on the other side of the sun light.

These boys are getten out. They could even be friends of vincents. One of them takes my arm at the elbow but gently.

Thanks i say. This sun light is blinden.

Your all right ive got you the boy says. I can see now he is tall another giant. He has two friends with him and they are laughen about some thing or other on one of there mobiles. It is a daft recorden a ring tone or some thing.

Thanks i say would you mind pressen ground floor for me i ask him.

No bother he says. He sounds like his voice is just breaken but he is still massive.

The door begins sliden shut when he steps back out.

Want a ride missus one of them says but i just ignore them. The door shuts and i am on my way. They are just boys i tell my selve. I always say that to my selve when boys worry me. They are just boys grace. They are just doen what boys do. Even so they frighten me a bit. I wander if vincent is like that when hes out and about with his pals. Probably yes. He would want to be part of the gang just like any body else. O please to christ i say a loud please to christ dont let him join up. I could not take it if he was to join up. Okay gracie dont think about it just now. One thing at a time. Let him do what ever he wants just so long as he dosent join the effen army.

The lift clanks all the way down but no body else gets on which is a relieve. Once it stops i am okay to get to the front door and out of our block. It is so dingy on the ground floor that no thing much surprises me no nuisance sun or any boys. I turn left and go on down the hill. It is so easy from here to the bus stop that i almost enjoy it and when i finally get to the bottom of the street i look up at our flats and i imagine i can see bud and sean waven and given me the thumbs up from the seventh floor which is wear we live. It isent true of course. They are way to far away for me to see even wether i have my glasses or not.

I go on over to the bus stop and wait for the first one to come along and hope it is the right one. Straight away i can make one comen down from past the library wear annette has her group. It will likely be a 42 or 20 but i ask some one an old lady the only person standen there.

Excuse me i say is what number of bus is that. A 42 the old woman next to me says which is mad because she sounds anshient but can probably see better than me. Well. Pretty much every one can that is not so unusual. But she sounds so old it isent fair. Then the old woman takes my arm and helps me board she makes sure i dont miss the step.

Will you all be right for getten of she says.

Yes thank you i tell her. I am fine if i sit near the driver.

She sits me down at the front in one of the elderly dis ability seats and i try to get a look around to settle in my head the way we should be goen. I ament nervis but i will be the nearer we get to my stop. A lot of these streets look just the same even if you can see. Be care full i say to my selve quite. Lucky for me it is a brighter day today but it is years since ive done this with these old glasses. Well two or three any way. The last time they gave me new ones i had to wait a week and that would be the last time i can remember. It is not easy tryen to get about with them it takes me back a bit i can tell you. Back then i was on my own to well not on my own but there was no bud. There was me and vincent and francis expecten all of us to gether in it. Well. We were okay. We were okay so long as we were to gether even though it was difficult some times. That is the way of the world for you bud says and he is right. It will always be a fight. Some times he makes you laugh with the way he talks i have to say. He is always talken about wanten to fight some thing usually the wrong thing i think. He would be on a hiden to no thing.

Driver the old woman says. Make sure you give this lady notice when we get to her stop.

She looks at me. Wear are you goen she asks.

Anniesland road at costigan house i say.

Give this lady a shout at the corner of dumbarton road and anniesland will you please driver.

I can hear the engine rumblen but we are not moven yet. It is warm in here and theres a smell of diesel which i like. There are a lot of people from the drum getten on which makes me nervis if some thing goes wrong. I dont want all my neighbours to see me make an eejit of my selve if i can not see them as well. This old lady is a hunched up thing she cant be more than 4 and a ½ foot tall. Some folk they are just tiny especially the elder lay in drumchapel though not all. The driver says some thing to her and she is sayen what was that back.

She comes over and sits down next to me. She has one of those old loud voices that wont get out of the road for any body. It is just my luck she has decided i am her good deed for the day.

The drivers not from here she says. He is one of they eastern europeans i think. He couldent understand what i was sayen the old woman says.

O i say. Well thanks for getten me on board.

The old woman grabs me by the hand and squeezes it. She gives me a bit of a fright to tell you the truth. What can i say i have never enjoyed getten grabbed by strangers even the very elder lay. The bus starts to move and she lets go again.

A dashed disgrace so it is the old woman says. There are folk from around here young folk that could of used this job. But they have given it to an eastern european. What do you think of that she asks me. I think it is a dashed disgrace she says. They ought to send the lot of them packen.

The bus starts to move i can feel it pull away from the stop im glad because i dont want to have to talk so i pretend to look out of a window. The old woman is talken in a way like a lot of people by not wanten much to here what you think. Even if i agree with her she will not here me i dont think. Well it is fine after a minute she is quite. I look out of the window and try to keep track of the turns the bus makes.

Somebody at the seat opposite a man is haven a conversashoun with some body in a seat behind shouten. He has a dog i can hear it whine. The dog makes an other mad noise and then sneezes and the man says all right calm down son your treats comen. I dont know what hes talken about but it is sort of funny the way he talks to the dog. The old woman says o hes lovely isent he what kind is he. She leans over to clap him and the dog makes the noise again.

Is he tired the old woman says. Is he yawnen.

Naw the man says he wants his pigs ear.

I can here a rustlen the sound of a plastic bag. The man says there you go son hows that and the old woman laughs like she is goen to choke.

He loves to chew them the man says.

O my the old lady says he fairly does.

The man goes back to his shouten conversashoun and the old lady says to me a pigs ears he gives it. Imagine that.

I dont know what to say to that so i say what kind of dog is it though i dont care. A mongrel of some description the old woman says. Like no thing she has ever seen before. Except that will be non sense. She is talken about a dog i dont see how difirent a dog can be. Even i can tell its just a dog. The bus lurches round a roundabout and i wander if this will be alderman road yet. It will be too soon for alderman rd but it must be some wear around here i expect. It is quite exciten doing this journey frightenen and exciten at the same time. The bus pulls up at a stop and a few people get up to get of includen the old lady.

Thats me she says. This is alderman rd she says theres a while for you to go yet.

Thank you i say but i am glad shes away now. I can here the dog is still growlen and chewen the pigs ear and sounds very happy. The man who owns it says now sit at peace will you buster. Thats it sit at peace ya maddy.

The bus pulls of again. It is not so far to costigan house now even if i get of too early or late it will only be a short walk. That is what im hopen for any way just a short walk. I will definitely reconise the builden even in this state with un satisfactory glasses.

We are passen trees i know because there branches rattle against the windows of the bus. We will be away down toward yoker now it isent far. Then we turn left and carry on a bit further with the shipyards and clyde on our right. Even i should be able to make out the cranes and then yes i can just about see the cranes. The bus stops at some lights and i get up and go over to the driver.

Is it the next stop for costigan house i ask him. Is this next stop the corner of anniesland rd.

He says some thing but i can not make out what it is.

Costigan house i ask him. He dosent know. That is no good to me i say. Wear are we now.

He says some thing about dumbarton rd about costigan house. I can not make out what it is he has an accent.

Then the bus doors open and he says some thing about costigan house about dumbarton rd. He is a menace this driver he would put me out in the middel of the street.

Next stop i tell him. After the lights.

That is just me surmisen though. There is no way on earth i will get out here away from any stop at some bunch of traffic lights i dont even know.

Some one the man with the dog shouts your all right hen its the next stop. He gets up and comes over and speaks to the driver and i say thanks sorry to be a nuisance.

Not at all the man says the driver just cant understand the accent.

I dont know what to say to that. It is to ridiculus to think of. Instead i laugh though i am not sure its all that funny. He is a foriner to this country but it is my accent that is dificult to understand.

The man and the driver laugh about some thing i just stand there waiten for the bus to move. The dog is winden it selve about my legs with its lead and maken me very nervis. I am not fond of them i have to say. It keeps rubben a wet nose against my hand or it is maybe tryen to give me a chew of its pig ear i ament sure which.

The man says it is all right. I wander if i know him from some wear. He says he will see me to the door of costigan house. Him and buster the dog are getten of here too. I am glad of that but i dont tell the man i just say no no i will be fine. He has offered now so i know he will insist which is a relieve except may be he wants some thing. Well. It will save me the bother of asken yet another stranger. It is stupid really because i would never let a wean go of with a help full stranger in fact i would tell them not to take any thing of a stranger not a lift not any thing. Even so it is just a fact that you have to trust folk now and again even if you dont want to. Grown ups have to from time to time. That is what i would tell sean if he asked. Wee boys should almost never trust a stranger but grown ups some times have to. In fact a grown up is mostly to place your trust in strangers some helpful others not.

I have had to trust a stranger on more than one ocasion and some times it was the wrong choice but there you go. It is done now. I still see some of those people about drumchapel but it can not be helped. Per haps this man is one of them. They will always be out there those men. If bud had his way he would batter some of them they make him so angry some times. You just have to live with them i tell him. Why he will ask. Because i have to so you should too. Of course bud is no threat to any one. On the other hand vincent is a difirent matter. I decide not to think about this as it will only worry me.

There you go the man says and helps me down of the bus. Do i know you he says. I am sure i know you.

I dont think so i say.

You are from the high flats arent you he says.

No i say. Not me im afraid.

He leads me up the road towards costigan house. I can make it out not far. A great big white builden you cant miss it.

I think i have got it he says. Its bud spence isent it. Your grace that bud sees arent you.

This surprises me. I thought i knew all of buds acwaintenses. Well i supose i must be i say. Unless theres more than the one bud spence in the drum in which case it might be some one else your thinken of.

Rid heided fella with a temper the man asks me.

If it is rid heided bud spence with a temper then it is the same bud.

The man says no thing he is likely thinken some thing good or bad about bud or my selve. Probably the latter in my experience. Maybe bud owes him money an old debt. Bud never gambles much now just the 2 or 3 pound we can afford. I tell my selve it is okay. It is okay gracie bud has changed. You have changed to you do not owe any thing to any man either.

The same bud the man says. No doubt.

Is this us i ask him to change the subject costigan house.

Aye so it is the man says. Come here buster and give the lady peace.

Hes very friendly isent he i say. He keeps tryen to put his ear in my hand i think.

The man laughs.

Oh aye he says. Buster likes everyone.

He dosent bite then i ask.

Och no. He might lick you to death but.

Well that is all right then. As long as he dosent bite.

The man sees me to the gate. This is you he says. Costigan house. He takes me up the path and says are you all right from here.

Yes thanks. It is plain sailen from here in i tell him.

No bother he says. Come one buster.

Thank you i say. The man waves a hand then stops.

Say hello to bud from me he says and i nod. Tell him gregor

sayed not to worry that bisnez its all forgot now. He will know what i mean. Gregor thats me he says.

Okay i say. I will tell him.

Cheers hen he says and walks away down the path with the dog beside him.

I am glad hes away. I do not trust him one bit if hes any thing like buds other pals bobby for instance.

He goes through the gate and then waves at me. I can just about make the white dog out. I still can not see any thing special about it except that it is a sort of white. If there is any thing special about a white dog then it is special i supose. I wait a few minutes until hes away and then press the entry buzzer. It is michelle who answers it. She is 28 16 year younger than myselve and she looks like a boy of six teen as well. She is all bones and angles jumpen out of her selve with a totaly white face like a clare voyent be cause she worries about her figure and no thing else except her stars. Oh she says when i say its me. Your not meant to be here grace your meant to be on holiday. I know i tell michelle. There was a mix up at the airport. Let me in and i can tell you all about it. Here we go i think better make this good gracie. I am thankful i wont have to see her properly today. She is nice enough michelle. I just dont like to have to see peoples faces when im elaboraten on the truth.

I wait til michelle has her back turned before i sign the register i dont like folk looken over my shoulder at my riten. She is a nosey type michelle. I have seen her try to tell people what they are like from there signature even though it is pure non sense her anal isis. Why dosent she just ask them i wander. It would save a lot of time. Once we are both sat in the kitchens with our tea and i explain about the airport and missen the whole of my flight to port adventurer and my glasses gone to. Michelle says oh thats teribel grace I am so sorry for you.

I tell it like it could of hapened to any one at all.

O dry up michelle i think but i dont say out loud. Well it is no wander.

To tell you the truth michelle i am about fed up with goen through this story and haven people feel sorry for me i tell her. It was my own stupid fault for putten the glasses in with the lugidge. It is my own fault for not readen the ticket properly to but i dont tell michelle that bit. It will be only a lot of troubel for me in costigan house if rumurs get about.

Michelle is quite for a minute thinken i would supose. Normally if shes thinken michelle has got an expreshoun on her face like she is holden her breath. She will puff air under her upper lip and sit with her hands clasped to gether on her chest. It is about the fattest thing about her whole body when she does this. Then she lets out a big suck of air and rushes back in to the conversashoun. It can be dis conserten at least for me anyway. It is totally mad. You would never know that she has not got some thing stuck down her throat.

But its odd just the same gracie.

How do you mean i ask her.

Well i dont know. Just that when you had your good glasses on you never looked at the ticket to see wear it was goen.

It is all right though. I am ready for this so i dont panic yet.

O bud had them and he just handed them to me at the last minute. He knows i will forget my head if it isent screwed on right. I had so many other things to think about i never thought.

I tell her that has been a long time since i went any wear on a holiday and was just to excited.

My mind was full of what i was goen to say to marie when i got there and what would the canary isles be like and wanderen wear she would take me.

I can see michelle nodden she is not convinced.

What has been happenen here i say to her to change the subject. It is awful quite. Michelle leans in all conspirashounal.

Old mr munro died since you were last in michelle she tells me over our tea. The ones that could go are away to the service. Theres not goen to be much work around her today grace even if you had been expected. You should have called and saved yourselve the trip.

That is a shame michelle i say he was a nice old man. It is over a week since I have had a shift at costigan house i wander why they havent asked me to do more. Well. That thought gets me worryen again too.

Humph says michelle nice my bum. He was a miserable old swine is what he was she says. He used to tease me about my weight. There goes the lump he used to say to me if you can believe.

He was not so bad i say. He was only pullen your leg. He called me things too.

O he did did he michelle says. What did he call you then. I bet he never called you the lump.

I can not under stand michelle. She is totally sensitive about her weight even though she is thin as any thing. Mr munro can not have helped much callen her lump. She will have layed of break fast after that if i know her.

Are we talken about the same mr munro old eddy i ask her. He would not of harmed a fly i say. It is true. All old mr munro ever did was sit in his chair and sing. Day in and day out he sang i cant remember the song it was some thing about the power of the union.

Michelle laughs. Yes he did sing that dident he she says. My that was funny. I had forgoten already.

I dont know how you could forget michelle i say. That was all he sang.

Michelle nods and i sip my coffee. It has sugar in it which i dont take but i cant be bothered to tell michelle. She will fuss away like an old woman. We are sitten in the staff kitchen next to the liven room. Theres only one other person on the nurse shes on sleep over so she is a sleep just now. Margaret will be in later to mores the pity. I do not really get a long with margaret because of her relidgous views. Her relidgous views are v annoyen actually because she is so keen on sharen the effen things with you. Not only that but she never is done talken about her home in the caribean wear she comes from.

Michelle is thinken so i dont disturb. She is quite all i can here is her spoon in her mug goen tinkle tinkle. Her perfume is v nice and i want to ask what kind but i stop myselve for the same reason with annette i told you about be fore. It will be too dear for me.

You dont get me im part of the union you dont get me im part of the union. That was what he sang wasent it i say to michelle. Till the day i die.

Thats right grace. He worked in yarrows the ship builders when he was young. He was very proud of that. His father was one of the red clyde siders. It was nice for him to live here so close to home. He grew up and lived his whole life within a couple of miles of costigan house.

That does not sound so marvelous to me michelle i say. I have lived most of my life in the drum but i dont much want to spend the rest of it there either.

Michelle laughs.

What were the red clyde siders michelle i ask her. What did they do.

O she says and waves her hand. Its a long story grace she says. They were very political.

Well i say. I could of gessed that. Dont you know what they did michelle.

They went on industrial action michelle says.

It is a shame for mr munro i think. Nobody here even knows what a red clyde sider was and now we cant ask the one we had.

Why dont you gogol it michelle says. We can see what these red clyde siders were all about.

I dont say any thing i have to think fast. I can feel a hot flush comen right up my neck so i get up and go to the sink and rinse out my cup.

Come on michelle says getten up. I can put the kettle on and you can gogol red clyde siders next door on the computer.

Do you not want another cuppa first i say. My hands are beginnen to sweat the palms.

O come on stick in the mud michelle says. I will put the kettle on you might burn your selve your so blind. Go and gogol red clyde siders for us.

The kettle is a big old fashioned kind with an iron handle that sits on a hob. The handle gets so hot you have to wrap a cloth around it or get burnt but i would rather take my chances with the old technology than new.

Michelle wont let me though. She puts a hand on my shoulder and ushers me into the other room and sits me down at the computer which is always on. It is blue enough to hurt your eyes even mine.

I can not get out of this now. I could of said i need my glasses but they use zoom text here a big magnifyen glass.

Red clyde siders michelle says. Type it grace.

I imagine i can here some thing malishous in her voice just under neath but i dont know for sure. It is like she wants to see me fail.

Im sorry michelle i say i am so slow at typen even with zoom.

My hands have got tremors the palms are all wet.

Whats the matter gracie you must be abel to see these letters they are huge.

I can see the letters up there on the screen i cant see the ones on the key board i tell her.

Oh for gods sake she says and takes my finger to press the keys and i let her.

She types by holden on to my index finger and pressen the keys. All the time i memorise the letters and there posishouns. It must be red clyde siders she has typed but i can not say for sure.

There michelle says that wasent so bad was it.

I dont know what to say be cause i feel so embarrassed so i just say thanks michelle though i ament thank full at all.

Michelle clicks the button and a whole lot of stuff comes up except michelle has not zoom texted it though. That is fine by me. I have about lost interest in red clyde siders. If that is what has come up. Thanks you michelle i tell her again. Look at all this stuff about the red clydeside.

Dont worry about it grace. Your secrets safe with me she says.

What secret i wander. But i dont say this a loud.

Oh i better get that kettle michelle says before it boils over. Then she rushes out of the room.

While she is out of the room i try to find the zoom text magnifier. It is no use though. I am still a bit shaky and sigh out loud be cause no one is around to here me. I have to get a bit of relieve. I know michelle is a friend well a colleag but it isent a good feelen. She does not mean any thing by that remark i tell my selve. She is just meanen about haven bad eye sight. Yes i say to my selve. That is definitly what she is meanen. As is the usual senario when this happens i cross my selve though i am not relidgous or a catholic. If any thing i am a not practisen prodasant which marie used to say was the same thing as a regular prodistant any way. Still i am wanderen if marie really knows any thing or if it is just of the cuff that remark. Michelle is a teribel one for gossipen and that worrys me to.

I get up and feel for the door handle and go through to the staff kitchens again. I try first to have a look in the tv room but i cant make out who is sitten there apart from lily eccles who never leaves her favourite arm chair and will start to make a teribel fuss if any one else ever trys to sit in it. Lily eccles is a sweet heart. I know be cause she is never done tellen you she is a sweet heart. I am still some ones sweet heart she tells you even though you are just asken if she wants some more tea or an extra cushion for her neck which is bent right down almost on to her chest.

Hello lily i say from the door but she dosent here me. Well. She is probably a sleep. The tv does seem to help some of them doze. It sounds like it is day time tv that is on.

Through in the staff kitchen michelle is fussen about with the cups and the tea.

Do you not want your tea through there and see gogol she asks me.

I shake my head no. I cant see what it says i tell her. I cant find the zoom text.

Oh well i could just of told you what it said if your haven any dificulty michelle says.

I dont know about any difficulty i say. I just can not read the thing.

That is what i was thinken gracie. I would have read for you aloud.

I dont say any thing be cause it will just make her suspicions worse. The other thing is i dont like to be read to. People have been readen things to me as if they are o so clever for well my whole life it feels like. If they are not readen to me they are asken have you read this grace. They are asken how on earth can you not have seen this gracie. Even vincent and bud do this though i have told them not to. Bud especially.

Well never mind then grace michelle says. To sugars is it.

A splash of milk as well i tell her.

Michelle is haven some kind of herbal tea like usual. I can smell some thing flowery that isent like my tea or even erroll gray.

Mmm she says you should try this. Its really good for you.

I ament keen but she makes me try any way.

Careful she says. We dont want you burnen yourselve do we.

The way she talks to me. It is the sort of thing that bud likes to say as though i am a baby or some thing as though i need to be looked after or i will do my selve some injury.

That is rank michelle i tell her. What is it meant to be.

Rasberry and elder flower she says. Do you not like it. It was a real favorite of old eddy mr munro she says.

It is no wander he upped and died then i say and michelle laughs. You should know not to give elder flower to an elder person. They are bound to come of worst.

You are so bad grace i thought you liked him.

I did like him but that stuff would of not helped him live any longer i dont think.

Michelle gigles a bit then is quite for a while. She sips her flowery tea and i sip mine.

You really never even looked at the destinashoun on the ticket michelle says. Not once the whole time you were sat there in that departure lounge. I cant believe that gracie. That is just nuts so it is.

Michelle i say suddenly. Michelle i have some thing i should of told you before.

Not even once michelle says.

Listen michelle i have some thing to say. Your the only person i can tell. I feel teribel about it.

What is it grace michelle says putten down her cup.

Okay i say to her and take a deep breath. If you promise not to tell a sole.

Grace of course i wouldnt tell. What is it you want to say.

I take another big breath. Well I tell her. It is regarden old Mr Munro.

Oh she sys. Go on.

Michelle i say. Yes grace she says. Michelle i have some thing to tell you. Please dont you tell any one else it will be so embarasen. Michelle is all ears she says. I am all ears grace what do you want to tell me. Well i tell her. It is like this. I used to let mr munro you know what. No says Michelle tell me. O i cant i say to michelle. It is to embarasen. O gracie come on you cant just start and then not finish she says. No i tell her i cant tell you. Honest. You will think i am teribel you will think me a bad person. No i wont michelle says its all right you can tell me it wont go any further. O all right then i will. I wait a minute before i tell her. I take a big deep breath and my skin is so clammy now.

I used to let mr munro touch me i tell her. For a second michelle says no thing and i think this is awful this is so stupid you should have kept your mouth shut gracie. You are a fool so you are.

Then michelle says really grace. When was this.

O i say it was just once or twice i came in for a shift.

Did he grab you grace did he hurt you.

No no no i shake my head. I wanted him to do it. I wanted him to touch me.

This is totally mad i am thinken. Mr munro was 90 if he was a day. He was an old old man.

You wanted him to touch you michelle says. Well. That is some thing else grace. How long was it goen on for.

I dont know i say just since before xmas.

Michelle is getten much more serious than i expected. I can feel my ears are getten red. Michelle will definitely tell every one if i go on with the lie but i dont care. If it means people forget about the airport then that is okay.

He dident hurt me or grab me i tell her. I would just sit with him in his room and he would tell me of his dead wife. I liked him all right he was kind and funny. Even if he some times wasent. It is true his medication made him do things he was ashamed of. He could not of helped it. I reckon thats why some times he would take his thing out in front of me.

I know that grace he used to do that to everyone. Even wee stevie in the kitchens.

I cant tell michelles expreshoun it would help the story i am tellen her if i could. I would know what way to make it go so it is a lie one that she expects. So that it is a lie that dosent go to far.

He was always taken out his boaby and waven it at wee stevie the kp in the kitchens michelle says.

I nod. I know i tell michelle.

That was why wee stevie left she says. He was traumatised.

I nod again. I know michelle.

It is horibel to see an old mans boaby she says though this time she uses the see word. The other see word. The one for a mans see.

I know i say. I am so embarased i say but im not. He used to get it out and play with it in front of me and he used to sing at it the same time. Especially when i had to bath him. You know wash his private parts.

I can not believe i am sayen all this tripe. It is a lot of non sense so it is.

O grace.

I nod. Please dont say to any one i tell michelle.

I wont she says but she will. Who wouldent.

Go on grace tell me what happened.

I nod. Then i take another deep breath and go on.

Well he would get his you know what out and then he

would start to sing to it in front of me and i felt sorry for him. It wouldent go very hard michelle i say. I felt sorry for him. When i was washen him you know his private parts he would talk about his wife and how he still fancied her even now when she was dead and start singen.

What he sang that song michelle asks me. You dont get me im part of the union that one she asks.

The lie has gone ahead of me now i cant think what he sang. All i know is surely it cant be a song about the union.

He sings stand up stand up for jesus ye soldiers of the cross. Because it wouldent go stiff like he wanted. This one time he started to cry and asked me if i could help him to carry this burden.

The story could go one way or another. It can go right or it can go wrong and i might lose even these one or two shifts. I am already in danger of losen them any way because they want every one to have qualificashions soon.

I wait a bit while michelle takes it in. I am a panten a wee bit but i doubt if michelle notices.

So you did michelle says. You helped him.

I nod. Dont be angry with me michelle i say. It was only the once or twice.

Im not angry grace she says. Im disapointed.

Please dont tell anyone michelle.

Well she says. Well well. Sheesh. You know i have got to laugh she says. I have done some manky thngs in this job. I thought I had done all the manky things in this job actually.

It wasent that manky it was in the bath i tell her. It was quite clean really.

True.

I mean if i have got to clean his backside every day what is the big difirence.

Well better out than in i supose.

Michelle is laughen a bit now. It is all goen to be okay i think.

You wont tell any one will you michelle. I only sayed be cause hes gone now and i had to tell some one. Now my conshiens is clean about it i feel so much better.

Dont you worry michelle says. Dont you worry about any thing. Your secret is safe with me gracie.

Except i know that is just talk but if it all goes all right then it will not do me any harm. It will just be a funny story care workers tell. I will be famous for a while.

Michelle gives a mad snorten laugh all of a sudden that makes me jump.

Oh michelle i say its not funny then i start to laugh as well.

Right michelle say. We should probably do some work now instead of sitten here chatten away all day. While theres no thing to do and we still have the place to our selves.

~

Costigan house is like a morg with every one away at old mr munros funeral. There is just no body about at all and so not much work to do any way. All the old folk that could have been huckled of in minibuses. The ones that are to far gone to notice old mr munro has poped it are to far gone for pretty much every thing. They either just sit there in chairs or lie in there beds maken quite sounds that dont mean any thing. It cant be to much fun liven a long long life i dont think when i see these old people gazen of into there memories of ages a go. I dont want to live as long as these people. I would prefer to leave with my faculities. Often i think it would be a relief just to go all your worrys away now flown of. It will be like in the song bud plays fly away o glory ill fly away fly away in the mornen. It is an old song. It is not copy rited bud says you can not copy rite beauty or truth. To true that to he is fond of sayen.

Just a few more weery days and then bud plays on his guitar sean burblen along.

I will fly away. To a land wear joyce will never end.

I will fly away.

Whose joyce he will ask littel sean who just looks and stares. Whose joyce sean she must be huge eh. To a land wear joyce will never end ill fly away. Joyce will never end eh sean she must be masive. Bud sings his voice is hoars from sigarets and his wheeze is always there. No one sings like bud does i swear he is an orijinal. How about that then gracie he says. How ye like them onions. Its a great tune eh grace he says. Wish i could record it on the old record thing eh.

When i die hallelujah bye and bye.

I will fly away.

Who are you kidden grace. You couldent even get as far as port adventurer the canary isles to see your sister marie but you had to come back. Well when i do fly of i am not comen back that is for sure. Not a chance of it i am about done in with this life as it is what would i want to come back for.

I have said to bud to just switch the machine of if it comes to it but he has told me it is against his believe sistem. He is a non practisen atheist so he says. Be sides he likes the idea of haven some one about who cant answer him back like i am want to do.

You will be my ideal woman then gracie he told me.

Thanks a bunch i told him.

Bud just laughed.

Michelle says watch your feet on that carpet at the top of the stairs there grace and i say what carpet then nearly go flyen.

Are you okay michelle asks me and i say yes.

This place is comen down round our ears she says. Look at the state of this.

She is down on one knee pullen at the flap of carpet.

Damp she says. And the nails come up through it to she says.

I am a bit shaky from the fright i got my mouth has gone all dry so i just nod.

Anyway michelle says there is a new person in mr munros old room. He is a paki i think. One of they wont speak to a womin brigades.

Who i ask her.

The effin mad mullahs i dont know. Mr munro would turn in his grave.

He isent in it yet i say. Or not long any way.

Well he was political he fought for your writes grace how would he be pleased about one of they wild lot in his room.

I dont know how but he would probably just show them his you know what like he done to every one else i say. He dident care what there religioun was.

Michelle laughs to true she says. Stevie from the kitchens is still shaky from his experiens.

Well even still i think it is fast work even for costigan house a new person inso quick. Mr munro isent even cold in the ground and his room is gone already. There is a waiten list for good rooms like this one but still i am surprised. It is funny to think of but i used to like mr munros room myselve i used to think about me moven in one day. It has a nice view over the road to the adictions forum and there is a bath room and a kitchen too. You have got every thing you need in there so its comforten to think of. You could of moved in when you are still able get about your selve and be selve sufficient gracie. No body would have to bother about you and you wouldent bother about them either would you grace. It would be as good a place as any.

We go in and sure enough there is some one else not old eddy munro in his bed. An old indian man of some kind in stead. Michelle bustles up to him in her way and talks to him like hes soft in the head. This poor old man is sitten up with cushins behind his back and a minichir table over his lap with a bowl on it this mornens breakfast i would think. It is pushed away of to the edge and he has pile of envelopes and a book or some thing in the middel. It makes me nervis straight of to see a book sit there. Any time you see a book about it will sure as any thing cos you some troubil in my experiens. Best to keep away from them graciegirl. The troubil is there every wear.

How are we today then says michelle all settled in are we.

The man grunts some thing and jerks his head i dont know what he means.

O come on says michelle its the same poridge every one eats theres no thing wrong with it.

The man jerks his head and says cold but he barks the word out. Cold he says again. Cold. Cold.

These old glasses of mine are rotten i cant see him to well but he has not got a mustache i think just a beard. Some how i always think of old indian men as haven a mustache it is a prejudis of mine i supose. Bud thinks so. You have got some prejudises there gracie he will say. Only some are true though. I have got my own he says. Be cause there mine they are all correct. Then he usually laughs and says it again like you never heard first time round.

This is grace michelle says she works at costigan house to isent that right grace.

Michelle i say.

Its true isent it. You do work here. For now eh.

There is some thing in michelles voice when she says this. I dont know what maybe im imagenen it. How long have i got i wander what does michelle know i dont.

I smile at the old man. Only some times i tell him a couple of times a week usually.

He grunts and sticks out his hand the left one and i think he means for me to take it. The other is curled up at his side and close up i can see his face is froze on one side. I take his hand wich is cold and bony and i shake hands i think its what he wants but he lets go.

He has wide eyes that look like they are beggen you but still proud. They look like they are sayen listen listen i have some thing importent to say. I am still here.

He says some thing and i say excuse me.

He says his name is osama michelle says and laughs. That not right mr bin ladin.

The old man rolls his beggen eyes up at me and then michelle and tries to say some thing else.

He says his names osama bin ladin and hes goen to blow us all up that not right michelle says laughen. I am only kidden you she says to the man and his eyes say no listen. Michelle plumps the pillows behind his back and helps the man sit up but he slaps at her with his good hand.

O now now says michelle. Thats enough of that sort of behaviour.

Eff of he says. It comes out like a hiccup. Eff of you effen silly bee.

Michelle stops dead. What did you say to me she asks him except it isent a question.

The man makes a noise like a moan.. Eff of he says. Then he says dead slowly maken the shapes of words with his lips i am sarwar tarick sarwar.

I am bond james bond michelle says.

I try not to laugh and the mans eyes roll over to me.

You can eff of to cow.

Michelle is anoyed he spoke to me like that. But even i can see even with my rottin glasses that mr tarick sarwar is the sort of man who will tell any one just what he thinks of them wether he is parilised or not. He has never taken any rubbish from any one not ever in his life. His eyes are only beggen be cause they have to do most of his talken now. Other people might have begged him though. I dont know i am prejudiced about old indian paki men ament i.

He is all yours grace do what you like with him. I am goen to change the linen next door. Misses merriken bust her hip bag just before the bus came for her. We had to bundle her in the shower and she wouldent come out after. She just sat there shiveren

and greeten. It took four of us to get her out and dried of and o she screemed the place down. We put her in with old maisie eccles in 2 1 8 she can always seem to get through to her when she plays up.

Okay michelle i say. Me and mr tarick sarwar will just get to know each other.

Fuch of effen cow mr tarick sarwar says.

Michelle laughs and says o he is troubel this one. You had better keep an eye on him grace. Mr tarick sarwar keeps his good eye on me and tap taps his tremblen hand on the book he has on the table top in front of him. He looks at me as if to say you should bow to me he is so haughty as if he is used to getten every thing his own way.

He taps with his tremblen hand on the cover.

Here is say to him and open up the book. I dont need to smooth the paper down so it will sit open for him the pages are thin like a bibles. The pages are covered in riten in an other langwidge it must be muslamic or some thing. He looks at the pages and his lips move he is tryen to say the words. Then a tear comes down from his frozen eye and runs right down his cheek.

I wipe it away with the back of my hand his skin is cool and dry. O dont cry i say. It isent so bad as all that is it.

Fucgh of he says pullen his head sharp to one side. I look at michelle who is draggen the hoover in though the door. She shrugs.

When she comes over i say is mr tarcik sarwar okay.

The old buggers daughters dident want to look after him she tells me. They were sick of him so here he is. They have pretty much left him to his fate. I think he might have been a bit of a tyrant in the old days. He just seems to want his koran now. He has finally found relidgoun in his infirmity.

Well that is some thing isent it i say to michelle. At least that will be a comfort to him.

Not on your bum says michelle. After the stroke he cant read it any more.

How is that michelle i ask her.

Beats me she says. Some times that kind of thing can happen to people who have strokes. He can see the words but he can not under stand them.

Mr tarick sarwar is tracen his finger over the words and repeaten some thing to him selve then he shuts his eyes his hand waveren static in thin air as though supported by an invisible string from the ceilen.

Later on michelle says it is okay if i want to go she can manage till everyone else gets back from mr munros service. Come in again next monday she says we will get you some shifts here and at mortens too. Then she asks me what i think of margarets job. Margaret is getten promoted even though she was promoted above me and michelle only very resently. She is asken me if i fancy doen margarets job when the vacancy comes up. She says this bringen me an other big mug of tea when i am minden the spy tellys that look over the back and front doors to costigan house the car park to even though there are only a couple of cars parked there. Michelle has hers parked there it has a long name japaneas per haps.

Just have a think about mortens she says. They arent so bad. Not really michelle says. It might be good for you to go there.

Okay michelle i say. I will think about it.

I look at the spy telly pictures all grainy and black and white and grey. Some times you cant even believe these camaras work at all the pictures are so hard to make out even with a good pair of glasses.

Michelle goes back to see about changen the linen and to speak to wee stevies replace ment in the kitchens about him arriven late again. Wee stevies replace ment reminds me of vincent a few year back even though they are both about the same age. Except that this new wee stevie is still just a nice young boy. That is some thing that my vincent has lost some times i think for good. Wear does that nice wee boy go i wander.

It is then i see some thing out in the car park a man. He is so hard to make out but he goes a round looken at the cars he dosent see the camara or dosent care. I get nervis be cause i am suposed to write details down if he tries any thing funny. The time on the camara the natchour of the bother the car regis strashoun if he tries to break in. But the man goes away again and i sit and stare at the screen wanderen when will michelle be back and i should try and call my sister marie on the canary isles port adventurer.

Then i see her. It is her i know it is. The mans feet are visibil at the top of the screen and some one else a girl has come in to view. It is so hard to make out but i pick up the pen and pad as she goes over to a car may be michelles car. O no gracie not michelles car any other car but that. The girl tries the door and then goes round to the pasinger side and i see a white face just for a second. She looks up to the camara and i see it i know it. It is in the way she turns her head and flicks her hair it is in that moment. It is in that second which is 10 37 and 44 seconds that i know. I know. Except it can not be her it isent posibill.

It is francis. My daughter.

And i stand up i open my mouth and say her name francis and she is looken staren.

It is like she sees me. It is like she knows i am there.

Then she looks back to michelles car the japaneas name car i dont know how to spell it. I look help less stuck here stuck still and she the girl francis tugs at the pasinger door and the alarm goes of. She is gone. She has disapeared like a ghost.

I can breath again but i cant move for a few seconds it feels a lot longer.

All that time i have waited 1 year and 21 days and 10 hours and 37 minutes and 44 seconds. That is how long it has been since i have seen her. I know exactly. Only now i think what if it wasent her grace. You dont have your right specs on they are in your bag on a plain to the canary isles they are half way across the world you could of been mistaken. Are you not just after sayen the camara picture is not so good plus you have on old glasses. Yes. Are you sure grace. Are you sure it was your daughter. Are you sure it was francis. How long have you wanted to see her grace. Well. You know how long. How long have you wished for it and hoped and hoped. A year and 21 days. 1 year and 21 days today exactly. You know be cause you have counted them every day every hour.

I have to get out of the room i have to move about.

Are you sure it was her grace. You cant be can you. You have only wanted it so badly and feared it. It might have been her but it wasent. Was it. It was just hope and you shouldent hope ever.

Not ever.

Just then michelle comes back in i have to collect my selve. I have to get my selve back to gether again. It wasent francis you are just thinken daft gracie.

Have you thought about mortens michelle says. O is that my alarm goen of down there.

 She muddels about not payen me any atenshoun.

O yes michelle i say. Some one had a go at breaken in the pasinger door.

Michelle jumps to life o did they now she says. Well you have got them on camara right grace. You have wrote down the details. You have got a record.

It was just this second i tell her. They have legged it.

They never got in did they she asks me.

No it was a girl but she ran of when the alarm sounded.

Good work michelle says. Effin theiven bees.

I never did any thing though. I was surprised. I got caught of gard.

No. But. It was a good job you were here though grace. What about mortens then.

Had you not better go and check on your car michelle.

O good point grace. Keep an eye out if they come back eh. Dont bother to call the polis we will get the new shef to bring a knife in case.

Mortens i ament so sure about though. I have never found that place to be very good for work. A few times i have gone and they acted like i was some sort of idyit who shouldent even of been there not some one whos there to help. I dont know what it is about that place i tell michelle but i ament to keen on goen there. Begars cant be choosers michelle tells me. That is very true i sayed they sure cant. Of course i will go if they want me. Stick by the phone michelle says and i keep quite be cause i dont have one. I use my son vincents number when i have to and like i sayed he isent to happy about it.

My son vincent is never to happy about any thing these days. It is that age he is at. A gun would maybe make him happy a gun or a knife or some thing of that nature. That is the way he is headed. If he joins the army o that will be my end. Joinen up will finish you grace you have told your selve that so many times. Even if it makes him happy a man even o grace. O gracie.

Francis o francis you could help. Vincent if not me.

Just vincent. Like you did when you were small together.

Remember how you gave him your tedy when he was born francis. Do you remember that of course not. You were still so small then your selve. But you did. You gave him that toy that you loved be cause he was new.

I wander what else we have forgotten the both of us francis.

Look at the sky francis i used to say. Isent it big.

Its so big the sky it has got to cover every thing thats why.

It has to cover the whole world in blue francis.

Its got every thing in it all the blue and all the world you and me and vincent as well.

Have you forgot that to francis. Of course you have havent you.

Yes. I think you must of.

But i worry i am forgetten to. There are times i can not picture her face any more. It is an other harder face that haunts me. The face of a dependent. That face follows me i see it some times in a crowd or a queue or out side a shop. Blood rushes up in me like a whoosh francis i some times catch my selve sayen. Francis wait. It is me francis. Your mother. But it never is her is it grace it is just a ghost it is just your mind or your eyes playen tricks.

When i get out of costigan house the wether has turned again.

It is blowy with big skirts of clowds and its so much darker but so far no rain yet. Our father me and maries used to say that. Look big blowsy clowds like skirts he would say there like ladeys under ware. He was a funny man for sayens though he always sayed the same sayens over and over. Big skirts of clowds and things like that. If it takes a week to walk a fort night. What is the difrinse between a sparrow. How long does it take to sand paper an elefant down to a grey hound. One of its legs is both the same. Those kinds of things. He would make me and my sister marie laugh that way sayen things over and over for our benefit though i dont miss it except these days. He was a kind man our father. To tell you the truth he was so kind he wouldent have let us go though we were grown up. If he could of he would of made us both stay with him. My sister marie left though i stayed. Well that is the way of it he sayed when i asked him why it was that my sister marie got took away from us and i stayed til the end. Some stay and some go our father sayed. You stayed graciegirl be cause you just cared more for your old dad. They couldent take you from me could they graciegirl. You just knew wear your place was while marie your sister had to go and find it her selve.

That was what he always used to call me graciegirl. I was impashent with him for that but now i dont mind it. Some times bud calls me that even though he never met our father but just thought of it on his own. I like it now when he does it but it makes me upset some times. Though i never tell bud. I just let him wander about it

The sound of him dyen.

O the sound of him dyen in that bed. I held on to francis my daughter so tight in those days. I said to her like he said to me dont leave me ever francis. Promise me that you will stay no matter what. The world will not take you away from me. I ament goen to let it. You will stay with me.

Promise me.

My daughter francis had curls then not straight hair like now. Brown curls and fingers that curled around my own. Never leave me francis i would say. You and me will just stay to gether and be old mades.

It was just the way i used to feel.

I can not stand to want her back and be afraid of it to. I can not stand what my daughter will take away with her the next time.

I turn down the path and bump into the gate at the bottom forgetten it will be there plus i am away of in my own head. It catches me on my hip ow i say for gods sake grace look wear your goen. Thats a joke with these use less old glasses and my others away to port adventurer canary isles. I guess i can expect another sore bruise there on my hip in a few days time. It is not even funny im covered in bruises all the time even with my desint glasses. Bang things batter into me all the time i am so clumsy. If there is a way to bang into some object you can bet your bottom dolar that gracie boats will find a way to fling her selve in to it.

Your like some kind of mad shoppen trolay bud says. Its like you have got a wonky caster .

It is more like things conspire against me i have told him. They see me comen and know i am a soft touch.

Well if any one can find a chair to trip over its you grace says bud. No doubt about it at all

I footer about for a while tryen to get the latch open and then footer about again closen it properly. I could go back the way i came for the bus but i dont think so just now. Shall we toss a coin for it grace i say to my selve. Heads we go back on the forty to tails we walk up the road a while till scotstoun station and go back on the train. If we go that way it will have to be back to hyndland first and then on to good old drumchapel. It is further this way and dearer to since i have a ticket for the bus but it will be more fun an adventure. Our father was always very keen on local adventures that went no wear to.

Marie my sister went of on real adventures to places but i stayed to look after our father. He had no won else then just me and my daughter francis and my son vincent not even born. I can not believe it has been so long since they were both born and even shorter since sean came along to.

Getten old are you gracie.

Though you have always been old compared to others havent you.

Havent you graciegirl.

I hardly ever take the train to drumchapel even though it goes near enough to wear we stay. Still it will be nice to walk along down through old drumchapel at least if the rain stays of. I can walk past saint benedicts church and the war monument which always has a wreath or some flowers there no matter what time of year it is. No body forgets in old drumchapel it would seem. If i was braver i would go to the old folks home up there and ask about work but i ament very brave not today any way. They might have some thing a register or some thing to sign and i can not do that so well with out my good glasses. I take a coin out of my pocket but i have already decided to go by train. I toss it and it comes up one or the other how would i even know. It is way to small for me to read. I decide it is sayen tails.

Just then as i set of there is a big crunch of thunder but still no rain. What the hell gracie i tell my selve the worst that can happen is i get a total soaken. I squint at the sky but it will not tell me any thing other than that it might rain. So then i just start walken along the pave ment and turn into anniesland road on the corner. Even i cant make a mistake about anniesland road it is a very distinct road with the kingsway flats on one side and near dumbarton road there is the grocer shop and the dumbarton road corridor adicshouns forum place beside it. I have been in there once a year or so a go to a group. It wasent one of annettes groups it was some body else. Bud dident like me goen to it though so i stopped the same as with annettes group in the drum libary. What do you want to do learn about computers for bud sayed. That was back when you could do things with out those machines in my job any way.

It isent like you use one at work is it he sayed. You dont use one at costigan house or any other effen time why do you want to go to a class. Your needed back here to look after the wean. Nobody else is goen to do it are they. He is your effen grandson isent he. He needs your help you cant trust vincent to do any thing can you grace. Francis has left him its up to you now. Vincent will just lie in his pit while the wee man runs riot. He could have an effen acsident or some thing.

So i dropped out be cause some body had to look after my grand son sean francis my daughter wasent up to the job.

The last time i saw my daughter francis was at the adicshouns forum. I left be four she could see me in there. I sneaked out of the door so my daughter wouldent be a shamed. She wouldent of reacted well to see me. She never does.

I can not even believe it has been so long already. 1 year and 21 days and how many more days will it be. How many hours.

She is comen back soon though i know. Bud knows to so does vincent. Now that tv camara knows to.

None of us says any thing about it though. We are all quite for the sake of sean. He is the only one that dosent know his mother is on her way.

Please god look after sean. Please look after vincent and sean and our francis.

Please bring her back. Please keep her away.

O gracie.

O grace.

I cross my selve and say a prayer for francis even though i told you i ament a catholic or religious any more like our mother. Thats all i can do and so what if it is all a super stishoun maybe it will help her it cant do any harm. It is not like i even say a proper prayer i dont know any other than the lords prayer. I just say i know you dont exist but if you do and im wrong then im sorry but can you look after my daughter francis and keep her safe away from us please. I will apologise properly if i can speak to you in person. Naturally if god does exist he isent goen to be fooled by that one but its worth a try any way.

Imagine if god spoke to you in person i say to my selve. That would be mad. If he did i would have to give him a peace of my mind for all the bother he has put me through. Even that old man mr tarick sarwar had his holy book there with him it must be a comfort. He showed it to me and asked me to read it to him i knew that would happen. The words in his book were forin. They were shapes like squigles. It was not my langwidge so it was okay that i couldent read for him. It made old mr tarick sarwar angry though. Im sorry i told him. It isent my langwidge i cant read it i sayed.

Alah shush on you he said.

That isent very christian is it i said.

Fugch you cow he said.

You or alah.

May owr profit destroy the house wear you sleep cow see.

You are an angry man.

Peas be up on him. Alah you fuchin.

I would of prayed to alah if i thought that he could help me. Of course he cant either he is just the same as the other god the same god neither of them any use. Still what harm can it do to ask.

So alah please help. You fuchin.

I find my way to the station without any problem and get on the first train that comes by since they all go to partick any way. Inside the caridge it is all redish and orange colours an old one i think. There is only one other person aboard that i can make out some one sitten with a paper in the chairs in front of me. The train slides of and we are on our way home the slow way. The trees go past and also houses which get more spaced out and bigger the farther along we go. The houses of people with a lot of money doctors and so forth. I wander who lives in these big houses. I have cleaned a few in my time done there toilits and kitchins. I dident mind i needed work. There was no bud back then only me and my daughter and my son and his father who i never knew well was not there either. That man never payed me any thing unless you count a bloody mouth. And left me pregnant in to the bargain.

I used to take francis with me to some of the houses francis who was small and quite and serious and looked at you with out fear isent that right gracie. She looked at you with out fear and stared right through you daren you dident she.

She sure did grace. She bunched her hands into fists at you. You were so stupid to think you could beat her grace. Marie your sister even told you. You can not fight that one and win. Not ever grace. You will come of second best every time. She was always smarter than you to wasent she. To smart for you to clever for her own good.

The voice comes on the tanoy and says this train is for milngavie the next stop is hillfoot. I panic a second because that is totally the wrong informashoun but it seems the recorden is faulty. When we get nearer to jordanhill station the tanoy says this train is for milngavie the next stop is hillfoot again. It is not just the wrong information it is the wrong effen line they are talken about excuse my swearen. It is then i think o dear grace you have went and annoyed god now he is tryen to put the wind up you. Well. I supose i do deserve it i shouldent of been maken my silly demands of him. He has a lot better things to be doen with his time except for gods sake gracie he doesent even exist i tell my selve. It is a faulty tape recorden is all it is. Get a grip of your selve silly.

It is lucky for me i know how many stops from jordanhill to partick ive traveled this route a fare few times. Even if i miss the right stop i just of got to get of and cross the line and go back one or to. That is the meanen of adventure our father used to say before he died. Even bud says it as well. Not knowen exactly wear your goen to end up or how to get back that is true adventure he would say. It is never as adventurous as you think but its better than goen back home in the middel of the day when you are suposed to be on holiday. I can get of and go to the shops and well not by any thing but look. Some one like annette or marie or michelle would window shop for fun except that is all i ever do. Now and then maybe once a year marie sends me clothes she dosent fit any more to wear. She is tryen to be kind i do like to receive these outfits on ocasion. Marie never really forgets me totally. She has given me dreses and blouses and things shoes even but i cant wear them be cause she is at least to sizes biger and there isent any occasion for me to wear them to. Still it is nice. They are some thing to put in the wardrobe and keep it warm.

Tickets the ticket man says. My father would of called him the clippey. Marie would of laughed at that. Our father would of done or sayed some thing funny. He knew every one that worked on the trains in those days. That was long ago in the past when he was a clippey himselve.

A single to hyndland please i say. I wish i could think of some thing funny to say some thing to make the ticket man think im a funny clever person. I can never think of any thing though. I ament funny except by acksident and im right fed up with that way.

Wear you comen from the man asks. The foxes are asleep look. We are comen in to hyndland station the train slowen down. What foxes i ask. More kinds of dog i think.

Ach youve missed them now the clippey says. Back there asleep on the bank of the rail way. Got to keep your eyes peeled or you will miss them. The urban fox.

O foxes i say. I see them all the time in drumchapel runnen about at night i tell the clippey although that isent quite true. If it is posibel i dont go out at night in drumchapel. I dont like the drinkers. I dont tell the clippey man this though.

Aye there asleep there on the bank every day to or three of them he tells me. Curled up. A wee family. You see them every wear at night now but seen them a sleep is not so usual. They dont bother about the trains at all.

He gives me a ticket and says i better get of the train this is hyndland now. So I get up and the train comes to a stop and straight away i bump my other hip into the row of chairs ahead of me. Just your luck eh gracie. Bang thump thats what our father called me to. It was either graciegirl or bang thump.

Here comes bang thump he would say. Watch your selve marie here it comes the runaway train bang thump gracie boats.

O marie.

Out there on the canary isles port adventurer.

Come home marie your needed here.

Your sister needs you.

Your sister grace.

O marie.

Here you are in the out side world again.

What would you make of your graciegirl now daddy i some times wander. Would you be proud. Would you be glad of her family here or ashamed of what a bad mother i have been at times. I dont know what you would of made of it. Was it your fault i dont know. I was not good at school you should of helped me or made me stay in stead of looken after you when our mother left and then later marie my sister. Then it was only you and me wasent it. Just bang thump gracie boats and roy the boats wanten all my atenshoun all the time.

Remember how you liked me to draw for you when i was a girl. You would of remembered that if you were still here to help me. You would of known what to do about my daughter francis. Should i let go of her. You would of known what to do about sean. Is it posibil to love some thing so much and not love it i wander. You would know. Just look at the mess you made of your life you would say. They should of taken you of with marie your sister.

You wouldent know how to help would you. No.

Per haps it is a reward for stayen that i can never go any wear it seems. Even that only time a way on the costa blanca marie wouldent let you stay with her in her apartment would she gracie. She had a man there so there was no room she asked me if i would mind finden some wear else just for the night. My first night a broad after marie got out. The both of us suposed to be to gether again. Some holiday that turned out to be.

Then again now years much further a head and your bag goen round the carousel on port adventurer the canary isles all alone. You cant even go on a holiday with out some disasteris events be fallen you.

Well this is hyndland stashoun and there are foxes near by. So stop your moanen graciegirl. Stop whinen you have just got to get on with it. You alone did not make your daughter francis a dependant. Every thing is not your own fault not all of it. You arent a bad person grace. May be you just made the same mistake as your father yours and maries.

You tried to keep things to close to you. So they wanted away.

You wanted them to stay with you and were jealous. That is all you have done its natural.

You were to rapped up with that bud you never cared you couldent see past him or the drink.

Bud is not a bad man you sayed to your selve. He is rough that is all. He has his own ways of relaten to people.

Well hyndland station and the rain seems about to come on it is spiten some what now. The sky is grey as any thing once again. There is not much use in tryen to look for the foxes with these glasses on now is there gracie. Not much of one i think but then no i see one. It is there on the other side of the train tracks lopen a long then another and another. It is hard to tell but there are two smaller ones and a big one at the front. It is odd they have got disturbed by some thing not the trains they must be used to. Boys i here some wear near. It will be small boys i shouldent think. They will have disturbed them with there racket. Foxes sleep duren the day and come out at night. Wee boys do the oposite they are natural enemys of one an other.

Then they are away sleekit is what they are and i smell coffy fresh coffy. There is a stand here on the plat form i would love a coffy. You dont even need desint glasses to see that that smell is so good. Any one can a blind man could.

I can just follow my nose to it.

How much is a small capo chino i ask.

A big solid semen girl says a pound and eighty five pence.

That is dear but i ament goen to come back from this trip emty handed. I have got my ticket now and can get back so i ask her to give me a capo chino.

Our father me and maries used to like coffy but not let us drink it til we were older. He had a sayen about it a song. See o eff eff ee ee coffys much stronger than tee. Better by far to be simply a drinker of tee. He would sing that some times.

What did you want to be when you were a young man i asked him once. If you dident work on rail ways what did you want to be.

He thought for a bit and said well i always wanted to play the piano. A piano player

That isent a job i sayed what job did you want to be.

You asked me what i wanted to be not what i wanted to work at he said. I would like to of played piano in a jazz group.

You could of done that couldent you i asked him.

No he said. I couldent have read the music. Maybe i could have been a piano tuner. They just use there ears dont they graciegirl. None of this messen about with sheets of dots and squigils. I am not much of a reader to be honest. But a piano tuner just goes from house to house tunen up the pianos and drinken cups of tea and chatten to difirint people. Dosent that sound nice.

Yes i sayed it does. I would like it i think.

There he sayed patten my hand. Let me rest a bit now gracie i am dead beat.

Ok i will bring some thing to eat for you later.

O dont bother your selve. I have no apetite. Theres a good girl.

So that is what i think of him as some times. A piano tuner. If he is any wear then he is goen from flat to flat drinken cups of tee and chatten and tunen pianos.

It is better than dead which is what he is.

Small capo chino says the solid girl. One pound eighty five.

I give her the change it is about right i think. I cant make out the coins to well with these glasses.

A penny short she says. I rumidge about. I dont have a penny i tell her thats every thing i have got.

A penny short she says.

I look at her. She looks at me. Then she hands me the coffee. You can owe the til she says.

Thanks i say. I head of to the other side to wait on my train and take a sip of coffee nearly burnen my tung of. It is effin hot. She has a cheek sellen it at that tempratchir.

On the next train home i stare out of the window and cant stop yawnen. I am always yawnen these days. I am always yawnen and fallen a sleep wear ever i go. I dream a lot but it is like when you are a wake odd be cause i dont sleep to well when i go to bed. Bud dosent make it easy to rest either wanten you know what or jumpen about in his night routines his maken the bed his routine.

Well. I ament to sure i would sleep even if i had the bed to my selve. Even goen through to littel seans room dosent help much. I am so care full not to smother him it is like i have fell a sleep on a window ledge. I am sertin if i dose of for a minute i will roll over and crush him to deth so i dont ever sleep i dont think not really. On this train yes i could but no clippey comes on so i wish i hadent bought a ticket i could of saved the money. Plus i also need to go to the toilit soon after drinken so much tea and the roasten coffy of earlier. It is okay though i can hold on til i get of the train. I have held on o so many times i have got holden it in down to a tea. It was a great coffy delishis so it would be a shame to let it go so soon that not right gracie.

That is to true i say to my selve. The coffy was great and delishous some things are.

There go trees out side but no sign of the urban fox in his naturel habitat towns yet.

How many times have you taken this journey i wander grace. It must be hundreds at least even though i usually get the bus. How many times have you gone past your old naybor hood and wandered about it. How it has changed. How the people who were there when me and my sister marie grew up there have probably all gone now. Our father is gone our mum is long gone no body knows wear. Some times i wander. It is no use though it would lead to hopen. After so long it would be daft to give in to the hopen even though it is always there to torment you. Well. What would bud say of course he would say it is a fight. It is always a struggel. It is always a fight gracie just re member. It is only one stop away as well from wear you are now.

Really it is only one stop drumchapel though you have all most never gone back have you graciegirl. Not after our father died and his house be came the counsils again. I can not even really remember our mother from that time. I try to think of her face. I can not what of her mind. She was all right she was okay. My selve to.

I look out of the window at the trees and the houses and stare at wear we grew up as the train goes out of the stashoun. Our mother was a beauty like my sister marie who my daughter francis takes after but not hard like my daughter francis. Thats what i some times dream of. She isent mean in my mind she is a loven mother a good mum to us. She dosent shout and threaten you with a knife. I dream she stays and our father dosent wallow in his own lonely mess.

Faithir. Or it could be fayther or even faith her. I dont know.

Marie would tease him with that name. She would tease him with his own sayens he used to ask us when we were small.

Faithir or fayther. If it takes a week to walk a fort night how long does it take to sand paper an elefant down to a grey hound. What is the answer.

Not now marie.

Or what is the difirins between a sparrow can you tell me faithir.

Marie. Give me peace.

Our father me and maries never moved from that place in knightswood. He only went from his chair to the bed he died in. That isent far to go if you are some one who has traveled all over on the trains with his work. Our father me and maries roy the boats never even went back to the emerald isle he was born in.

Other people would have gone further. Marie for instance your sister who wanted to be an ice danser.

For petes sake father sayed. Put some clothes on marie.

Some thing was funny about marie then not right.

For petes sake marie will you put some effen clothes on.

Marie my sister walken about with no clothes on the bare linoleum.

In the all together our father used to say. In the bare buff.

You arent a lassie any more he would say.

You arent a wee girl. Put some thing on.

And marie with all her goen out make up on doen one of her spins a pirowett a double axel of some kind on the red kitchen lino and with the sun shinen in the window in the afternoon. I watched her i thought she was a beauty. I thought she was the worlds most beauty full woman or girl. There isent any thing wrong with the human body she sayed to our father. It is beauty full we shouldent hide it.

The look on his face was difirint to hers my sister marie dident see what he saw. What he saw i was to young at that time but it was some thing not right about it. He must of knew then there was some thing not right about it. Except it is true she was beauty full she was like a holy thing come down through the light of the kitchen window to shine on us. Spinnen then slippen and fallen on the wet pool on the lino behind her all naked the sun shine laughen at me and him .

So he went out and got a blanket and wrapped her up in it o she screemed. She screemed effen see and scratched and effen kicked and he wrapped her up in the blanket. For christs sake grace go to your room he said. Get out of here. Except i just stood while he held marie my sister she was cryen and he was callen her a name. Not in my house our father was sayen not in my house do you here. He held her mouth between each word and her face was red with the words he was scwashen back in to her. Her mouth was scwashed in to a red bow. I couldent move though my mind was full of wander.

Then he was looken at me grace he sayed quite both of them down on the floor in a heap. Go to your room now grace theres a good girl. Your sister is upset. Go on now graciegirl.

Of you go and look at your story book or some thing.

Except i dident feel like looken at any story book. I dident feel like drawen or playen with my toys or any thing. I just pulled the bed covers over me and went to sleep wear it was warm and away from the light. I some times think i have been a sleep ever since. Some time duren the evenen i got up looken for a drink of water there was our father moppen the kitchen floor. Go back to bed gracie he sayed. I will bring you a drink. He spoke as though he was away some wear him selve as though he was no longer present. Marie was gone no wear to be found.

Marie left you stayed gracie that is be cause you cared more. Thats what our father sayed when he was ill o the sound of him dyen in that bed. You stayed be cause you cared more about your old dad more thats all gracie. I couldent make you go if you dident want to. Except after a while it was to late and stayen was all there was isent that right dad. You can wait to long the moment passes and you are left stuck.

Your ship sales with out you eh gracie. Is that not right roy the boats.

Yes.

Out side the window it looks like that rain is finally comen the sky is so dark o grace it is lucky you brought that plastic bag isent it. The train pulls up at drumchapel really old drumchapel near st benedicts and i footer about getten the bag out of my pocket. I can never be bothered carryen umbrelas i will likely lose it. Well it would be no surprise if some body could follow you about every wear you had ever went grace. They would be like bread crumbs for hansil and gretil all the umbrelas you have left lyen about in places. It is embarasen how many you have left lyen to go to waste.

Buds pal bobby has all sort of con spirasy theorys about the wether and the government and other forin countrys. He says likely the chinese get them all in the end umbrelas. He says just think about it. Just about every thing you have ever bought or thrown away is probably in the hands of the chinese right this minute. They are a mad lot for re sicklen dis carded rubbish which they made in the first place the yellow devels.

Ach shut up bud would say to him if he was there. Its just the wind like your full of bobby.

I was only sayen to grace bobby would say. You agree dont you grace. Its got a lot to do with the chinese.

Numpty bud would say.

I wouldent say any thing.

I roll the plastic bag up and wander if its made in china. It dosent say on it so i put it on my head and hold it with one hand to stop it fallen of. The sky is low and angry now all the trees by the stashoun are blowen about and the leaves and rubbish in the gutters beginen to get rest less. The wind is starten up but not a regular wind that just blows you. It is the kind of wind that just frightens you that some thing mad might happen. It is a july wind in the middel of febuary which is not right at all. It is global warnen i will bet.

It is the reason why we should of re sycled all your rubbish grace buds pal bobby would say. Global warnen ha ha. We should never have bought all they cheap clothes of the chinese. We should of bought local thought global that not right gracie.

It was july wether to that time vincent my son and francis

his sister run of and tried to lose you grace. There own mother. That was july wether in july but still. They ran away and left you lost. You had to wander back through drumchapel at night with out glasses.

It was hot though to wasent it gracie. Hotter than in years and so close. It was so close you felt like you would of sufocatid if you couldent get some air that not right.

My son and my daughter vincent and francis. Imagine tryen to get there own mother lost. It is that sort of wether today. Its the kind of wether wear your own children cant be trusted. O grace you shouldent even think of such things it isent any ones fault it is just the wether. It is just this wrong wether.

I walk down past the pub on the corner and go to the monument with the roses under neath leanen on it then theres a big crack of thunder and a few minutes later the rain comes on lashen down. It is comen down in mad fat hard drops it bullets on to me and my hand gets cold fast numb and then its starts thinen out and goen in gusts.

My hand is getten froze from holden the bag on my head so i decide to go back up the hill and shelter at the chippy near st benedicts til it passes they will probably not mind if i dont by any thing. I start to run and am bursten for the toilit by now but i also wish i had the money to get a chip role and a pick killed onion as soon as the vinegary smell hits me. As i get in the door of the shop i here a voice i reconise behind me.

Grace its you again i knew it. Look at this wether.

Hello annette i was just ducken out of it in here.

Well come on with me annette says. The group is just starten round the corner we can get a cup of tea.

This is just tipical of Annette. She dosent know when to stop sellen with some people.

Annette is flusteren about with a giant blue white stripey golf umbrela half taken it down half puten it back up again while the wind is blowen rain in to the chip shop in those gusts. I can here the wind rattlen her chip wrappen paper.

Come in or go out again will ye says the girl behind the counter.

I look about and the chippy has to or three others in it come out of the rain.

Are you getten any thing annete asks me and i shake my head not abel to think of any thing i can afford other than a few pickilled onions.

Well come on now round to saint benedicts. Annette grabs me by the arm and leads me away. I pull my hand back sharp may be to sharp she says oh.

Annette i say i dont like getten grabbed by people not even friendly ones like your selve.

Annette hold up her hands o im sorry grace. Your right i just forgot. Come in to saint benedicts out of the rain and take the bag of your head.

Then she laughs like she is goen to burst and i just stare at her face blurry from my steamed up glasses.

Well she says. Styled at tescos. You have to admit it isent the best look is it.

Rory you wanted to say some thing this week dident you annette says. Rory is an elderly man maybe 60 with a blue growth on the back of his neck that im glad i cant see to well this week. I have to admit some times it can be a blessen not to have my desint glasses with me. I just sit not even looken at any one just down at my nease and wipe the steam out of my specs. We are all in a half moon round a circuler table every one with pens and paper except my selve. Annette passes some paper a long to me and there are colored pens and more paper on the table all ready. When the paper gets to me i can hardly see the riten on it but it must be my own from last week.

Dident you rory.

Rory dosent say any thing to this but starts to stutter and then annette tells him its okay he can take his time. Another fifty years goes by and annette says shall we start with some one else just now and come back to rory.

I keep looken at my nease i dont want her to start with me. No one says any thing and then annette says sheila how about you. How have you been getten along this week.

I look up at sheila and back down again. She still has the yellow streek through her white hair and is agitatit be cause she can not smoke in the church hall. There are only me sheila rory annette nan and bridie here this week. That is to less than last time i was here a week ago. Dug and bren are gone this week. Well they wouldent have wanted to be here. They were neither over 16 or 17.

The church hall is drafty and smells of old peoples cloths and the wet dog which rory has brung in with him. It yowls suddenly it is sayen a loud what im thinken. Well. What can i do i have tried to let annette down gentle by not showen up but she some how always manages to catch me.

A bit better i think this week sheila says. I mean last week was my jordans birthday as you know. So that was hard.

How old would he of been annette ask. If hed been alive.

Well sheila says. He would have been 32. If hed been alive.

She makes a wee drawen in of breath and annette says its okay sheila just take your time.

How long had he been dependent annette asks.

Sheila sighs. He was dependent as long as i can remember. Ever since he was a young boy. He got in with a wrong crowd early on in life.

I look up at sheila. I would lay odds she is gaspen for a sigaret in this place so am i and i havent smoked in years it would drive you to drink.

So its been better this week annette says. Why is that sheila. Whats made this week better than last. Whats changed.

Well. Sheila says it isent his birthday this week so that helps. I dont know what else is difirint though. I have tried to look to the future not the past though it seems hard.

Annette says hmm yes. It is always hard. It is always a struggel to be the ones left be hind. How do you think your son would feel if he knew how this was affecten you now.

I listen for this my glasses cupped in my hands wanderen what francis my daughter might think if she knew.

Sheila sits up and crosses her legs. She has got on a brown skirt of some kind is it wool. Wool would be a comfort in this wether if it was ordinary wether for febuary and not july wether in febuary.

If he was here now he might feel bad about what its done to me. But hes gone some wear he cant feel any thing about it. So it dosent matter does it.

Annette says no thing for a moment then says yes. Is that really true though.

I can hear rory tryen to stutter some thing out and annette sayen wait now rory. Its true your son isent with us any more

Hes not with any one any more rory shouts at last and his dog yowls again. I can not quite make the dog out it looks like a black one of some kind.

Nan micknulty laughs and says o ha ha. Not with any one any more. My.

Annette says thank you rory for that.

Then there is quite and just tea spoons in cups and me dyen for the toilit except now dosent seem like the best time to go. What can i say i have always been rottin at ex cusen my selve at the best of times. I decide to give it a minute longer i will sneak out when there is a lot of talken and every one is interested in the sound of there own voice.

Sheila says i ament sure if he is with any one now. She sounds so sad sayen this like she is ashamed of it. She says i havent been sure in a long time though i want it to be true. Of course i do who wouldent.

I am not sure who wouldent annette says. I think every one wants to belief there loved ones are in a better place after there passen.

Sheila says but i still want him here with me.

She starts to snivvel a bit. She snivvels quitely and annette passes some thing i cant see what over to her a cross the table and i here her blow her nose.

Annette says to nan what about you nan how old would your to of been.

Nan micknulty is about 80 year old and cant talk about any thing with out laughen. If you say to her nan how are you she will go och you know ha ha getten by ho ho. It is just her way of dealen with it her troma annette has told me. Her eldest son was dependent and so was her daughter and they are both gone to. I cant see her to well today but i doubt she will be any bigger she is so small like so many elder lay of drumchapel.

Ha ha says nan he would of been och its either 50 or 51 i think. If hed of been alive today that is. Dawn would of been 47 ha ha.

If shed of been alive shouts rory. And wolf gang amma day is motsart would of been about 2 hunderd and effin 50 if hed of been alive today. What is the point of aw this effin rubbish he says.

Rory annette says in her best quiten your selve down voice. Calm down. We are only tryen to put nans childrens lifes in perspective. Talken about them is some thing people in here get used to not doen. In a sense nans children are a life be cause they are still a life to her. Isent that right nan.

Ha ha well no exactly.

Well do you talk to them. Do you think of them every day.

Eh ha ha i some times forget there no with me now. I some times think my neybour ewan is my son he re minds me of philly so much he he. I like to think philly and dawn are just away some place and theyll be back soon to tell me all about it there ex plorashouns. Instead of me goen away some place and maybe joinen them one day if im lucky he he.

Rory is stutteren and getten all worked up with his dog the same yowlen and girnen. It gets up and yowls and annette says does kylie need to go to the loo rory may be you should take her out side for a minute. In fact why dont we all break for another brew does that soot every one here. Bridie has brought jas min tea as well we could have some of that. You are a big fan of green tea to arent you bridie.

Effen green the point is what says rory

Every one here murmers and gets up to stretch there legs except bridie goodwin who is already out the door for a sigaret. Sheila will not long be be hind her.

It is an un fortunate name for her i think bridie. It is an old old persons name and she is only out of her teens plus she is even quiter than me. She has been that way ever since she found her mother and her mothers boy friend dead on the couch she was a dependent and so was the boy friend. They used to in volve bridie in there shenanigans annete told me. Bridie never says any thing but she is always here she has been comen regular for years not with her mother or boy friend of her mother just on her own.

Annette comes over and whispers do you feel like con tributen some thing this week grace. Then she takes a bite of some thing may be a biscit.

Every one else is waiten for the kettle to boil some are even talken in a quite way.

What can i say annette i am a bit short this week.

O you know what i mean annette says. Do you want to say some thing to the group this week.

I dont know about that. I ament really prepared for talken.

You dont have to prepare. Just speak from the heart.

Annette puts one hand on my shoulder and gives me a squeeze but it in no way helps. I nod and say no thing and annette pats me on the shoulder.

It might help you greve annette says.

It is one thing to say annette i say it is another to do.

Thats okay grace just say how you feel to the group.

I will have a think about it i tell her.

Okay grace she says just you have a wee think about it she says and goes quitely over to join the others maken tea.

What can i tell you. Between our selves i have been comen here on and of for ages. Bud dosent like my comen so i dont say any thing to him and only now i know i cant come longer. I just have to find a way not to let annete down.

Then i here her clap her hands and say shall we get started again has everyone got a fresh cup of tea.

Excuse me i tell her i have to go to the toilit and then i nearly trip over rorys dog.

Watch your selve there kylie he says.

Well. That is charmen. Not only have i got to look out for chairs and doors and steps but i have to watch out for animals to.

Mind wear you step grace he stutters at me.

Okay rory i say. Its just as well kylie isent a guide dog isent it.

Rory sticks a finger in my face about to say some thing but annette tells him to take a seat. She is very determin sounden and rory does what he is told.

Of you go then hurry up we will start in a minute annette says.

It is so dingy round the back of the hall wear the toilits are i have to feel my way a long with my hand on the wall. When i get in i can not find the light switch for the life of me and have to get in a cubicel in the dark. There is only yellow light comen from a small window very high up so i have to feel about in the dim ness to find paper to wipe the seat and lay all over it. What are you like grace i say to my selve. You are like a mad woman with your a blushins and your paper seat decorashins and your worry of germs.

It takes me ages to get up the courage to use the toilit as if some thing will jump up out of it and bite me as soon as i relax.

It is like i told you i must be cracked in the head.

You must be cracked in the head graciegirl. You have got it so you cant plant your effen bum on a public lavy seat with out maken it in to crismas.

I feel about at the sinks after for a hot tap but only cold runs so that will have to do me. I just try not to think of the germs from others who were here be fore which isent easy for some one like me. I fumble about and find the door and the world comes gogolen back with the light from the far end and voices. There is the hall way all bare wood or formica. I put a foot forward and straight of a step trips me up. Over i go and stop my selve with a hand but it makes one hell of a smacken noise. Up once again and dust of my hands which i just washed o what is the point i some times wander.

I get back round to the hall again keepen a hand out on the wall except this time i pick a difirint seat nearer to bridie at the back. It isent any use though. Annette pounsis as soon as i have got my selve composed.

Grace would you like to add any thing to that. Bridie was just sayen that comen here helps her come to terms with her loss.

I look at bridie. It isent like her to say any thing annette must have got her.

Isent that right bridie.

Bridie nods her head actually its more of a jerk.

Do you agree grace. Has comen here made any difirins as to how you deal with the grieve of your loss. You dont have to say any thing if you dont want but im sure every one here is very interestid to here about your uniqe situashion.

I doubt it i say. It isent so uniqe as all that.

Uh huh says annette. Go on.

I shrug. I havent got any thing to add i tell her.

There is silence for a minute annette letten folk think about things.

No body adds any thing so she says ok. Lets do some thing difirint.

I dredd this kind of thing this role play that i know she is goen to introduce from last week. I dont want to play a role or any thing like that. I dont want to draw a picture of how i am feelen or what i hope the future will bring.

You have all got what you did last week in front of you havent you annette says and every one murmers. What have you got bridie.

Bridie is next to me i can feel the heat come of her she is so worked up.

Rory is stutteren.

Rory a minute annette says. Let bridie speak. Its okay bridie take your time.

Bridie is twisten about in her chair i can not see her do it i can feel it of her the tenshin.

Rory is waven his arm about from the other side of the table. He is totally hyper. He stutters some thing every time bridie tries to speak. It it it he says.

Bridie exs hales and fans her hands to her face.

It it it rory is stutteren.

Bridie says i was goen to rite about this week comen she says.

This week now and how it was goen to be a good week. I was picturen it like we have been taught i was doen our chant in my head and every thing asken the universe for it to be good. I was goen to rite that last week except i couldent think how to rite it.

Thats interesten annette says. Go on bridie.

Rory is tryen to stand and annette is getten him to sit back down again except then he tries to stand again sayen it it it it.

Well that was all bridie says her voice all un even her breath not steady. I just couldent think how to rite that down.

You could of rote it like you just told us annette says. Couldent you.

Bridie says she suposed that was true she just dident know how and any way this week turned out to be not so great her healen prayer to the universe hadent worked so well.

It was effen shite this week rory explodes. Aw this asken the universe is effen rubbish. Look at it out side. It is pure pelten down. The universe is rainen on your parade bridie.

O ha ha says nan micknulty. Rainen on your parade ha ha ha.

Rory annette says. Calm down and let bridie speak.

The universe dosent give an eff about what you want he shouts at bridie who burst into tears.

Rory could you please stop annette says sharp and he shuts up sudden. Its okay bridie just take a moment okay she says. Grace she says turnen to me what about you how are you dealen with your grieve. What did you do last week.

Bridie is snivvlen be sides me and i have had enough just the same as rory. I shouldent be here with these people with there problems. I am in the wrong shop.

I dident do any thing i says. I shouldent even be in here.

Why is that annette says.

Its effen rubbish is why rory says.

Go on grace. Dont you need help like the rest of us.

I nod yes annette i say tryen to be nice. I do some times. But i dont need to grief for my daughter francis any more just now.

No one says any thing for ages.

Then annette says why is that grace. What is so difirint about you that you have no place in your heart for griefen.

Be cause i saw her i tell annette.

You saw her bridie says turnen to me. Your daughter.

Yes. I saw her. She is alive.

O says bridie it it says rory well says annette.

Oh ha ha says nan micknulty. Thats a good one alive ha ha. O you will be the deth of me so you will. Ha ha ha.

Annette drops me and nan micknulty of in her car even though it isent far for me. Nan only lives in the next street to st benedicts but she takes a lift if one is offired. Well that is fare enough. She is getten on. Annette drops nan of first and then we wait til she gets up the to steps to her flat an end terrace flat on the ground floor. I have never lived on the ground floor my selve. I have never lived be low 4 floors. Just now me and bud and my son vincent and littel sean are on the 7th floor for as long as the counsil wants us there. Of course only a few more years they say. Then they will pull down the builden and we will be moved again. So bud says. We have got 5 years max gracie he says. Then these big effers are getten pulled down. Just as well the state of them.

I try not to think about it my selve. It is almost to much the worry of it wear they will move to this time. Likely it will be farther out again so that we will be in the middel of no wear.

No wear bud says. Wear do you think we are now the middel of gay paree. The new york hilton.

It is our home bud i have told him it is no laughen matter.

All the time i wandered about our lifes. How will my daughter francis find me if we have to move. How will you ever know what happened to her if they knock down your house and you have to move away some place you dont know. O it is teribel to think of. Vincent my son vincent will leave he will join the army and we will never any of us be to gether again. Only me and bud and littel sean who will never see his mother. Only me and bud and littel sean who can not even remember her.

Annette drives the long way round my selve settled in to the warm of her car. It is gone 2pm now and the sky so dark and the rain comen in rushes then dyen back then comen in rushes. Neither of us is sayen any thing perhaps annette is angry with me i dont know why she would be.

Thanks for the run i say to her. Annette dosent say any thing back she is quite thinken i would think. She is thought full that way she dosent say any thing until she is sure of it. She is like the oposite of bud. She is definetly the oposite of my selve.

Grace she says after a bit. Dont take this the wrong way but you have sayed you have seen francis be fore havent you.

We slow down at traffic lights all this rain batteren on the wind screen the wipers swishen against it no use.

Youv thought youv seen her a few times have you not.

I nod i dont know what to tell her. It is true i have thought ive seen her in difirint places be fore now. At hecla square in drumchapel near greggs i was so sure it was her i shouted her name. In partick train stashoun on the other plat form getten on a train except i dident have time to shout. Another time i thought she was be hind of me in a q at the shops except i was afraid it was her this time. I dident try to speak or look at her i just felt she was be hind me. But why would she be here i kept sayen to my selve. Why would she be here if not for littel sean and i left that q with out turnen to look and crossed the road back to our flat up the hill my heart jumpen in side of me. Bud i sayed when i got in bud wear is sean. Has she been here. Has she taken him.

O bud wear is sean and then i saw him playen on the floor just as normal just the same. Gracie bud was sayen gracie calm down he is all right the wee man is fine. That not right sean. You are grand there arent you.

Yes i say to annette. It is why it is to early for griefen. I saw her today even if it wasent her those other times. I cant belief she is gone just be cause it is best to think that way.

Annette says grace it has been over a year. Dont you think you would of herd from her if she was okay.

Annete is right of course you would of herd some thing gracie. That is un less she dident want to be found if she dident want any one to know she was still a round.

What can i tell you annette i say. She is a dependent. She dosent think like you or me would in her situashoun. Perhaps she dosent want to be found or perhaps she left our city. Perhaps she dident want to come back until she was ready.

Okay annette says. Okay grace. If you think you did then maybe you did.

I dont think i saw her i saw her.

Okay annete says laughen a bit though i dont know whats funny to her. If you say you saw her then you saw her.

I did see her annette. I would know my own daughter wouldent i.

Of course you would. I just wander.

Why do you wander.

I just wander wear on earth goes the sort of a mother that dosent try to see her son for over a year. Thats how long its been isent it grace. Its been over a year.

I dont know i say to annette. It has been 1 year 21 days 14 hours and 46 minutes. I dont tell annette that though. I kept it to my selve.

What sort of mother would not see her son for so long.

Maybe one who is dependent.

Uh huh annette says. That would probably do it.

We turn round kinfauns drive and along to the next set of lights the street light already on some of them. It is so dark out. I cant even see the tele phone wires above our heads the ones that have pairs of shoes and boots slung over them from childrens games. I know they are there though. I have seen them in the past it is usual to see several difirint pairs hangen down. I wander why. Who can have the money to let there kids throw shoes away no one will ever get them back down. It makes me think of when marie and my selve were young in our fathers house there was a tree below the liven room window. I used to think when i got big enough i could lean out and touch its branches but i never did get so big to do that. Our father used to hang cloths of ours from the kitchen window he would jamb them in it so they would dry. He was not so house proud once our mother me and maries left. There was dust and dirt every wear and dishes always in the sink. It seemed there was no end of laundry washen in the bath we had no machine. O and my sister marie and my selve bathed in with the washen often.

All year round the tree was there just out of reach so it wasent any surprise when some cloths a pair of red under pants got blown from the kitchen window on to that bare tree. In winter they froze solid in the branches for years those red under pants hung up there like a flag. Our father roy the boats used to ask if it was fine out or blowy.

Which direction are they underpants pointen he would ask to our laughter. Is it a north wind marie. Is it an east wind grace. Which way is the wind blowen.

He did try to fish them in with a mop handel but they were not easy to get. The naybours across the landen misses brown and lees used to complain of the sight of them. They are an affront those underpants misses brown and lees would say. We are black affrontit every time we see them. You ought to be ashamed so you should. And you should get that girl to cover up always runnen around half naked. At her age to.

Well our father me and maries dident like to be told what or not to do so he told the misses brown and lees to mind there own and he would mind his.

I am black affrontit to have to old mades liven together up the same close as my selve and my girls he told the misses brown and lees.

O sayed misses brown and lees.

And theres no thing wrong with the human body either. She is nearly a grown woman how can i tell her what to ware.

O teribel sayed misses brown and misses lee con cured.

So he just left the red pants up in the tree. He sayed they could be the barcos flag no body was goen to tell him that his red underpants were a black affront. Roy the boats barcos and marie the boats and gracie boats there flag is always at full mast be cause we are a team arent we he used to tell us.

Were a team arent we graciegirl he sayed to me even after marie my sister had gone and our mother as well long be fore. Its just you and me now gracie. The to of us. But were the best kept secret any way arent we.

It was true in his mind that we were doen okay even with out marie my sister or our mother who was gone.

Well then here we are says annette your stop grace.

Thanks annette i say you have saved me from a soaken.

Ahem excuse me says annette. I have saved you twice in to days actually.

O thats right. You spotted my espadrill. And you drove me home. You are right thats to times.

I go to open the door and get out i have my plastic bag ready to cover my hair when i make a dash for the front door of our flat ours and the counsils except then annette puts her hand on my shoulder she sits me back down again. Next she takes my hand in her to and squeezes them she is close to me i can smell her perfume v strong in my noze.

We can still save you a third time if you let us you know. It isent so hard just to make that leap youll see.

I just sit and am conshous of my hand in her own hands not knowen what it is meant to be doen with it selve. Should it just sit still and wait or should it be doen some other thing.

I dont know annette i ament sure what to tell you.

Annette sits there not sayen any thing just holden my hand stroken the back of it. I dont say any thing either just sit there waiten for it to be over.

Annette sighs after a while.

Okay she says. Okay grace. I will let you go on home now.

I look at my hand she is still holden it.

Thank you i say. Im sorry.

Her hands fly apart suddenly and let me go and i slide of the seat in to the rain.

Annette is sayen some thing after me i cant make out. What is it i say about to close the door.

You know grace one day the spirit will just leap out and grab you. It will grab you and it wont let go and you will be power less to resist it. Thats what the spirit will do and you wont have any say in the matter grace. Then you will know true grace grace.

Okay annette i say. Thank you for the advance warnen.

Your just determined to fight it arent you she says sounden a bit dis appointed.

I dont know about that. I just have no ex periens with the spirit thats all.

Okay grace. But a bit of faith would help you no end. Like

with your other dificulties they would benefit from some faith to. It would help with that. You have to believe you can do a thing to be abel to do it. Faith in some thing other than your selve can give you that strength to carry on with present hard ships.

I dont under stand what you mean.

The readen and riten grace. We could help with that at the group. There are things that can be done about it.

I feel my ears get hot straight of when annette says this and i have got no anser for her. Even though i know that annette already knows i am still a shamed as usual.

I know you dont like to here it sayed out loud like this annette says. But admitten you have a problem is the first step to finden a solushoun. Well the church can help with that to. Just say you will think about it. We arent goen to try and brain wash you or any thing. We just want to help. That is what we are for.

I dont know i say after a bit. I have tried be fore.

You need the strength to keep on tryen. Thats what we are for we are here to support you. We are here to lend you some strength when you feel weak.

I would like to i tell annette but it isent so easy especially when bud dosent like me goen to groups.

Well look she says. We just wont tell him. How does that sound.

I laugh. It sounds grand but it is asken for troubel. Bud isent any dafty he will find out.

Let me think about that one for a while annette says. You just think about comen along on Monday.

Can i bring my grand son i ask her.

Theres no cresh grace. We dont have funds for one just now.

He can sit on my lap he is a quite wee boy.

If your sure that he wont bother the others.

He wont annette.

Then is it a deal.

If i can bring him it is a deal.

Whatever you say she says. Good. See you on monday then. See you i say.

She pauses a second be fore shutten the door over. I am beginnen to think she is never goen to leave me alone what else can she want now and the july wind in febuary is flingen my hair all over the place. I am getten wet standen here plus what if bud comes along. He will give me hell for talken to annette. No thing is surer than his temper goen of as it is want to do.

Grace. It would be a good thing if your daughter came back. Francis i mean. No matter what youre a fraid might happen. It will still be a good thing. Okay.

I know i say i am just bein stupid. Of course it would be good to have her back.

So long as you keep that in mind then.

I nod to her of course i will keep it in mind even if it is not so simpel.

At last she shuts the car door. I stand there i dont know what i have done to offend her. The engine burrs into live a gain and the car is pullen away. I un roll my bag half way over my head it is still lashen down. This july wind batters my tesco hat so I have one hand against my head keepen it on. It seems like the rain comes in swooshes with no fixid direcshoun. Now it is comen from north now east. Now it is comen from south then west all at the same time. You can almost see the patterns it slashes on the ground then they are gone and new ones are getten made and disapearen all be fore your eyes even if they are stuck be hind old glasses. The early light from the street lights makes the rain flash and flutter if you see it from the corner of your eyes there is even a rain bow by the door of our flats and the counsils. Could it be your glasses that made you see a rain bow i wander gracie. Was it really there maybe others saw it or was it re fractid from your lenses. Well. Who knows gracie. Not you any way dafty. There isent any thing in your head silly.

I stand and wait for the lift to come down there are no boys about so good. There is no one around to give you any bother not that they always do. It is probably a prejudis of mine. Bud would wave his stick at them and act like a maddy they would just think him nuts thats how he gets away with liven around here. Woah here comes that mad guy they must think. He is of his rocker waven that walken stick about. Out my road bud will say. Bud spence express comen through woop woop. Yous lads better watch it the bud spence express slows down for neither man nor beast. Out the road numptys woop woop woop.

I hate it when he does this im terrified they will catch on and bring him down it would be easy. Bud is all racket and smoke and mirirs he is the wizard of oz so long as no body stands up to him. One day they will it has happened be fore. Till then he will likely just go on with the bud spence express show.

The light is flickeren on and of in side this lift it gives me goose pimpels on my neck some thing to do with the strange wether maybe. Still the door opens at the right floor which is dingy as any thing but even in the dark with no glasses at all i could find our door. Still i hesitate to step out with the light flickeren and no body to be seen even if my eyes were good enough to see them. All i can see is shadows at the best of times just gostes. Any body could be up here waiten for some one unsuspecten like me to come buy.

Well. Even as im tellen you this the lift door slides shut and nearly traps the back of my coat but i snatch it away just in time be fore the lift goes down again. Or up. I dont know which. It is a deth trap this builden it has always had it in for me. Some times i think it will be good when they tear this place down and we are put some wear else if they dont just throw us all out on the street i wouldent put it past the counsil. Bud has been goen up to there offices on and of for over a year tryen to get us a better place nearer the ground. Unfortunetely he is just him selve i am no use to him.

Gracie come on we have got rights here he says to me. You an me we should be on a ground floor flat with an extra room. It isent right for the wee man to sleep in a cup board is it.

I have told bud it isent just a cup board its a walk in ward robe but he just snaps.

It is an effen cup board with a bed 8 times to big for the wee man in it.

Well. Bud is right but sean is littel it will be years be fore he minds. He can play on the bed just as well as on the floor i think well he has no choice so whats the point in getten upset about it. Vincent will go spare if we put him back in there with him and it isent a good environ ment for a toddler. Vincent is nearly a man he needs his own space his own things about him.

He needs a kick up the arse bud says. You let him get away with murder so you do gracie.

I know bud is right about that to but i was hard with francis look wear that got me. She is gone she is dependent and we have littel sean to look after. You tried with the first one dident you gracie i say to my selve putten the key in the lock. You tried with the first one and no body tells you how its done. No body gives you a class on how to bring them up. So you try again with the next one even though you dont know if you did it right with the first one. And you dident get it right did you grace you were to hard on her you tried to fight her all the way. What a thing to think would work. No body can fight francis. Only a numpty would even think that was goen to work.

So what if vincent is spoilt and treats me like dirt. He is only a teen age boy they are all like that. It will pass. All you have to do is wether it like the rain gracie. It is like july wether in febuary it will pass even if it never seems to stop. It is just the same. Until it passes you will just be a libel ity to your son vincent the body. He will be ashamed of you and that is okay. He will laugh at you with his friends but thats okay to.

So what if him and francis your own daughter francis tried to get you lost that time. You asked for it graciegirl. You owed them a better life than the one they have got. So quit feelen sorry for your selve gracie. Quit your silly moanen graciegirl.

It is quite in the flat theres no one in yet. Not even my son vincent who often brings his friends back though i dont like it when he does. Well. What can i tell you they are a rough lot not only vincent is obsesed with joinen up. I pick up some mail from the door but dont open it i will let bud. I am afraid of openen letters they are a terror for me. I havent debts but theres always money to be paid for some thing that scares me since we are always so broke. Of course bud has had some money troubils to in the past he has owed people who dont send letters. The kind of people bud owed just let there dog lose on you. What can i say i have never been to keen on dogs now bud is the same. He gives them as wide a berth as possibil now i can feel his hole body stiffen when we come upon a dog. I dont have to be touchen him either i can feel it just through close ness to him.

He dosent like you to menshion it though. I have sayed bud its okay he will growl at you. I know its okay im not an effen ten year old he will say.

The flat is so peace ful with no one home. Bud will be down at play school waiten for littel sean he will be kicken about with bobby his pal. I ament to keen on bobby but they have been friends for years. It is hard to trust bud not to start selve medicaten with a pal like bobby it is always a risk.

I go in to the kitchen and put the letters down on the work top. Bud will read them for me we will club together to pay whatever it is that needs to be payed for counsil tax or electrc or gas we dont have a phone any more. It got cut of but its better this way i was afraid of it ringen and some one i dident know answeren at the other end. Always it seemed to be some one wanten money for some thing. To have a phone is a horror to have letters come through your door is a horror. Now vincent answers calls for me on his mobile except i some times find out days later that some one called. My sister marie for example. She might call from port adventurer canary isles and i wouldent know if vincent dosent bother to tell me about it.

Just then who comes in the door but vincent. I can tell be cause of the weight of his steps comen down the hall. He goes past the kitchen and just says alright then straight on to his room. What can i say it is just typical be haviour for him these days. All the men in this house either grunt at me or are effen and blinden there isent any in between. Vincent i call to him but he has already shut his door be hind him selve.

I put the kettil on for a tea and stare out the window at the sky so dark so early in the day. Vincent i shout again but he cant here me he has his stereo on playen that rotten music of his. It is some sort of horribel techno music that i would be embarased to be caught playen. Bud calls it nosebleed techno it is all high pitched helium voices and cheesy shouten over horribel plastic beats. No one who isent 17 can listen to it and think its good. I go down the hall and knock on his door but no body ansers. I knock again and then open it a crack. He has the music on loud and is lyen on his bed with his shirt of suroundid by all his wreck age.

Vincent i say did my sister marie call yet.

He dosent look over he has his eyes shut.

Vincent i say again louder. Turn it down please.

This time he looks over what is it he says.

Turn it down vincent. Please.

Effs sake he says am listenen to it.

Just turn it down please it is blasten out.

He sits up and turns his stereo down. I can see how much he has grown up even in the last few months his boys body is a mans now. He looks like all he does is go to the gym even though thats not the case. I am speech less for a second i cant believe he came from my body. He must get it from his father who ever he was. I dident know him very well francises father either. I was fool ish with men in those days i went for the ones who i thought could get me some thing. None of them did though. They all left. Except bud he stayed he has a good heart. He stayed be cause he cared more. Also he was heavily medicated he wasent capable of leaven.

What is it he says he looks stoned or like he has been drinken. What ever it is i dont want to know i cant stop him from doen what he wants.

Did my sister marie call yet.

Eh aye she did. I forgot to say. This mornen. She sayed can you call her tonight.

Did she sound angry vincent.

He shifts about scratchen his arm and stroken his belly.

Naw man he says. She sounded like she was expecten it. She just sounded disappointed man.

O.

Vincent sees i am wellen up im goen to cry and he looks afraid.

Listen you can use my phone he says. I can leave it here for you im away out later.

O thanks vincent i say thats a great help. It would mean an awful lot to me son. Just as vincent surprises me with his considerashoun i surprise my selve by nearly keelen over in a faint.

The next thing i am aware is vincent looken in my eyes

scared scared.

Mum he is sayen mum are you okay.

It takes me a minute or to to get my faculities back together. I am not quite sure wear i am in the room for a bit then i see i am sitten on vincents bed. As soon as I am abel i start to snivvle do you have a hanky i ask vincent and he jumps about looken for one. He hands me some thing it looks used no thanks i tell him your all right. Instead i wipe my eyes on my sleeve. I can not help it but i can only imagine a teen age boy usen a hanky for one thing.

You okay mum vincent says again.

Yes i tell him i am okay now. I havent really eaten today my stomack is to nervy.

You want some water or any thing.

No im okay vincent. Thanks for taken the message.

No bother he says and i get up. A bit shaky still and ive got a sweat on. Some times it is beter to have people angry with you than disapointid. I know marie my sister she will find this hard to take.

Want me to make you a bit of toast or some thing vincent asks. Well. It must be the first time he has ever ofered to make any thing for me and i have to laugh. O vincent i say.

Whats funny he says all defensif.

Just you. Look at all these muscles your sprouten your getten to be a man now.

He laughs yeh he says. I need to get some new cloths every thing i have is neat on.

Well okay i say. But things are a bit difficult at the moment.

He nods. He is used to hearen this still it isent nice to have to always here it.

Vincent has gone quite.

How about the end of the month i tell him even though i know no thing will be difirint then. He wont ask i know him he will wait and wait and i will have to disapoint him like every one else.

Okay then i say to him. I will leave you to it just now.

He nods again and i get up to go.

How are you getten on any way i ask be fore i go. Is every thing okay.

Aye man its all good.

Are you haven any luck finden work.

Nah man. Theres no work about here.

You could see if bud knows if any body needs some body. He knows a lot of people.

He cant even get him selve a job how can he get me one.

Well you arent dis abled are you. Bud walks with a stick in case you hadent noticed. Im sure if you asked he could find you some thing.

Im no asken him for no thing.

Then i just stand there quite and vincent sits there quite. We are likely at stale mate with this one.

You know he is all right really i tell him. If you tried to get to know him you would see that. Look at every thing he does for littel sean. He will be down at that play school waiten on him now when its me that should be.

Then how come your not he says.

Well of course i dont have a good answer for that. How can i tell vincent im afraid. How can i say i am afraid that i will lose him that his own mother will come and take him and then he will be done for. I cant tell vincent that or any one else. They would think me a bad mother except i ament his mother i just look after him for his own mother who is dependent.

Be cause i had to go and see if i could get any shifts at work if im not away to the canary isles. So i can buy cloths for you to wear.

Whatever man. Im still not goen to be mates with that guy.

Hes cracked in the head.

Hes not so cracked that he thinks joinen up is a good idea i say then regret it straight away.

At least it would get me away from this shit hole he says.

O vincent i say. I wish you wouldent talk about joinen the army. I have lost one daughter i couldent stand to lose a son as well. At least tell me you will think about it properly be fore you do any thing.

Vincent dosent say any thing he takes a shirt from of the floor and puts it on.

Vincent i say.

What.

Promise me you will discuss it with me first be four doen any thing.

He grunts.

Vincent promise me.

Okay man effs sake i promise.

Good thank you.

I go out the door and close it quitely already vincent has turned his music up again but not to the volume of be fore which is a blessen i supose. I go through to get my tea from the kitchen and wait for bud to get home with littel sean. I think about marie my sister on the canary isles port adventurer waiten for me at the air port then haven to go back home all alone. I wander how she is if she is well if she is still a beauty like in our past. She will be nearly 50 so she must have changed a lot. She has sayed in our few conversashouns how she has put on wait but i cant picture it not really. I only see the girl who danced on the red lino spinnen around and around and then our father coveren her up with the duvet. And her screechen to let her go the human body is beauty full the human body is beauty full we shouldent hide it. We should display it and be proud. Our father dident see it like that though. But that was be four she went to the hospital. That was when she had her hole life ahead of her.

There am i again in seans cup board room tryen to make it nicer when there goes the door and bang thump laughen and mens voices buds voice and another. Then comes a squeal of a child it is littil sean. I here them humph about in the hall talken but i will have to wait to get out this cup board since when the front door is open you get stuck in side just like the place me and marie my sister grew up in. Well. One of the places we grew up in we moved about a lot.

Bud i say is that you but of course it is him. Who else would come in usen a key.

Hullo there grace says an other voice. Long time no see sweet heart.

The door of seans cupboard opens a bit and i see two faces looken at me. Bud and bobby.

Come one out of there bud says i can smell the drink of him out his every pour. Bobby to. His face is leaner than last time i think. Yes.

Seans face presses against the crack in the door to laughen.

The door shuts so they can get properly in to the hall and close the front door. Then they open the cup board door again and i squeeze out till bud grabs me and presses his cold face against my cheek o lovely and warm he says.

His clothes are sodden and smell of stale wet smoke. I have to stand there while he hugs me then sean tries to squeeze between.

I touch his wet hair it is so soft his curls francises curls.

Bud kisses me. O you are reeken of booze i tell him. Wear did you get the money.

Bobby is quite i cant tell who is responsible for this. It could be either.

Bud jerks his head backwards at bobby.

Your man won a couple of quid on the horses. So we thought a wee celebrashion was aproprishous. Its just a wee bottle of whisky grace. We havent been goen daft. That not right bob.

How are you grace bobby says.

I am all right bobby and your selve.

Good grace good. Then he goes quite. It is a while since bobby came up here to our house.

Well bud says. I thought you were comen down the park with us today. How come you never showed.

I was busy i tell him. I couldent of come if i wanted.

Aye you must have been snowed under there at that place says bud.

Bud i says. Stop showen of in front of bobby

Ach bud says and then trudges on through to the liven room. Bobby shrugs he looks abashed i think though i cant be 100 per cent sure since the bulb has went in the hall.

Sean thunders along after bud his hero.

Every thing okay grace bobby asks.

Yes bobby every thing is okay.

I walk ahead to the liven room. Bud i say i need to talk to you.

Except he has already got his makens out he is rollen a joint and tryen to tune his guitar one handed the bottle of whisky there on the coffee table open. Bud i say im talken to you. I can here bobby come and stand in the door way he doesnt know weather to come or go.

Bud i say.

Grace.

I need to tell you some thing please.

Wear were you grace. Me and sean were waiten on you werent we wee man.

Sean is looken up at him from the other side of the coffy table.

Bud slumps back in the sofa with his joint and lights up starten to strum his guitar. Now i know there is no point in talken to him. He will not even remember it.

Take a pew bob man he says.

And that is when bobby saunters in and sits down taken a drink from the bottle on the table.

Oof he says droppen onto the couch. My feet are killen me.

On raglan road in september bud sings way of tune. Bobby nods along and sean claps his hands on the coffy table.

You know this one grace bobby asks.

I saw her first and knew bud sings. He has found the right key now.

That her dark hair. Would weave a snare. That i would one day rue. Thats you graciegirl. Your own dark snare ha ha. Would weave a hare.

You know the words gracie bobby asks laughen.

Yes i tell him. I know all the words. Ive heard them all before.

One singer one song bobby shouts and i get up and take sean by the hand. Come on then sean. Time for your dinner.

Gracie bud shouts after me. Wear you going. I just ignore him.

There carousen goes on till bud falls asleep on the couch. It is still early though not even 10 o clock. Littel sean is in bed asleep to vincent is out that leaves me and bobby. Bobby is not so drunk as all that he dosent drink like bud. He just always drinks in stead. When bud is snoren away he talks to me low and quite like he used to.

Dont you want a wee drink grace he says. Your not still off it are you.

Yes i tell him. It has been a year.

Thats good. Thats great. I wish i could say the same.

He says this even as he lifts his glass to his mouth. Bud stirs in his seat and nearly knocks over his guitar except bobby catches it and rights it against the wall.

A whole year he says shaken his head.

We are quite for a bit.

Im about done with it my selve he says. Or it is about done with me one or the other ha ha.

It is not always what its cracked up to be i tell him. Some times i wander if i will go mad with out a drink. I think i would like to get good and drunk some days bobby. I would like to get so drunk that i forget every thing in my life i forget bud and sean and francis and vincent and you and costigan house and marie and my glasses and this house. I would like it all just to go away.

Bobby sits looken at me.

Give me a drink bobby i says.

Except he just sits there.

Bobby give me an effen drink.

Grace maybe thats not such a great idea.

Bobby how long have you known me.

I dont know grace.

Its a long time though isent it.

Aye i supose.

Give me a drink bobby.

Grace think.

Bobby.

All right. Here.

He gives me the bottil over and i fill up buds empty glass.

Take it easy on that stuff will you.

I pour the whisky in to the glass and swirl it. It has been a whole year nearly as long as francis has been gone. I drink the whole lot down in one go and i can feel it spread it selve through me and then it is up in my head high up pushing out through my four head and i close my eyes and give in to it..

We are quite in the room bobby sayen no thing. I can feel him looken at me though. I can always feel bobby looken at me.

Bud shifts in his sleep shouting and barks at his dream.

Hes some man bud eh. Some sleeper.

Yes i say. He is always like that drunk or not.

I pick up the bottil and pour an other drink and bobby says eh hold on a minute there grace you sure you should be doen that. Ones enough is it not. After all this time. It will knock you for six.

I dont down this one though i just sip. I dont like the taste so much i always pre fer a sweeter drink like a rum and coke or even lemonaid. The feelen is good though. My eye sight and my mood match when i have a drink i am boyed along by it. It dosent matter having bad eyes and out of date glasses just now. I can feel things begin to ebb away just as i take one sip after an other. I can feel bobby staren at me i can make out the glow of his joint even in this dim room.

I here vincent come in then close his door and bring the glass close to me so he can not see it from the door be cause my back is in the road. I know him he will never come in to the room not with bobby and bud both here. Only if for some reason sean needed some thing only if littel sean was here to.

Im away out he says.

Okay i say.

But he dosent go he waits.

Marie dident call he says. I need to take my phone with me now.

Thats okay vincent thank you any way. I guess it is late for her now.

I have my back to him and look over my shoulder.. He is big in the door frame to big for this small flat.

Bud roars out effen bees you lot and then shifts again

Bobby laughs. It is nervis laughter.

Some state bud eh he says.

Is he going to stay there all night vincent asks me. But it is not a real question. It is him wanten trouble.

I dont know vincent likely he will make his way to bed eventually. Why.

Vincent is surly he dosent want to say to me. I dont need good eye sight to know that.

Hes wanten on his x box arent you vinnie bobby says.

Shut up bobby i say what is it vincent tell me.

I half turn a round care full to keep the glass hid from him. Vincent i say to him.

He huffs. Just dont freak out or any thing he tells me. Hes just comen up to talk to me about it thats all. I havent signed any thing yet.

O vincent what is this what are you thinken.

Its just a chat thats all man.

A chat with who about what vincent o it is the army i know it.

Its not the army effs sake. I knew this would happen.

Who is it then who is comen here. Tell me vincent. Tell me please.

It is just a guy i know who used to be in the forces. He is goen to tell a few of us what its like. Its not just me.

I try to be calm about this. I try not to panic. Grace you have got to calm down i tell my selve. You are his mother. You will drive him away if you dont. You have lost one child already you dont want to lose another. O but the army. There are wars on and you lost francis but now she is alive she isent lost maybe not totally. Like comen back from the garscadden woods we were lost but not totally you dident totally lose them grace. Not that time not finally.

Hes just a guy who knows the score. Hes not like even in the army any more.

So how do you know this man vincent how old is he even.

Vincent shifts about.

He is about 35 or so i think. He was in the guards.

What guards what is that.

The dragoon guards it is a unit in the army. He is retraining.

So how do you know him he is to old for your friends isent he. Why would you trust some one of that age.

Its not like that. He is in comunity work now he says.

O he is a drug dealer then is he. That is all the comunity work that goes on round here.

Effs sake vincent says. I shouldent of told you. It is a waste of time talken to you about these things.

I turn right round to look at him and spill the drink be fore i know it i am soaken wet.

Here dont worry about that grace i will get a wet cloth from the kitchen.

Thank you bobby i say then just sit there dumb with the glass in my hand. Slowly I put it back on the table as bobby gets up and goes to the door.

Me and vincent are alone.

He does not say any thing for a few seconds.

I dont say any thing either. I can not bring my selve to look at him.

Vincent i say at last.

Dont he says. Dont even say any thing. I cant believe this. Why should i listen to a word you say about any thing. You can not be trusted with any thing.

I can not think what to say. He is right.

Im out of here he says and turns to go.

Vincent i say. Wait.

But he dosent wait. He goes leaven me it will be no use to follow. I hear the front door bang shut. I put both hands up to my face and hold my head o he is right. Vincent is right it is what they always tell you. You can not trust a dependant. There words are not true they will lie even when they mean not to lie. They will tell them selves what they say is true and that they mean it even as they lie right to your face.

It is late at night. Wear can he go i wander. Who will take a boy his age a man in to there house at this time of night. No one i would think. He must just wander the street. It is a wild night out to be wanderen empty streets with just your friends. Of course there isent any need to worry for vincent my son he can take care of him selve. Except you do dont you grace. You will worry any way. Well. All he wants is for you to here what he wants. It is better he is talken to you about it isent it grace. Yes. But the army. It is the army the guards he wants. This man will tell him it is o so great. It will be all adventures and playen with guns and then its best not to think what. Wear will they even send him these days do they still go to northen ireland the emerald aisle. That was wear our father me and maries was from. Was it the northen part or the emerald part i dont know i dont re member the name of wear. He used to be funny about it sayen he was irish but dont let on. Or was it northen irish. But dont let on.

I remember asken him wear he was born and wear had he lived.

Acht all over he sayed. We never stayed put for long.

Did you go to school i asked him.

I was never in the school to tell you the truth. I was no good at my books but i have never needed them. Your better of with out all that non sense graciegirl.

Marie dident believe him they fought so much when she was older. She liked to go to the school our mother wanted her to stay there for us to stay put in one place not be on the move for ever.

There better of here he would say. Our mother argewd they fought from what i remember. Our father and marie were always butten heads.

The rest of your family the barkers they worked wear ever in the world they could get it our father sayed. They all had to leave. Who knows wear half of them ended up eh gracie. Some went to scotland some to england they followed work. Do you know the name barker grace.

Yes i told him it is our name.

Well it might be an older name even than from the emerald aisle.

Older from wear.

I ament sure gracie. But i heard it might be a spanish name or portugese. So may be we are all from much further a field than even the emerald aisle of northen ireland.

What does it mean then our name i asked him.

I dont know gracie. Some one told me once it was like a word for boat. Ho. That was when i was worken the ferrys they all thought it was funny. Roy the boats they called me and i liked it enough to let it stick. If i dident like some thing some one sayed about me in them days they would know about it. But i liked roy the boats well enough. Its more my own name now than my own name.

That is good i sayed. I like roy the boats.

And your gracie boats my girl.

Thats good i like gracie boats.

Even when he was dyen in that bed he called me gracie boats. Im off soon he sayed taken the ferry once again ha ha. Your a good girl gracie. Stayen with me. Gracie boats and roy the barker. The fair ground barker eh gracie. Round and round we go eh.

Even after he had gone on o wear to grace what are you talken about. Theres no wear to go on to. He just died that is all. You were left. O that is non sense as well you werent left. He could only of left you if he had been goen some wear and he never went any wear. Your mother got taken away your sister marie left to and you dident you stayed. Our father me and maries just died. He just died.

Bobby sticks his head round the living room door.

Every thing okay grace.

Yes i tell him. It is okay. I just worry about vincent.

Bud shifts in his sleep.

Oof he says and looks up his eye lids flutteren not really here. Francis he says. Is that you francis wear you goen francie.

I look at bud his big shapeless body moven in the dimness.

Bobby says should i go grace. Do you want me to leave.

Bud shifts again and lashes one arm out suddenly this time the guitar goes over and i brace my selve as it begins its jangly slide over waiten for the thump when it hits the ground.

Stay for a bit bobby i say.

Are you sure.

Yes. We can go in the kitchen.

As i go out past him i can not smell the drink of him any more. It is be cause i have had a drink to. I brush against his jacket which he never takes of a leather jacket.

Do you ever take that jacket of i say to him.

Eh i dont know. I feel a wee bit exposed with out it on to tell you the truth.

Well take it of if you are goen to stay.

Right you are then grace bobby says fanklen with the zipper it is stuck he says.

He makes a big production of getten his zip stuck just below the neck and even i cant get it un done.

It is no good bobby you are stuck fast. You will die in that jacket most likely. You wont need a shroud they can bury you in your jacket.

Thats not funny grace that is a morbid as eff thing to say. Take it back.

How can i take it back i tell him. Its been sayed. It is out there. You cant take words back once they have been sayed.

Well its not very nice to say some thing like that to some one. You will bring bad luck on them.

Bobby huffs and groans and thrashes about pullen him selve out back wards through his jacket. He has got it up over his head and then half way up over his head then just his four head and hands are stuck in the neck and the cuffs respectively.

I can not help but laugh it is like he is wearen some sort of mad instrument of torture.

Grace it isent funny he says.

Im sorry bobby i say. Here let me help you.

And the 2 of us are pullen him one way me the other until his jacket lets him go and he falls back saved by the door frame at the last second.

He stands there all red in the face. I can not tell if he is redder in the face than be fore or if he is worser now.

Better now i ask him.

Its not funny grace that jacket has nearly kilt me.

I can not help but giggle then so does bobby.

There you are then i say. Your good as new.

Ooft he says. Totally born again eh. Now i need a drink.

Me to i say.

Do you think thats a good idea gracie.

To tell you the truth bobby i am just about all out of good ideas for today. I am about ready to give the bad ideas a run for a while.

Okay he says it is up to you. But dont go tellen bud it was me that made you. Or vinny. Christ.

Your secrets safe with me bobby. Come on.

Take it easy with that stuff christ bobby keeps sayen to me. Grace you have had a long lay of just be care full. Except i am not in a mood to be care full. I am in a mood thats difirint now the old mood it is back again. Hello wear were you. You have got to be gentel with me its been such a long while since we were to gether. You have got to take your time with me.

Me and bobby are leanen up against the break fast bar with my old tape player on quite. Bobby is laughen at all my old tapes from years ago just as bud is wont to do.

He is slurren a bit now though he normally dosent show the drink to much. Generally he just reeks of it. I have hardly ever known him to be drunk not to look at any way. But he is. He is drunk all the time these days. He even drives his taxi that way it is a wander how he gets away with it.

You like this he says. Dusty in memphis.

I like to here it some times yes.

And you like simonen garfunkel to. Do you grace.

I am nodden I am used to buds laughen at me.Yes i tell bobby i do like it so what. Simonen garfunkel are not importent bud tells me. But i dont care if its importent i still like it.

He just laughs and tops up his drink.

I dont listen to music be cause of its importens i say. I listen to it be cause i like it.

Bobby is nodden. I know he says buds the one who like to argew about these things. You know what i am quite fond of sheena easton.

Sheena easton o bobby that is bad.

He is laughen i know he is sayen. Its beyond the pale but i have always liked sheena easton. For effs sake dont tell bud he will nail me to the cross.

Bobby i say that is one secret i can not keep for you. Bud i say loud but not to loud come and here this.

Bobby is laughen o no grace please he will never let me forget it. But i make to go to the other room and bobby puts his hands on me to stop me and next we are both laughen to gether he holds his hand against my back. Grace he says and we just stand there i am breathen he is breathen. Then he goes to kiss me and i turn my cheek. He puts a kiss there on it but it is my mouth he wants.

He sighs and drops his hand from me and i go to turn dusty in memphis down a bit.

Bobby is quite now sippen his drink. Then he laughs and says it isent you grace its me.

I know that i say to him. It is you and bud is your best friend.

He comes over to me again. I know he says. I cant help it grace. Ive never been able to help it. Your special you know.

I take his hand in mine and pat it but not that way.

Some would say i was special needs bobby.

He laughs and shakes his head and sighs again. He is just looken at me in that way of his again when i see there is some ones dark shape standen in the door and me and bobby snap a part like pieces of littel seans lego. It is littel sean as well. He is just in his top he has kicked of his jammy bottoms once again. That can mean only one thing he has peed the bed.

I can not make him out so good in the door way come here sean i say what is it. My heart is pounden sean comes over and tries to push between my selve and bobby. He is girnen and buries his face in my legs.

I think the wee fella might need a clean up says bobby. I better get goen down the road. He leans over and gives me a peck on the cheek and i pick sean up sure enough he is wet and pee smellen. Bobby zips his jacket up you are all set i tell him. Your back inside your survival gear. He laughs and i put sean down come on i say lets get you cleaned up. Bobby sighs again and pauses and then says night grace. Then he goes. I here him goen down the hall and the door close quitely and it is just me and sean and the sound of bud snoren in the other room. Sean pulls at my finger tips and i stand swayen a bit the music quite. Dusty and me and sean. Then i am taken a sip of my whisky all of it down in one go and feeling it carry me and sean take us in its arms me and sean and dusty and of we go and sean tugs my fingers and i follow him his move ment his dance. His littel body warm his breathen. It is him carryen me through to the bath room he is dancen me leaden me a way with his tango and i reach down for the tap and run the water warm in to his plastic basin in the tub sean half a sleep next to me until i take his top of and lift him in. Mummy he says. Mummy water. No sean you should be tellen him grace. No sean gracie isent your mummy. You have got to remember sean. Do you remember sean. No. Of course you dont remember. You have long forgot her. Francis your mother so called. And she has long forgot you to or she would of never left. Would she grace. No. Never. You would never of left your son vincent no matter what would you grace. You would of stayed no matter what. Even if they had made you leave you would not of gone if you could of helped it would you gracie. You would of done any thing any thing at all to keep your son vincent safe from harm safe from trouble. Your mummy never did that sean. She dident keep you safe she left you. Do you here me sean no not at all.

Yet you still can not keep them all safe can you grace. You can not keep them from harm. Not even vincent. You can not stop him from joinen up if he wants to. You can not prevent him from goen away may be getten hurt some wear a broad in a fight he isent old enough to under stand what it is he will be fighten and what for. All be cause he cant find a job here in his own city his own country. It is better than signen on he says. You can travel. You can go to other countries. It is better to do that than stay here and die of bore dom doen no thing in stead.

Later after i have turned the matress and changed the linen. Later after i have washed the baby and put him down and am looken at him his sleepen face the light down low in his cup board his bed room. His and the counsils. I run my hand through his soft hair which is francises my daughter. Francis who is near by some wear i know this. Francis my shadow always be hind me every wear. Sean breaths his chest warm and i am leanen over him. I would like to pray for him except i am a non practisen protesint. What good are prayers they are for the superstishous. I am putten my hand to his cheek it is so warm and soft. I am leanen down close i am almost touchen his face with mine his breath is sweet with milky ness and sour ness to. He has no thing to worry him just now. He is never un happy just now. He can not be un happy at his age every thing is new to him. If he falls over and hurts his knee he cries until only a second then he is happy again. He has bud to take care of him until his mother my daughter francis comes back. He belongs to her so she can take him. That is only fare every one would agree with that. If she is well. If she is no longer a dependent. She has made her selve well be for and she has made her selve sick again to. It is all relative for dependents. They are never stable it is always a struggel for them. Every thing is a fight bud would say. Is that not right gracie. Every thing is a battel.

Do you remember her sean i say but of course he dosent here. He wouldent under stand any way. No thing can worry him he is to young. Why would he even worry about his mother. A wean should not have to worry after his own mother. That is the wrong way round. It is the job of the mother to worry for the child that is how it should be. But grace if you could you would keep this child safe wouldent you. You would keep this littel lamb out of harems way wouldent you. You wouldent see him un safe with a mother who depends would you. No.

So it is maybe better. To keep him safe what would you have to do grace.

How could you put littel sean out of harms way.

You could do it couldent you grace. Do you think if you had to you could.

You wouldent have to let this child suffer the way francis your daughter has suffered. Or as you your selve have suffered. It is why you have always kept your distance isent it. You have always stayed wary of hope havent you. Havent you grace.

Look at him. He is so small. He is so fragile.

I put my hand over his mouth and nose. I feel his breathe struggel through my fingers. It would only be a moment. It is only a moment. How long a moment.

I breath out.

I lift my hand i spread my fingers his mouth is openen. He turns over in his sleep. Littel sean. I get up and put of the light. then pull over the door so it is still open a bit. My throat and mouth are dry.

I get up and go through to the kitchen and pour another drink of the whisky. I put it to my lips and taste. O grace. What is this you think you are doen. Why. But you still want it don't you. Dont you grace. Yes. Yes you still want it so much. You want it more than any thing not to have to deal with any thing. For one night. For one whole day even perhaps to be away some wear port adventurer the canary isle with your sister marie. Except you had your chance dident you grace. You were so use less you couldent even manage that.

I stand in the kitchen looken at the sink. I pour some water in to a mug sitten on the counter. It dosent matter to me weather its clean. It is of no importence. I sip the water and then pour it away. I go over to the door and switch the light out and stand there. I look up out of the kitchen window in to the night sky but there isent any moon or stars to see there is no thing up there to night. So i just stand there. I just stand in the dark staren at the night thinken about the song of simonen garfunkel the one about the darkness my old friend. So i am reachen for the whisky and pour an other drink i can feel it runnen over my fingers i ament sure of getten any in the glass but some how in this pitch i can perform this funcshoun better than in the light. It is some thing i was good at be four drinken in the dark when the money for the meter was spent. You are so good at this gracie i tell my selve. You are the best. Probably there is a competishoun some wear in the world for pouren drinken the dark you could enter and win.

After i am sitten alone in the dark in the kitchen hearen a siren i just keep taken one quite sip after an other one after an other.

You know wear this will get you bud will say. Dont you grace. You have been down this whisky road be four. Yes bud. I know. I know wear this will get me. So here you are now in the dark kitchen grace and next in the dark liven room leanen over a man on the couch is it bud. Yes his face is rough the con tours are the same rough dents his stubbil the same rough stubbil that of bud spence his face staren up at me a sleep in the dark to. He was here be fore he is always here. He is always here isent he gracie. Your man bud. Yet you can hardly even see him this face of his with its dents and stubbil. He is just a man on his back. I see you i say to him i see you i see you. What are you doen here why are you here in my house. What are you doen you big baby back here in this house. I am holden him by his hair i am nodden his face up and down i see you i am sayen. I am slappen his dirty effen see of a mouth with my other hand yet why dosent he a wake i am hitten his stupid face what an ugly face what an ugly man an ugly baby. Yet why dosent he wake gracie. You should ring his stupid neck you should smash in his drunken teeth grace. Smash in his drunken face with a bottil it will be his own fault he can not even tell you are here. He can not even wake up to see you. He is just like your baby lyen there among the nettles isent he grace. His body still red and raw. Do you remember. Yes. Yes. And this baby here to. You are never done either. You are never done asken me when when. Isent that right bud. Yes. You are never never done asken when. When grace it has been so long. When when. You should give him some thing grace shouldent you. You should give him what he is asken for you should take out that floppy thing of his and do some thing with it shouldent you. That is what to do. Take it out give him what he wants. Go on grace.

Jesus eff whatre you playen at. He is sitten up all of a sudden he is zippen him selve up. He is rubben his eyes who is that there.

What are you doen. Who is that there. Is that you francis.

No bud. It isent francis. Its me. Grace. Your gracie.

I reach for his face in the dark and he jumps at my touch.

Holy eff grace. What a scare you gave me. Holy jesus. I thought you were francis.

I know bud. But it is just my selve here. Im sorry I gave you a fright.

He is breathen a big sigh of relieve. Wear is bobby what time is it he is asken. There i was dozen of again effs sake. You should of woke me grace. You shouldent have let me sleep like that. You should of woke me. What are you doen kneelen down on the floor like that any way.

I put my hand on his leg. It is okay I tell him. It dosent matter.

O i need to go to the lav man. Jesus effen christ. Have i been lyen here with my flies open all night. Effs sake the baldy man is hangen out as well. You could have woke us grace. This is what you get grace. This is what you get for bevyen. Your lucky to be out of it.

I am out of it i tell him. I am one of the lucky ones. You should think of quitten as well bud. You will be a stronger person for it.

He clicks the table lamp on and starts footeren with some

thing on the coffy table his makens i would think. I see his arms
the shapes of them goen through his familiar motions i here the
russel of his papers. And there again his matches bloom orange
and yellow and flex of green. Then the red ember his rolly the
smell of the sulfer and the tobaco.

Bud laughs. He is okay with a few tins and a joint he says. He
is your classic binge drinker but he says he dosent need to quit.
He always behaves the same way wether he is drunk or sober. I
supose that is true i say. You are a creature of habit that is for sure.

He picks up his fallen guitar.

So long as your dry thats the main thing he says.

Yes. Thats the main thing.

Fair play to you though graciegirl. Youv done well to get as far
as you have. Im proud of you so i am. Really really proud.

I am drunk. Really really drunk. But bud can not tell as he is
also drunk and the drunk are imune to each others drunken ness.
He puts his rolly in the ashtray and strums.

Quite bud i say to him. Its late sean is a sleep.

He plays a cord very soft and hums leanen over. His voice is
a rough one but some people say that its good any way. It is true
i think he is no dusty in memfis but he is good any way like grit
on ice under your shoes it is cold and hard and brittel and warm
a comfort all at the same time.

Big eddy knew he says.

Big eddy who i say.

Now there. Are just twelve. Steps to heaven bud sings. Big eddy
cochrane he says. Wah wah ooh. Thats your tune isent it grace. The
twelve step program ha ha. One foot forward one foot back. The
twelve step program the hokey cokey program. Your song.

Yes bud i say it is my song. Thank you.

Get with the program sister. Just listen. And you will plainly
see. There any thing left in here to drink. No. Forget it. Need to

be up in the mornen any way. Grace youll have to take the wee man to nursery. Bud spence is a man of gainful employment as of tomorrow. Did i not tell you.

I jump up to my feet o bud you have found some thing tell me what is it.

You are looken at the new gardian of knowledge.

What do you mean what is that.

Worken the doors at the college.

Worken the doors what is that you cant work doors.

Course i can work doors. I got in here dident i. Im there new concierge the man in charge of garden the information the mane meeter and greeter. The boy who says aye or naw to the comers and goers of our fare citys west. Im worken the doors. Look on my doors ye mighty and beat it. The knowledge is not for the likes of you. Nor neither mine own selve. But its almost a liven wage.

O bud that is great news i say. That is great news. I could cry i say to him. And i do. I cry a loud right there in our own liven room. Ours and the counsils.

I wake up early out of a dream wear i am readen a book a loud and i am abel to read as well as any body. The book isent a readen book though its a jotter a school book. The words are like a diary full of private entrys ritten in pencil almost a childs riten babyish riten. I am abel to read this book and under stand not only the words but other things to like what is goen on between the words in the spaces. It is like i can read this person or child through what there arent sayen even to there diary. Not only that but in some cases i find my selve rubben bits out with a rubber then changen the words. I can write as well as any body and i can not stop changen the words in this diary to my own words. It is then i know it is all my own work it is my own jotter of thoughts. They are not right some how they have to be made better to say what is between the words between the lines. In the dream i can do this but there is so much to change it will perhaps take some time. The jotter goes on and on i get angry frustrated that there could be so much to change. Just when i am about to go crazy a phone rings it is a phone sitten on a table in the room i am in which is just a room. In this dream i answer the phone what i say who is it. It is marie says a voice your sister marie. And when i go to answer i do it in an other langwidge a langwidge i can speak better than english my own langwidge. It must be spanish the langwidge and marie agrees it must be to. Of course it must be since what other langwidge would they speak on port adventurer the canary isles. At the time i know what all this means but not after waken. Well i supose that is the way with dreams. Do they mean some thing or do they mean no thing. It is dificult to say.

Littel sean has clambered on top of our bed me and buds and want us to get up. He cant say get up yet he says o my which is his favourite thing to say . O my and o my golly which bud taught him by letten sean copy. It was his tryen to limit the amount of swearen around sean when he was starten out speaken. He started sayen effen see be four he was so much as three year old. I have to say i was black affronted. That is your doen i sayed to bud. That is enough to bring the social up here as any thing else. You should of watched your langwidge around him he dosent know any better. Do you want him to use langwidge like you do. No. Of course you dont. So it is your responsibility to teach him how to speak properly not like some body you would be ashamed to be seen with.

Bud was very sorry about it. It was of no use to argew. He is the only one in this house that talks that way although vincent is also bad. Vincent dosent do it around sean though. He just does it around me. So every time he was goen to swear bud had to stop. He would say o my o my golly. So that is what seans favourite thing to say is mainly i think because bud swears so much he had to say o my o my golly a lot.

I am up now any way. I dident sleep to well. I had to get up and clear away the bottles and glasses and then i sat. I wandered if i should go and see annette today for some spiritual guidance of some sort to help. Help of some sort would be good. All dependents need help from time to time it is the way of things. Annette would say i was in need of spiritual nurish ment and who am i to say no. I am pretty well famished for spiritual nurish ment and havent had any spiritual guidance for a while either.

It is early and bud is out cold curled in a ball under the duvet.

Suddenly i am very tired. To late for that now how ever. I put on these old glasses and try to get as focused as i can. I have got a mygrane comen on now it is in the post. The light is affecten my left eye it is super sensitive to it.

I get up and take sean through to get washed and dressed. I can here vincent snoren in his room back from his wanderens. I look in there is a shape on the bed. Vincent the body my son. I close the door quitely and go in to the kitchen wear straight away the bin bag bangs my toe. It has been lurken be hind that unit all night gracie waiten just for you. You know better than that a woman with your bad eyes. It was a sayen of our father me and maries.

If you put things wear they go then theyll be wear you put them.

That is what i am thinken now about my other glasses. They are in that bag of mine wear i put them some wear may be port adventurer the canary isles may be with marie. If she has that bag she will see my things in side. They will ask her to check. She will see those glasses of mine may be she will see if they fit her what the world looks like through her sisters eyes glasses. From port adventurer it will surely look a lot better but then they are a reason able quality of glasses.

Marie had good eye sight compared to my own. She had

talents. Yet i never envied her them be cause she was beautiful to me she was a wander ful creature to me. It seemed im possible that she could be my own older sister so beautiful and bright like that sun light that brought her down in to our kitchenete and lit her spinnen on the linoleum.

She was good at figure skating and at maken things i remember. Often she would get me to help her make things. Of course i have not got any great talents. Only caren our father used to say. You stayed be cause you cared graciegirl. That is talent enough

It isent true though. No. I dont think so. Is it graciegirl. You dident stay be cause you cared any more than marie or our mother. It was only be cause you dident want to move around any more. You were sick of moven even as a girl you were sick of haven to be the odd one out every wear in school after school. You were sick of haven to start all over again. It was only be cause of that and not being brave enough to go.

If you put things wear they go then they will be wear you put them that not right gracie. Isent it.

I pick up the bin bag and take it over and put it in a corner. I wouldent like annette to come in here now and see this mess. It is probably a mess any way. If i had my good glasses on i could tell. It most definitely dosent smell to wander full. Of course it is better some times not to know. The dirt has to get to an awful size be fore you start getten tripped up by it. So says his nibs. So says bud.

When our father me and maries was dyen in that bed i asked him if he remembered her dancen and what happened after. I wandered wear did marie go that time.

What dancen he sayed. Though i could tell he knew.

The time in the kitchenete in knightswood. I went to my room and when i woke up she was gone. She was away a long time.

He took my hand and held on. Your mistaken gracie he sayed.

She dident go any wear.

Yes she did i sayed.

No grace your mistaken. She never went any wear. She stayed with us. Your mind is playen tricks on you gracie.

And i was goen to ask was he sure but he pretended to be to tired.

Och he sayed they have got me so tight in this bed i can not move.

They had him in a nurses tuck. He could only move his chest and head. The rest of him was pinned there. They always seemed to do that the nurses.

Did marie go away some wear. I dont know now for sure. Why would he mis lead you your own father grace. Well. He was of that older generation. He dident like to talk of upsetten things.

Aye when they nurses make a bed it stays made he sayed. No matter whos in it. If they put things wear they go then they stay wear they put them. That not right gracie. That not right graciegirl.

It is likely he thought that of me to. If he put me wear i was meant to go then i would know wear i was meant to be. But did he mean your whole life grace. Are you suposed to go your whole life wear some one else has put you. Just to feel safe in your selve.

Littel sean is playen with buds ear and he rolls over half awake. O he says is it late. He picks sean up and lifts him over his head then brings him close and nuzzles his stubbel into seans neck which makes him laugh with glee. Hows my wee pal bud says. How is he. Hows my wee pal sean.

Sean grabs at his nose with both hands sticken his thumbs up buds hairey nostrils.

Ooyah says bud. Give me back my nose. You have got my nose sean. Look.

Then he tickles his neck with his stubble again.

It is nearly eight i tell him.

Jesus effen christ he says and does not exactly leap from bed but puts sean down on the floor and hobbles up with the duvet draped over his shoulders in the usual style.

I need a wash he says. Any chance of a slice of toast and a cup of tea graciegirl.

Bud i say be four he gets out the door. Bud i saw francis.

He stops in the door way. He dosent turn around.

Francis he repeats like it is a name he hasent ever heard be four. Are you sure.

Now he turns round and though i can not make out his expreshoun i know he is afraid and embarased and not ready to give in all at the same time.

Yes i tell him. I am sure bud.

He nods his head slowly.

I ament sure may be i imagine it but it is like bud gets smaller in that door way. It is like he is stricken. Well. So be it. Let him be stricken.

We have not got much to say to each other this mornen it seems. We move a round each other careful. Bud boils eggs for break fast and we eat in silence with the radio blaren. It is classic fm in the mornen bud likes the classical music normally i ament bothered by classical music but to day its okay. It is soothen what needs soothen most. We eat toast and eggs and say pass the salt or pepper or do you want an other cup of tea. Yes please. No thanks. If it isent to much troubil. Bud is quite not even sayen hello when vincent comes for his habitual corned flake break fast. There is an atmos fear of some sort but it is easier just to let it continue than to con front it. In my experience con fronten an atmos fear is a fraught business. Especially since this one has been a long time on the horizon.

Bud looks out difirint shirts and tries them on. His one good plane white shirt is covered in burn holes from his rollys and joints. He has hardly any proper shirts it seems.

He comes in with an other on this time a purple one.

No bud. Purple shirts arent any use for the concierge of a college builden.

Vincent laughs over his corned flake break fast.

Your never going to wear that are you man.

Bud ignores him and goes out again comes back five minutes later with a blue shirt which is to small around the middel. The buttons are parten for the seas to spill.

Vincent laughs and so does sean even though he dosent know why hes laughen.

What bud says this is all ive got.

O i say is there no thing else not even maybe a plane polo neck or some thing.

Naw he says. That is all i have got. The rest is just t shirts grotty t shirts.

Vincent is still guffawen away.

Right vincent you will have to lend him one of yours.

Not a chance man. Im not haven him rune my gear man.

Vincent i say to him. I ament asken you i am tellen. Lend him one of your plane white shirts so he can go to work.

You would be doen me a big favour bud says.

Vincent sighs.

It is true vincent. You would really be helpen. You know how it is here. We need the wage.

Vincent clatters his spoon in his bowl and huffs a bit.

All right he says. But he better not get fag burns on them or ill go mental.

Bud says dont worry buddy dont worry. I will look after it as if it is my very own.

So i go with vincent to find a shirt to fit bud and we get him into one which is big and loose on but when its tucked in and we find a pass able tie and put a jacket on him it looks okay. Yes every thing looks a bit big but okay. Okay. Even if bud does look some what under nurished in it.

Okay bud says. Okay okay. Ready to rock and roll. Ready to hit the road.

Have you got bus fare i ask him. He nods.

Okay then i tell him. If your ready to rock and roll better get a move on.

Bud is nervis now i can tell.

Dont worry i tell him. It will be fine.

Okay okay bud says. Okay okay. Effen rock and roll effen rock and roll man. Lets rock. Jesus christ i think am going to feint.

Aye man vincent says. Better take a mop and bucket if your going to be a janitor. The sweats lashen of you.

I fix his collar though i cant tell if it is in a fankel i just fix it any way. I want to say good luck bud but some thing is stoppen me. Bud is breathen near my face it is un settled. He gives me a kiss on the cheek and says okay well time to go. We walk to the door him determined not to limp. As he goes out i take both his hands and squeeze them. It is then i realise he has forgotten some thing importent. He has not got his walken stick.

Bud i say to him. Arent you taken your stick.

No.

Why not.

I cant.

But why.

He takes me by the shoulders. You know how it is gracie he tells me.

No bud i do not know. Why arent you taken your stick.

He is sighen.

I had to tell a few wee white lies to get the gig he says. You know the sort of thing.

Bud i dont know. What lies.

No thing much grace. Just that i wasent a cripple. Im meant to be worken the doors here. You have to be abel bodied for that. So the man i spoke to sayed to me.

What man. Who are you even talken about.

The fellow from the college. Bobby put me on to him. I spoke to him on the phone. So he sayed to me are you crippled or in sane be cause you have to be mad to work here.

He dident really say that your joken.

Aye well more or less. The job is equal oportunitys but there are sertin fisical reqirments.

Like what sort of requirments. You are only to open doors and welcome people in are you not.

Aye grace bud says. That is right. But in theory.

In theory i say what theory.

Bud is getten anoyed now his voice is risen a gain. Jesus grace what do you think. In theory i might be required to refuse a troubel maker entry. In theory i might have to help get the students out if the builden catches fire.

Why would the builden catch fire bud it is a college.

Its an effen libary grace. Its full of books. I just have to drop a match and the place will go up.

I look at bud and wander. Surely he wouldent set fire to a libary. He is always on about revolushoun and against a lot of things. Any thing to do with instushions any thing to do with the state he is against it. Even educashoun he is against schools and every thing above that. Money is money though his principels never survive our needs. It is funny he has taught him selve all sorts of things from books he is a beter reader than you grace yet he isent one for books really. He dosent read a book if its just has some story in it only if theres some thing else like an idea plus it seems like he just reads them to see if he is right about some thing. Then he will take great de light in tellen you all about it isent that right grace. It sure is. See he will say its here in this book what i was sayen about relidgeous indoctorinashoun. It is here what i was sayen about the effen state and the goverment. Right here it says it in this book right here. It isent like bud even goes in to the library we have down the road. May be to get out of the rain or if he is betten but cant afford a pint in the pub between races. He will go up there and sit and fume.

Of course he has books of his own but he is always spillen wine on them or tearen wee bits of the covers to make dowts for his rollys. Not only that but you will quite often seen him throw a book at the wall if it annoys him. He will also try to break the spines of books that annoy him. If the spine is to strong for him the book gets an other chance but its days are likely numbered. Sooner or later that book is a goner.

You should use your stick you will hurt your selve with out it. It isent any good for your leg i tell him. You shouldnt be putten to much strain on it. What will we do if you hurt your selve and then you cant work at all.

He is nodden. I know he says i know. Its just for to day. I will take it tomorrow when i have had a chance to see how the land lies.

You promise.

I promise graciegirl. Come on. Dont worry. I will be fine. One single solitary day cant hurt. I just have to get to the bus stop and from there up the hill to the college.

Im comen with you then. You can lean on me.

No grace let me do it by my selve. Please.

He sounds so like a young man like vincent when he says this. Let me help you on to the bus at least.

Grace no. I want to do it by my selve do you under stand.

The light from the close window falls in a big dull grey square about the stare well and landing. An other dreich day but no rain as yet. Those teen agers arent about just now the close is quite. Well. Let him grace. He is a grown man it is up to him if he wants to do this in his own way. He would of let you wouldent he. Yes. Most likely he would.

Okay bud. Be care full though please.

Okay gracie he says. I will.

The walk to the nursery is a lot easier be cause i have sean to lead the way. All i have to worry about is him getten to far a head and out of sight all to gether. I have to make my way past the usual throngs of people by the shoppen centre which i dont like. I am always wary of meeten some one i know especially some one like annette or some one else who knows my business. Of course annette has only good intenshions it is true she has helped me a lot in the past particularly when i was haven dificultys.

I am not so sure now though. I was haven some dificultys at the time. I am not so sure i was ever dependent. Not the way francis is dependent.

But of course here in the grey in hecla square there are other people who would say difirint. There are people here who have there own reasons. Some of those men i used to know are still about. Not every one is to be trusted except if you are littel sean who will go of with any one. Of course bud would batter them for taken advantage of some one vulnerabel. So he says any way.

Sean i shout come back here. I am sure that is him about to try and cross the road.

Then i feel a hand reach for mine it was not sean ahead at

all but trailen some wear be hind that makes me break out in a sweat. It is odd for him to reach for my hand how ever. Some thing or some body must have given him a fright and then i see it is a big dog a white one comen. Sean is scared of dogs of course we all are after buds experience. He will never walk right again be cause of it i dont think.

Sean whines mummy and we stop he is hidden behind my legs.

Sean i say it is okay though i am not sure.

Then i see a man comen up buster he says. Here buster and buster skips away he dosent seem agresive more like he is just curius and play full.

The man says dont worry doll he wont bite he is a big wean. O it is you you are bud spences girl arent you. We meet again.

I just stand there with sean danglen on my hand.

You want to give him one of these to chew son the man says to sean who is not normally shy but is now.

Aye he loves to chew these. That not right buster wear would you be with out me maken a pigs ear of things for you.

Of course it is that man from the bus yester day.

Hello again i say. I am sorry i have forgotten your name.

He is a tall man as big as bud but more solid. From what i can tell he is not afraid of any thing he is confident walken and talken. That makes me nervis of him plus like i told you i ament keen on dogs of any kind.

Gregor he says. Your grace arent you. Mad eh. Thats twice in to days.

Sean is still shy of the dog but seems not so scared he is quite now not panicken.

Well i tell him. We are in a bit of a hurry arent we sean we are of to nursery so we better get goen.

Ha ha laughs this man gregor. I might see you again soon he says.

Why is that i ask. Is it some kind of threat he is maken.

Im goen to see your boy. Vincent isent it. Him and a few of his friends. I see them at the community centre some times. They were wanten to know about joinen up. I am away up to the high flats just now to talk to them so if the place isent in order i will have to put you on a charge grace. Ha ha.

I have not got my glasses my proper glasses so of course the place is not goen to be in sparklen condishoun. He has a cheek even to say this. He has a cheek goen up to talk to my son.

I have went and done some thing be four i can even think what to say to this man. I have gone to hit him a slap just lightly not a real one and then the dog barks angry in to life and the man gregor yanks him back on his lead down he shouts down buster. It is to late though sean is screamen and terrified behind my knees and the dog is still now but growlen.

Get that animal away from my son i am sayen though of course sean isent my son.

Its all right gregor says he just dosent like people getten fysical. He wont touch your son. It is okay.

Now i am flustered and sean is screamen. My breathe comes and goes in funny rithems taken my heart with it.

Shush buster the man says. This gregor.

Shush sean it is okay i say. The doggy wont bite you.

What did you do that for any way gregor is asken.

You are the man that is goen to talk my son in to getten him selve killed in some war he isent even old enough to under stand.

No grace he begins to say. It isent like that.

Well what is it like then. You are the big man you tell me why. Why should i let you speak to my son. Why should i let you in to my house at all.

Sean is pullen at my fingers but i am holden on tight keepen him away from the dog be cause now he has lost his fear of it he wants to pat the thing.

Give him this the man gregor says. Its his pigs ear. He kneels down and puts his hand out to sean. Just then buster yowls all excited and sean hides be hind my knees again.

Look the man gregor says. Youv got the wrong end of the stick doll. I just know them from that community centre wear they all hang about doen eff all. I just get other kids in to play foot ball talk about whats goen on with them try to get a few wee classes arranged for them. Thats it. Im not a gangster and im not representen the armed services. I just try and tell them what its like if there really interested.

I am nodden. Of course i want to believe in him but he is a stranger to me.

So you arent tryen to persuade him to join up.

Not at all gregor says. I do some work for the community centre like i sayed. These boys come in looken for some thing to do. We try and get them interested in things you know other than runnen about wild. It isent my job to say what they should do with there lives just try and point out the whys and wearfours.

And you were in the army. How long were you in the army.

I was in nine year he says.

Nine years i say that is a long time. And here you are still breathen.

Ha ha he laughs. Yep still here still breathen. Just about. I reckon i have got a few years in me yet.

I try to get a good look at his face by squinten hard through the good eye of my glasses. His head is square and he has blond hare very short. I can see his teeth when he grins but not much else. His teeth look okay though. So that is some thing i guess.

How old are you then.

Me im thirty six. My names gregor.

I know you told me yester day.

I dident think you would re member. Are you headen up the nursery.

Yes i tell him. Then i am away to see if i can get some shifts arranged at work.

Oh aye he says. Wear is that then costigan house.

Yes i tell him costigan house.

That is some place that costigan house isent it he says to me.

I supose yes it is. I say this but i dont really know what this gregor means by some place. My left eye is beginen to squint now i can feel it the mygrane is on the way. It is like a bright shaft of light shinen directly in to it my eye even though it is an other dull grey day. The light seems to slowly get stronger and stronger. Soon it will be over poweren it will lay me low. There is no thing else for it but to keep goen just now. It will follow you wear ever you travel any way grace.

Getten some thing of a reputashoun that place isent it.

I dont know about that i tell him. It is easy for some wear to get a reputashoun.

Gregor laughs you would say that wouldent you. Worken there. The place is crumblen though. Even you could see that was the case eh grace.

O i say to him angry again. Dont ask me any thing about it. Obviously i cant see to put one foot in front of the other. If the place is fallen down it will probably be down about my ears be fore i am likely to notice it.

He is quite for a few moments and then says i am sorry i dident mean it that way. It was just a re mark.

I am quite to then i nod and say it is okay im actually not feelen my best this mornen. I should not of snapped at you like that.

No bother he says. May be we should get goen eh buster.

He leans down to clap his dog which littel sean is almost patten but not quite. He is stretchen an arm out but he is still a good two foot away from this dog.

Then he straightens up again. Your man he says. Bud isent it. Is he up there at your house. I was goen to say hello if he was in.

No i tell him. Bud is away to work today. He wont be home till later i ament sure when.

It is strange the feelen of pride i get when i say these words. Bud. Work. Bud. Worken.

Worken is he thats great. I know he was wanten to get back in to it again. Great news that wear is he worken.

I ament sure i should be revealen informashoun about bud to this man but i cant seem to help my selve. Be four i even know what im sayen i have already sayed he is worken as concierge at the college. Then i start maken excuses for bud for some reason maken it sound like his job is not real or no thing to be proud of. I dont know why per haps it is a kind of selve defense eh grace. If you dont want to raise the expectashouns of others to high may be it is be cause you your selve dont want to expect to much. Yes. That sounds about right dosent it gracie. Not expecten to much or to littel is just the way people in your posishoun have to live isent it. Other wise you would go daft.

Ha ha this gregor says he is a bouncer for the educashounal establish ment. That is ironic isent it. Him with his politics as well. Maken sure the knowledge is safe from the local bams.

Yes i say. I am hopen he will not have an out burst of any kind while he is there. I am hopen he will be on his best be haviour.

Aye that is a worry gregor says. It is his temper that you have to watch.

How do you know about his temper i ask this man gregor.

He is shruggen. He was up at the community centre a week or two back. He was shouten and bawlen be cause some of the young team were harasen him as he went by. Because of his stick. They were callen him names so he came up the steps.

He never told me about that.

Well he wouldent it wasent his finest hour. The other staff were for callen the polis but i says no. He was for cracken heads with his walken stick. He nearly clattered your vincent. We had to get him out there be four the young team set about him. They would have kilt him.

My son vincent was there i am asken this man gregor. My son vincent was goen to batter bud o. O grace he would have kilt him. He would have murdered bud. You know bud is no match for vincent only an eejit could think so. Only bud could think he was a match for your son vincent.

I am not abel to here this just now i have to go i tell my selve. You can not stand a round and listen to this sort of thing grace you will have a heart attack. You will keel over here right here in the street in front of every body. All these strangers goen by staren and you dead on the ground with your grand son thinken you are playen a game.

I have to go i say. I need to get sean to nursery.

O i shouldent have sayed any thing gregor says.

No you shouldent. You shouldent say any thing to vincent either. I dont want you goen any wear near my son do you here. He isent joinen any army be cause of you or any one.

I am turnen away pullen littel sean by the hand and the dog goes yelpen back i have stood on his toes i think.

Hey mind the dug this man gregor says.

You shouldent have an animal like that out with out a muzell.

Buster isent a biter he says sounden as though i have insulted his mothers grave. If she is even dead. How would i know.

He is an animal i say. How can you be sure what an animal will do.

He wont do any thing if you dont stand on his paws.

It is times like these i think contacts would be a wander full thing knowen wear you are putten your feet. However my eyes can not take them. Like i told you be four i did try them out years ago but i couldent get used to putten them in and taken them out again. The troubel with your eyes is that they are very resistant to change the optishoun sayed to me. They are resistant to these hard lenses but they dont seem to care for the softer ones either. Of course my eyes were swollen and red from tryen difirint lenses over the days and weeks. So of course we just decided i would stick with my ordinary glasses until such time as technology could adapt to the demands my eye balls placed on it. May be your right doctor i sayed. Except i dont like goglen at the world through them. I dont like the atenshoun be cause they are such big thick milk bottles.

Im afraid your stuck with folk goglen for now grace he told me.

Look gregor says i think we have got of on the wrong foot here.

I can feel my ears and face all red.

How about we call a truce.

I am taken deep breaths. Just take it easy gracieboats i tell my selve. It is not easy though. It is never easy to take it easy in my experiens. Not when you are flustered and bothered.

How about it gregor says. I ament goen to tell your boy any thing he shouldent here. That is the truth of it.

You promise i ask him.

I am a bit long in the tooth for maken those kind of promises but i can assure you i will not say any thing that will glamorize the army or the navy or the air force or any of that non sense. It will just be about what it was like for me and may be dispel any daft ideas he or his pals have about it.

And is that all. There isent any thing in it for you for instance.

There is no thing in it for me grace i can assure you. Im not getten payed for it and im not the press gang.

Of course i always tell sean not to trust strangers and especially not to go with them any wear but as an adult you some times do have to. Bud dosent trust any body he says but of course he has to as well. He has trusted bobby to get him safely up the road when he has had to much and it turns out he has had to trust this man gregor to a stranger. So it would may be okay to trust him to wouldent it grace. If you want to keep vincent here you shouldent try and get in his way. He will do what ever he wishes any way but if you try and stop him he will surely leave and join up.

Look gregor says ive no thing up my sleeves.

Then he shows me his cuffs and his wrists. I pretend like i can tell if he has any thing up there.

All clear i say and he laughs.

Friends he says and puts out his hand.

Okay i say and shake his hand. He has a very masculen hand shake very firm and dicisive.

Thank christ for that he says then stops. O sorry. You arent religious are you.

No i tell him. I am a protesent but i am non practisen.

Gregor takes it up on him selve to walk me up to the nursery school gate and talks away to me while i try to ask questions back. I can feel the preshure builden in my eye the light is beginnen to crack the vishoun on my left side. There is a feelen of fracture in my face to on that side. The skin it selve is beginnen to feel pain ful to the touch. My mouth is slowen to accommodate it. That is the order first your eyes and then your mouth isent that right gracie. It was like that when your own children you left them wanderen away. They were tryen to get you lost they knew how to take advantage of you there own mother. The garscadden woods were so bright on that day the green was pain full to you wasent it. Yes it was. Your daughter francis and your son vincent thought that was funny dident they. To play hiden seek to stay hiden so long. Your face was like it had split that day. Re member it grace yes. Wanderen along with no thing left to drink your children lost. Bobby in the car.

Grace this is a teribel situashoun get in the car.

It was like your face your head was cleaved into halves.

You couldent even speak to bobby.

Grace he was sayen. Get in. Get in the car.

Buster growls we leave littel sean plaen with the other weans in the nursery playground and go back out and he walks me back down the road and says would i like a coffy he isent in any particular rush.

Im guessen your son vincent isent an early riser he says.

No i tell him. He is sertinly not.

There isent any wear to have a coffy at hecla squre except to stand in the street with a cup from greggs the chip shop isent open yet.

There isent any wear i tell him.

We can get one from greggs and sit on a bench here he says.

This gregor dosent know you at all grace i say to my selve. You would rather do just about any thing at all than sit on a bench here in hecla square wear every one and there dog might see you. Every one and there dog could wander past and know you had been there at that time. That was the area you worked until the polis got involved wasent it. Yes. May be even this gregor knows you from then. It is posibil isent it. It isent as if you payed any atenshion to there faces once you had a drink in you. No. A date was a date.

I would rather not to be honest. I have a bit of a mygrane comen on to tell you the truth.

Well there is the regenerashoun centre round the back of the square he says. We could go there. There is a tea shop.

This is a surprise to me. I dident even know about a tea shop in there. I thought it was just a place the dole sent people like my son vincent with no qualificashouns. I am sure he did go to some thing in there some sort of course with no job at the end of it.

So we walk along to the regenerashoun centre. It is an ugly builden like so many of the buildens here in the drum. I can not even think of a single nice builden apart from our flat well ours and the counsils. It is just a huge sky scraper but of course they are goen to demolish it in a few years. Then who know what will happen to us whether we will even be abel to stay to gether our family. Grace it is best not to think of the future dont you think. Of course. If you could do a single thing about it about any thing in the future may be it would be worth the worry but you cant so forget it. Be sides it is enough to deal with just this present.

Gregor comes over and puts down to teas in poly styrene cups with some thing on top paper plates with a yum yum and a square of some thing.

Take your pick he says. But im willen to fight you for the millionaires shortbread.

I smile. He takes a slurp of tea. We sit at peace.

After a while gregor says you were a bit wary yester day. On the bus.

I take a sip of tea with milk and no sugars in it. Yes i say. I thought you were some one bud owed money to.

Gregor is shaken his head. Buster sits quite at his feet he is lyen down gregor got him a bowl of water.

No no he says. I was just meanen not to worry about the business at the community centre. About the polis or those lads comen after him.

Now it is my turn to shake my head. To tell you the truth gregor now i am conserned be cause of my son.

Well. Aye. It is a worry.

We are quite a few moments again but there is a pressure to

say some thing i think. There is a pressure to do some thing.

If it isent him joinen up it is him and bud at each others throats.

Gregor is nodden not sayen any thing. It is a good quality i think. There is not so many folk who just listen and dont jump right in to what you are sayen and try to interrupt by inserten there own tail.

You know they will have to learn to get a long or one of them will have to go grace.

I know that.

And if vincent really did join up how do you think you would deal with that.

I am shaken my head it is not some thing i want to think about gregor. Not just yet any way. I will deal with it when i come to that bridge.

Gregor breaks a piece of the millionaires shortbread of and puts it in his mouth.O my god he says and laughs. He is nudgen the paper plate to wards me. Go on he is sayen. Be cause your worth it.

I smile at him no thank you i tell him the dentist has swore me of sugary things. He says my teeth will be for the bucket if i dont keep good care of them. My father had false teeth while still in his youth i say. I dident want to follow suit.

I reckon it is all genetics gregor says. You got his weak teeth and vincent got his strength.

Vincent will weaken his teeth any way i say. He is sugar dependent.

Aye we are all dependents of one kind or another arent we though eh.

I feel my cheeks flush some what at this and wander if he can tell. He does seem to understand things about people. Would gregor judge you grace perhaps. Perhaps again no.

It was only last night you were stupid grace but it was only once. You are back on the wagon again this mornen. No one is any the worse for your mis deeds. Your sister marie in port adventurer the canary isles would not be proud neither would your father.

Vincent wouldent be proud o vincent.

Did he come in yes he saw. O grace you are an idyit.

Vincent saw you he guessed. He knows he isent any fool.

How could you forget that.

What will you do. No thing there is no thing you can do except wait and see. Vincent has heard your sorrys and lies be four. He has heard it all. He wont care for what you are goen through grace. He wont. Why should he. Is he not goen through it him selve to. Does he not live under the same roof is sean not his nephew more like a younger brother even. Is francis not his sister to yes. What about francis her selve if she is alive. What if she is like you grace what if she is no longer dependent like you are no longer as dependent. Then she will take littel sean with her and leave. People like annette will try and help but there wont be any help. They will read you pieces of paper laws and acts and things like that. Read this look at this. Do you understand. Do you under stand your situashoun. It is there in the small print. It is quite obviously there in the small print it states clearly. We sent you the informashoun you needed look it is here in this pile of male you havent opened yet. Why havent you opened it miss barker it is in your interests. It is your responsibility.

I get up i have to go i say i dident realise the time. I will be late for work.

O well let me give you a run gregor says.

I dident know you drove a car i say. What were you doen on the bus if you can drive a car.

Gregor shrugs what can i say grace. Some times it is cheaper to get the bus if your just goen down the road than to fill up the tank. Im paid today so ill run you up if you can wait.

What about my son vincent are you just goen to leave him in the lurch.

Your goen to costigan house right.

Yes.

That will take us twenty minutes at the out side. I will text vincent to say im delayed. I sayed i would be there some time be four twelve. Plenty time.

So we are out again at hecla square the streets still wet from last night. There are a lot of people about as usual but no faces i recinise if i could see them. Hope fully no annette though she is like marlys ghost bud says. Always trailen after wanten some thing from you. Rattlen her jewelry at you. It is better not to trust these kind of people he says. If they are worken for the counsil or for social services or from a church or from some interest group keep out there road. Except i ament so good at tellen folk to leave me in peace partly be cause i can not tell who they are until they are up close even with my good glasses and partly be cause they can see me comen. That is in fact how i met annette she door stepped me in the street next to the bus stop and of course me being me i couldent tell her wear to get of.

It was near here i was sitten on the bench. Out side of the bookies. I dident know what the eff i was up to or any thing i was in some state as vincent would say. O hello there this woman sayed to me she was a big plump woman with a feathery scarf a round her she reminded me of a big fat pigeon with its feathers puffed up.

Are you okay there she asked me.

I am fine i told her i just need to sit a minute. You looken for a date.

A date no. Is every thing all right.

Every thing is good i sayed every thing is super.

I cant mind what happened next i went to rise from the bench and felt my legs wobbly under neath me. Of coursed it was be cause of those shoes with heel i wore i wasent to steady be cause of the heels.

O my she sayed look at that.

Here let me help you up.

And she put her arm around me to steady me.

There were a group of those boys near by i could here them laughen at me. They had been laughen at me for a while. I had been sitten there for a while. I dident know what was so funny but they were laughen. They had come up and sat down be side me one on either side and asked me for a cigaret. You looken for a cigarette how about a date. It is only 25 quid. But they were not looken for any date just cigarets. Of course i had no cigarets then i found one boy tryen to go in to my pockets. I stopped his hand and the person jumped away but i knew him. It only took that half a second but i knew. It was vincent i stared at him he just backed away not sayen any thing. Vincent i sayed come here. But he dident come here he disapeared. It shook me up a bit i have to tell you.

So there i was sat there these boys laughen i shouted things at them from time to time. 25 quid for that one shouted back. I will give you a fiver.

It was a cold night i remember i dont know why i dident go home there was no money to be made. Annette came and helped me up and took me a round the corner and i dident argew.

O dear it looks as though you have had a wee accident love. Why dont you come with me and we will see if we can get you cleaned up.

So of course that was what the boys were all laughen at the sight of me a woman old enough to be there mother who had wet her selve in a public place.

She got me to the library and in to the bath room there she got a key from some one. I remember be cause i have once or twice tried to use there toilets but come away disapointed be cause they were locked to the public. There was a sign on the door of them i couldent read at that time or couldent under stand one or the other. So i just had to leave un satisfied. Annette told me later that the sign sayed please ask for the key at recepshoun. Or rather she dident tell me she helped me work it out my selve. When she per suaded me to come to her group. That night though she helped me get out of my wet things and gave me some soapy towels and even managed to get an old skirt from a box in one of the back rooms some one had left there for some reason. She washed my things in a sink and rang them and gave me them back to hang up at home in a plastic bag.

Next she got me a cup of tea and produced some stale pieces that were in the staff fridge from a do the day be four. We sat and ate them at a table in a corner of the library. It was warm and quite and so restful. So restful i would of fallen a sleep there if i could. There were some single individ duals at computers in the centre of the library but also individ duals at tables readen books or papers

Left over from my group she sayed offeren me a piece. We meet here on thursdays. We had a wee party to celebrate one of the groups success in winnen a prize for riten a poem and readen it a loud in front of an audience of other groups.

I drank my tea and did not say much. I was in some state but i have never got any thing to say when some one menshouns poetry. They are the worst kinds of books of all i find.

Annette dident need me to say any thing however she is some times good that way.

You know she sayed it is only the first step admitten you have problem. That is the start of it yes. But it is only a first step.

Yes i told her. Thank you for the tea and sand wiches.

Well. It was difficult to follow what she was talken a bout. I thought she meant drinken to much and wetten your selve on a public thorough fair but it turned out she meant readen and riten. Or may be readen and riten as well as wetten your selve i wasent so sure at the time.

After the first step of admitten your difficulty there is the desire to do some thing about it to. I ament sure if that has occurred to you yet. Has it grace.

No. I am pretty sure it hasent yet.

Well then she sayed. There isent any point in me goen on and on about it to you. After all we have only just met.

Annette laughed at this as if it was the funniest thing and i caught a waft of her perfume which smelled v expensive.

I like your perfume i told her it is very nice.

O this she sayed i think enjoyen that some one had noticed. This is my favourite i coudent say which one it is so expensive i am leaven hints to my husband to get me a refill at xmas. Chanel no 5 it has always been my favourite. So expensive though isent it.

Yes i told her it is very dear. It is to dear for me at the moment but i have liked it in the past.

O yes she sayed. A boy friend must have got you some did he.

That is right i told her. And then i found my selve just talken to her with out any worrys or concerns a bout it worries and concerns which would normally have persuaded me to keep my mouth shut. I began to talk about my selve i opened up as annette would say.

I had this boy friend from a young age just out of school really. He was the sort of boy who would buy you things give you flowers and so forth. I think he saved and bought me some of that perfume once. It is funny but i can not even remember what his name was now. Isent that teribel to not remember his name. I do not even know most of there names isent that teribel. They are just blank faces to me i hardly remember them after wards. I had a few boy friends some gave me to re member them by than others.

I hesitated for a second looken at annette. She dident seem to have any kind of judge mental face on even through good lenses.

O i dont know sayed annette. It dosent seem such a crime to me. Im sure i have had the ocashounal forget able boy friend to.

I remember thinken how nice it was in that library with the tea and the sand wiches and the warm. Even all the books dident see so intimidaten perhaps it was be cause of annette haven been so kind. I have often found that weather you like or dont like a place is to do with acts of decency from others or there lack. And there was annette already haven helped me already not tellen me what i had to do or had not to do. I re call thinken that may be it could be time to give it an other go. I re call thinken i might be ready to try one more time and that this would be the last time i would give it a shot if it dident work this time i would just have to live with it no matter the cone sequences.

I menshouned this to annette who laughed but not a laugh that was dismiseve.

O i know but wait till the mornen may be. You will likely want to have a re think when you have sobered up a littel bit. Dont jump to any conclushouns just yet grace. It is a big commitment to admit your dependency.

I meant improven my readen and riten annette.

O she sayed. O ha ha trust me to get the wrong end of the stick. O dear me.

Annette seemed to me to be a kind person a lady of a difirint background than my selve. Her accent was difirint to mine but it would have been difirint to other people of nearer my own age from even her own area. It was like an accent you here in sertin kinds of church. I am sure i have heard those accents in a church or some other relidgous place. That was the only factor that caused me any worry at the time. That there was goen to be some sort of catch to the whole thing she was about to try and con vert me to her believes.

It was not enough to stop me from tellen her all about every thing our hole situashoun. It wasent enough to prevent me from tellen about francis and her dependence and bud and his trouble with owen money and vincent haven just left the school no better of qualificashoun wise than his stupid mother that had walked away from them near garscadden woods. Of course there were other things to. Buds temper and his bad leg. The roof over our heads.

Annette just listened. After a while i began to get uncomfort able with the sound of my own voice talken. You just blether on and on dont you gracie i told my selve. Why can you not just shut up. Why not just shut your stupid mouth you idjit. This woman isent interested in listenen to your tales of woe. And what tales they are to grace you make it sound like there is no thing in your life good. That is what you sound like to this woman isent it. Yes.

It is odd about annette she always seemed abel to help you out of your selve. I supose that was an other reason for goen to her group. It isent like i had all these great friends there or any thing.

There must be positif things in your live she asked me. No thing is ever entirely nergatif is it.

I couldent think at the time though.

There must be some thing grace. Just think for a minute.

Annette was nibblen on one of these a bit stale sand witches. They were all tuna which i am parshial to. I remember she had a littel smidge of mayonase on her cheek at the side of her mouth.

She stopped for a second to get out her inhaler and huff on it.

You know i have a confeshoun to make she sayed. There

is so much good in my life so many positif things i havent any complaints. My husband the church my daughter nina who im so proud of. But to tell you the truth grace im a very shallow person.

I was surprised at annette for sayen this. She is hardly shallow for a woman of her stature.

Its true grace im so shallow you know what makes me happiest. Not really.

Well let me tell you. It is haven a time table. It is haven a time table and sticken to it. Isent that daft. First thing when i get up i consult last nights time table for this mornen. I am so organised i plan out the day the night be four. In the mornen i check it and make any tweeks and adjustments. And what is more i will re right my timetable constantly over the course of a day. If i am runnen late it will not only throw me in to a total panic it will be the most exciten thing that can happen as well. Imagine that grace.

Annette seemed as pleased as any thing to be tellen me this. I could not think of any thing that i did that might be similar.

So it isent the big things that make me happiest you see. Of course they are the importent things they are the hinges of your life if you like. But it is my own small obseshouns that seem to give me most pleasure. If i can find a way to cut a minute or two here it will make me almost stupidly happy. When i arrive at my group i am always the first there but i cant allow my selve to cheat i must take a certain amount of time. For instance i can not leave the place wear i have been early to get there. I have a regular meet with an elder lay gentle man of certin means who prefers to commune in the privacy of his own home. Well he is un like most of my clients and groups in this but that is okay. It is his preferred way. But i cant leave early un less he requests it. If he wishes to go over the agreed time i wont allow that but i cant stop short by so much as a few seconds. This elder lay gentleman often wants me to give him a few more minutes but im very rigid this way.

However the soshial pleasantrys of comen and goen often take up preshous minutes and i some times have to tweek my planned route. I have got to en sure i arrive no later than ten minutes be four the group arrives in order to make sure every thing all the materials are arranged and the kettle on and the room is warm and so on. Then i have to settle down and look at my time table and my notes for the group and arrange my selve so i am comfort table. When all that is done i will say a few spiritual words to my selve just to focus on the positif keep an open heart to the future and em brace what ever it brings. Then i am ready.

I remember wanderin what a complicated live annette must have but it must have been a round that time i started to be come over conserned about getten around between public conveniences so may be we are more alike now than i first thought.

Still i couldent think of the things that made me happy.

What about your home then grace annette asked.

I thought about that and after a while i sayed yes i supose that does make me happy. I do feel relieved to get inside our own front door ours and the counsils. I like to be at home when there is peace and the worrys have gone for the moment. And bud to i enjoy his humour he can make me laugh so much some times.

What about your children grace do they not make you happy.

Annette was leanen for ward and i wanted to wipe the smudge of mayonase of her chin but had to control the im pulse.

Your son and daughter do they not make you happy.

I shook my head no my son tryed to steal from me he dident help me his own mother. He left me there in hecla square he prefered to look the big man in front of his friends.

O that isent so good. No that is a shame full way to be have to your own mother. But may be he is just at that age may be he is rebelling and it will pass. I am sure he isent all bad is he.

No i had to admit. My son vincent was not all bad. Neither

was my daughter francis be four she be came dependent. She was not all bad though we have never seen eye to eye not even when she was littel. She would try and lead vincent a stray. Of course she was the ring leader in any troubel. Vincent looked up to his sister which is why it was such a worry that may be he would be tempted to. It was enough to worry about the other people he hung about with it was to much to worry that his own sister was likely a worse influence.

I told all this to annette and she listened.

Isent there any thing about your daughter that has ever made you happy or proud she asked me.

When she was younger she used to make up stories and right them in the back pages of her school work. I would get angry with her for de facing the jotter and sayed you will get in trouble from your teachers for this. Bud it was that red me what she had righten once. You cant stop her from righten gracie he told me. Look how good she is. She has righten these stories and you know what. They are great. She has a great image inashoun. You know she is like you to you have a great image inashoun just of a difirint kind. But francis can write what she imagines down and you will never stop her from doen that when she is bored in her class. She has got some thing here that no body can teach. Let her write what she likes in her school book. If she gets in trouble then so be it. But one day she will make you proud of her if you en couradge her.

And did it annette asks me.

It made me proud and happy when he told me how well she could write stories. Yes. But im afraid i dident encouradge her very much. I found it hard even then to en couradge her we were so often at logger heads.

O annette sayed. Well grace we are all just human arent we. We arent always able to do the right thing at the right time. It dosent always make us bad people just fallible. We are just people after all we are weak and dont always do the right thing at the right time. May be we should look to be better rather than dwell on our mistakes. We should ask our selves what we can do to be better and give thanks for what we have.

You have got some thing at the side of your mouth annette i told her.

O have i. Well may be i should give thanks for that she sayed laughen. Yum yum.

Gregors car is a small white one to match buster he says. It is quite cramped and un tidy with crisp packets and empty cans of juice lyen on all the seats so he has to clear them on to the floor so that i can sit down. There is a distinct odur in this car no dowt about it. I was goen to sit in the back so i wouldent have to talk but unfortunately he insists i sit up the front with him.

You dont want to sit in busters place he says. It is possible he has pished it once or twice ha ha.

I supose dogs are inclined to do that kind of a thing i say.

So i am sitten up the front with my knees up a round my ears. Buster yowls away in the back he is an odd dog. His yowlen seems un conectid to un happiness. He yows away as though there is no greater fun thing to do in all the world. He does not yowl loud though only a quite yowlen as though he is digesten some tasty morsel like his pigs ear and wants to tell you of his enjoy ment. He is a bit like littel sean that way with his noises and burblen. It is a simple enjoy ment of his five or however many senses i think. Neither littel sean or buster is thinken to hard about what is on there mind they are just in the moment most likely. I think it must be a wander full thing. It is like freedom.

Sorry about the state of the motor gregor says. He is tryen to start the car and it is whinen away competen for atenshoun with buster who suddenly sticks a cold wet nose in my ear from be hind which makes me start but the car dosent.

Give it a minute gregor says. This girl needs some four play be four she puts out.

I am pretenden not to here a bit embaresed looken out of the window the dull light splitten my eye now. Just the community pool builden oposite to see but then the engine coughs in to life and we back out of the regenerashoun centre car park. The sky is still grey but i wander weather it will rain like yester days whether did. Your sister marie will be in the sun shine to day worken in the hotel may be given up on you grace. She will be engaged in what ever a house keeper in a hotel does at this time of day collecten the linen or some thing of that nature. At least vincent has spoken to her so she will know the problem. May be she will have picked up my bag except of course she wouldent know what it looked like would she. Likely she wouldent even think of it.

Marie has never even seen littel sean has she gracie. No. She has been away that long not in port adventurer the canary isles but other places in and out of them.

It would be so good to here her voice today. So you must make that extra effort to contact her gracie. It is your own stupid fault you are here and not there speaken spanish like in your dream. That would be wander full haven the ability to speak in a difirint langwidge of course you did have some lessons in school. French it was and even latin. Naturally you dident show any great aptitude for either as well. Marie of course will speak spanish now she has been there a while. Remember how she told you of the delishous spanish foods there gracie they sounded interesten even though you are a fussy eater. There was potatos boiled dry in a pale of sea water. They dident sound so marvelus right enough. However there were other delicasies marie talked of that may be you would like to try like sea food of difirint types and meats to. You have always liked meat havent you. There is no doubt about that one is there.

We are okay for time just now i think gregor says who dosent make you fear for your life when he is driven like some people annette is one. I can not see so well but it is more of a feelen of security no thing sudden happens no sudden jerks or stops or any thing like that. It is nice. Bud used to be a driver to be four his leg. That was his main job driven a van. He used to love it he sayed. He got a lot more regular work driven than any thing else he did removals and deliverys and carten things about the place. How ever he could not afford to keep his van after his leg. He was layed up so long that he had to get rid of it for the money which of course got him down. He would just sit about all day with no apetite for any thing not even to play the guitar. He just watched telly all day day time tv with shows about arguments no energy even to shout at the telly like he used to. Need less to say my son vincent was not to under standen since they have never got on well. Also bud was very hard on francis to whom he was fond of. Bud is smarter than me he could tell what she was getten up to he knew. I was blind to every thing. It was only when i found her with to male friends tryen to drag the telly out that i began to realise. O course francis never had any girl friends only men she could wind round her littel pinky. I never have had any female friends either so in that regard she has took after my selve.

Wear are you taken our telly francis i asked her. She dident reply. She and the to male friends just quitely put the telly down and walked out the door. They dident dignify me with even one word of response. I was not even worth that her own mother. She simply shook her head as though it was my fault she had to take the telly. And do you know what i thought it must be. It must be my own fault for not providen for her better. You should of looked after your daughter francis better than this grace it is your own fault you are a bad mother to her. It is stupid that she has had to do this be cause of your own indequacys as a parent.

Bud sayed it is absolutely not your fault grace. That is just plane daft to say that. Your effen daughter is dependent and is sellen your gear to buy her own. Are you effen nuts or what. Jesus christ. Have you not tried grace. Can you not see how she is for effs sake. I have tried to tell you but you will not see it. You just can not see that your daughter is a dependent and you can not see that she can not be helped any more things will only get worse. So bud sayed.

You cant help her any more grace you have been blind to what has been goen on here and it isent helpen for effs sake. There is a limit to what we can do he sayed. After that you have to say no more enough is enough.

We dont have to say no more she isent your daughter. It isent up to you i told him.

Of course she was not his daughter but she could still wrap him a round her littel finger couldent she grace. Yes. She could get him to do any thing just give him her look and let her hair hang over the way she used to be always brushen it over to one side. She always had the brush she was always brushen brushen. What beauty full hair she had grace that was yours you gave her that. You and her father who ever he was.

Aye i know that bud sayed. I know how effen welcome i am a round here. You think i dont grace be cause i do so. I am the expend able one a round here no doubt about that. Bud spence is the one that has to go if the shit hits the fan.

I remember that rant all to well we ended up screamen and throwen things and bud sayen calm down grace. We were yellen fit to burst and some one called the polis a naybour or some one. There was shouten and swearen and the next thing was vincent was there in the middel to and boom the next thing after that was bud on the floor and me on top of him.

Vincent you hit him i was shouten why did you do that. Vincent why did you.

I never even touched him vincent sayed but there was bud on the floor of the kitchen with his mouth all blood.

I was benden over him bud i sayed are you all right. Are you okay.

Get of of me you he sayed. Some thing like that any way. I ament to sure to tell you the truth what happened. I had a mygrain and had took a few whisky toddys.

Then the polis were asken us all questions and bud was angry he was refusen to go with the ambalence. He was fine he was sayen. Leave us alone i am fine. On the good ship lollipop he was singen. Thumbs up doll he shouted. Double thumbs up gracie. The polis are simply an army disined to protect capital and the mechanisems of state so called. Isent that right gracie.

Vincent was in an other room with an other polis man. A polis lady kept tryen to get me to stand in the hall while bud was given a state ment. I am fine he kept sayen i am fine. Leave us alone i am fine. On the good ship lollipop he was singen its a short trip to the offy shop. He was tryen to dance.

Man i love driven gregor says. He is clicken on the radio and it is heavey metal music comen out. He says do you like that i loved that when i was growen up all they hard rock bands. Buster you love it to dont you pal. Give us a song.

I can feel busters pause on the back of the seat scratchen.

Sing buster gregor says. Sing.

So buster begins to howl and howl it is funny for to seconds then i want it to stop.

Sorry grace gregor says and turns the radio of. Buster goes back to his happy yowlen.

You and buster are inseper able arent you i say.

Gregor dosent say any thing for a second.

You know what gracie sorry grace. Buster saved my life. He saved my life. I mean he took me out of my selve when i was so low you would not of believed it.

You do not seem like the sort of person who gets low.

I ament that sort of person but when you spend a long time on your own you can get that way. I couldent find work i was separatid from my partner my kids i was just goen down the toilit as a person. It was as if the army had been the real family to me and my own i couldent even deal with them. They dident be have like the family that had been looken after me for nine year. I just couldent hack it the family i did have. So the ex wife the partner says right thats it we are of out of it. And i went mental for a while.

I am looken out of the window but can not see to much on this dreich friday in febuary. Just trees travelen past and wet drops on the windows and my head feelen fractured now. We are on dumbarton road i think but i ament sure. I wander have we past the cranes of red clyde. I could ask gregor if he knows what the red clyde siders did he does seem like the kind of person who would know.

So buster came along and it was love at first sight isent that right pal.

He is driven with one hand and reachen back to touch buster in the seat be hind which makes me a bit nervis.

How did you get him i ask.

You know there was an evicshoun and a crowd of us volunteers went up to try and stop the bay leafs throwen the folk in the flat out. We heard about the evicshoun and we were all ragen and formed a posse and went up there and tried to show some solidarity and get the evicshoun preventid.

Who was it getten evicted did you know them.

We dident know them well or any thing. But they were people.

They were folk who had come here looken to create a better life for them selves and there familys.

Did it work.

Gregor is quite again.

It got publicity and it delayed it but no. The folk liven there still got evicted. The polis came and re moved all the protesters and dragged them out. But one of them had a young pup he asked me to take and i says eh. How can i look after a dog. But the chap says please just take him. So i did. And thats how i met the love of my life. Christ i had to stop and really think about things. But it was one of the best things i ever did isent that right buster pal. Sing pal.

Gregor says aaaawoooooo

and buster bursts in to song right there in the back of the car and it feels like the to of them must be smilen away to gether it is truly a meeten of minds.

Oof sorry gregor says suddenly pullen the car to a halt. Got carried away.

What is it i say looken out the front wind screen. Have we stopped to avoid some thing i wander.

Your stop grace gregor says. Costigan house after the lights change.

O i say. I am relieved there is no thing to worry about but am not really looken forward to costigan house. Gregor drives on and up to the front of the builden after the lights change and we stop. The engine dies and we sit there a minute the car warm and comfort able even buster quite and settled.

Listen gregor says i will give you my phone number. If you are worried about any thing give me a call. I will not be given your son any illushouns about the forces but if you are conserned just ring. Any time grace okay.

I nod okay and he rummages through the debris for a piece of paper he can write on.

Shall we sing a song he says after he gives me the number. Its very healthy very zen he says. Come on grace. Buster sing.

Aaaaahoooooo gregor sings wear wolves of londin

aaaaahoooooo buster sings to

come on grace sing it aaaahooooooo

he takes my hand and raises it aaaaahooooooooo grace come on

i am laughen no i am no singer

come on he says wear wolves of londin

aaaaahoooooooooo.

then there is so much racket from the pear of them that i can not help but join in as well.

It is margaret who lets me in to costigan house and i know this can not be good if she has taken it upon her selve to answer the door. What can have happened i wander. Is there some troubil.

Grace come in she says. Her voice is not tellen me any thing though it is flat not given any thing a way.

I can not really see her face to well at all she is standen in the shadow of the door and the day light is comen back at me from the lenses of her glasses. I am haven to squint now really to keep the light out of my left eye my head ache is so bad. It isent really like a head ache at all it is more as if my skull has cracked from a place above my left eye down around it by my nose and down to the tip of my chin. It is as though there are two halfs of my head. The vishoun be comes so pain ful i can not hardly even bear it some times and there is no thing for it but to lie down and stay still till it passes.

I go over to sign the book but the pain of my head and the intone ashouns of margaret prevent my usual fear of getten seen riten from taken over. When ever you put your name to some thing it is proof of some thing isent it. It is a record it can be used against you. It can back fire. You can run up debts and lose even the roof over your head just by doen that small semen thing. That is wear all your troubels begin that small signature. It is as if you are signen away bits of your selve you can never get back. Halve the time you do not even kow what you are signen up for when you put your name down on a piece of paper do you grace. Not understanden what the small print says if how you end up destitute or in jail. Well. I wish just now to just be at home in the dark ness of my drawn curtains and to sleep and sleep.

No need to sign grace margaret says to me. She puts her hand on my shoulder and i step out of reach but not rudely. What can say i have told you already i have never cared for bein man handeld even by a woman like margaret.

O sorry grace she says. Its just we dont need your signachure to day. The shifts are full up on the schedule.

Margaret says this in that lilten accent of hers she is from the carbean. Her skin is shiney some what like the light reflecten of some thing i ament sure what. Not her glasses but that is how dark she is it is so shiney. I have not always got on well with her she is an other relidgous person. She is the senior worker who deals with my selve and michelle her white slaves ha ha michelle says.

I wasent expecten to work to day margaret i just came by to see when there would be shifts i tell her.

I know she will ask then why not phone but be four she can i add that

i was on my way to partick to get some messages so i just dropped by.

Uh hum uh hum margaret says it is her thing. That and tryen to put her hand on your four head so that you will let in the divine light. That and always tellen you about her home in the caribean saint some wear or other. I have heard about this place from her so much i just switch of.

Of course grace of course. Come through and get a cup of tea in the kitchen. Some thing has come to the light that we need to talk about.

My head is so pain full i ament even worried i just follow her like a littel lost lamb halve a sleep. I wander if my sister marie ever has been to the caribean there was a time she used to send post cards from all over the place. Port this and saint that when she was crewen on a crews ship. I was never sure weather to belief that she worked on a crews ship i was so sure i saw her once right here in this city. Except wear would she have got the post cards. I was not always sertin about my sister maries wear abouts to tell you the truth.

O hello michelle i say she is standen by the hob waiten for the kettle her arms crossed.

Em hi grace michelle says. She also seems un like her selve. She dosent move from that hob in fact she seems to be stuck there.

Grace sit down please margaret says and pulls a chair up for me. Michelle is that tea ready yet.

Did you ever find out about the red clyde siders michelle i ask her when she comes over with my cup.

No grace i dident. Did you.

I take a sip very hot and sweet sugar in it again. Thanks i tell her no i never found out. I guess it is lost to history then eh.

I guess so michelle says.

Margaret sits down and i can hear her breathen out through her nose. I am waiten. I can feel michelle is waiten to.

So grace margaret says it seems some thing has come to light that the whole team here feel needs to be talked about. So we have been talken it over and it was decided by the whole team that i should talk to you about it since you are the one it conserns.

I nod i can not think just nod.

Be four we start this mater dident come to light until michelle menshouned it in conversashoun with an other member of staff. She has volunteered to be here with me to talk to you about it be cause she feels

and maragaret looks up to michelle back by the hob and asks her how do you feel michelle.

Em i dont know says michelle.

If i might put some words in to your mouth michelle perhaps it is that you feel responsible is that it.

Michelle dosent say any thing. She shifts then says mmm.

What is this about i say hardly able to lift my head any more.

Are you all right grace margaret asks me leaning over and very gently placing her hands over mine on my lap.

I am fine margaret i say. I can not believe that michelle. Is it even that importent to the job. Is it more important than the hands on skills to be abel to rite as well as all that. Per haps it is. I can not believe that michelle would tell on me though. I have always considered her a colleag her at costigan house.

Margarit seems un sure and says no thing. I can here michelle footer about with cutlery spoons or some thing.

May be if you had an aspirin or some thing margaret i say. Perhaps that would help.

Of course grace margaret says. But it is michelle who goes to the medical supply room. She opens the kitchen door and i see some one getten wheeled by in a chair of to the liven room. I can not even make them out but then i here a voice struggelen to get out eff eff of it says. I think that must be mister tarick sarwar settlen in. They are of to help him watch day time tv in the liven room.

Michelle comes back and gives me to pills to take with water and then we all sit there waiten.

Grace margaret says this matter is quite serious. Do you know what i am talken about.

Yes i tell her. But i will do some thing about it. I will get help.

Margaret is shaken her head. Im afraid it is to serius for that grace. There are proseses.

I will see some one margaret.

Margaret shakes her head again. No grace not this time. If this has been happenen be four it cant continue.

I have already taken one or to classes i say i am sure if costigan house gives me a chance i can improve. I can bring my level up to a beter standard.

A beter standard margaret says. A better standard of what.

A level of improve ment i tell her. Of readen. And riten.

Readen and riten uh huh hmm margaret says in a flat way as though the words are round smooth pebels rollen round the in side of her mouth.

Did you know about this michelle she says.

Not at all michelle says like she has been insulted. As if her spyen has not been adequate to the job.

Grace this isent about weather your readen is up to par. This concerns your relashounship with mr munro who we buried yesterday.

I just sit there. O no.

Old eddy i say with no other words feelen every thing crumble away from under neath me.

Yes michelle says. You were abusen old eddy munro. You told me you were so dont deny it.

She comes almost runnen to wards me as though she wants to knock me of my chair. Then margaret waves her hands and says o please michelle calm down. I would like to here what grace has to say.

I never abused old eddy i say. I never. That isent my style at all.

But you had a relashounship with him margaret says. A physical one. That is what michelle says you told her. Did you tell her you had had a physical relashounship with mister munro.

Of course i had a physical relashounship with old eddy i say to her.

Margaret throws her hands up dont you realise what you have done she says. How on earth did you conseive it would be accept able. That is it grace the matter will have to go to disipliniry. You are suspended until we can establish exactly what happened. If you had a physical relashounship with mister munro im afraid your whole career will be in jeopardy.

Margaret i say. Of course i had a physical relashounship with eddy munro. Of course i did. We all did.

Michelle shouts o that is untrue i never had.

Yes you did i say. Every one who worked with him had a physical relashounship with eddy.

I realise though my head is cracked in halve that there isent any point in deny ing any thing it will be michelles word against mine.

Every one who bathed eddy or changed his under wear or got him dressed or un dressed or took him to the toilet or put him to bed or greased his sores had a physical relashounship with him. The same goes for every person under our roof here at costigan house. If i have had a physical relashounship with eddy munro i have had one with every person liven in this building.

That isent what i meant margaret says and you know it.

I stand up i am goen now i say. You can take me to disciplinary hearens if you want but i dident do any thing wrong. Who is to say that it was wrong what i did we are in the job of caren here at costigan house. So if it is okay to wash and change him why is what you both are accusen me of wrong. Wear is the line. If eddy needed some help some soothen help then per haps it is some times right to give it.

I think you need to leave now margaret says. I am just so shocked. I am so dis appointed in you grace. Go on get out you will be informed of the proseses by male.

O that is wander full. O that is the icen on the cake. They are goen to send me a letter. I get up and walk out of the kitchen i can see mr tarick sarwar in the liven room he is looken a round his hand is in a fist he is looken at me through the door imploren but there is no thing i can do to help.

I set of walken but i dont know wear to it. It is as if i am in a kind of stupour just wanderen my head bursten but not able really to think much about what has happened. It seems likely i will lose my job. It seems likely i will be un likely to ever get more work any wear else after either.

I could lie down here in the street and pull the covers over my head and never wake up again it is all to much troubel. How many jobs have you been through gracie. Not many thats how many. Not many jobs since you stopped bein dependent on men and there money. But this was just about the best one wasent it. Even though you dident do that many shifts and they passed you over for margaret even though she had been here in this country hardly any time at that time.

Even though i am so done in i dont want to go home yet. Then i will just have to sit and think on this until it is time to pick up sean.

O gracie how are you goen to look after them now. How will you ever keep sean safe.

I wander if it really was francis on the cctv the other day. Or was it your imaginashoun grace. Perhaps you just see what you want to see. Your children leaven you be hind when you left them and walked away. Vincent and those boys did you really see that. Bud and francis to gether. Under your own roof. Yours and the counsils. Was it even francis you saw those other times.

Tell me marie. You would of know what was goen on if you were here. Wouldent you. Yes.

Marie your sister that used to send you post cards. Every time she went away you would get one from some far of place. Some difirint country you never believed her though did you grace. You always had doubts about it. Even port adventurer the canary isles you were not sure. Per haps she was there per haps she wasent. Even sitten in that air port you were un sure you thought it was all made up dident you grace. Yes. You thought she was maken it all up and you would get of the plane and there would be no body there to meet you there would be no body at all. So what if francis is the same grace. What if it isent her on that cctv. You were sitten in that air port and you dident even want to go. You were afraid. It is like every time be four. You stop be four you even start. So you put your ticket in the case and sent it in stead. You never believed marie would be waiten for you so you found a way not to go dident you. Dident you grace.

O my head is comen apart. Well. It is temporary it will pass. Wear are you goen grace. Wear are you taken your selve. Wear was even the last place you saw her.

Wear grace. Think. You know dont you. Yes.

The last place you saw her. What have you got to lose.

No thing. No thing and every thing. If she is a dependent still. If she comes for sean.

She is still your daughter to grace. Sean is her son. You can not stop her if she wants to take him. She is his mother. She is your daughter. So you should go and find her.

I start walken to wards the train stashion at hyndland. I turn on to the steps and walk down on to the plat form headen in to town.

Some thing is not right about this. Some thing is not right about this stashoun. What is it gracie boats. What is difirent. What shore have you gone and fetched up on. My heart is goen mad in side of my chest. It is this place not right the bilden the stashoun is difirent. It was a grey block before now its a see through box except i can not see through it. I can not see the bilden any more. I can not see the other side just dark shapes.

For a second i see lugidge goen round on a carousel. On port adventurer in canary isles. Here there is a bangen and construcshoun noises. Sparks jetten up from some one a machine. The shapes of people are moven about on it builders and i am thinken what have they done with partick stashoun. Wear have they put it. Some one be hind me asks to get by i move for them my hands shaky my hands not right in them selves.

This must be the wrong stop grace. You are at the wrong stop. What have they done with your stashoun.

There is a bad smell like burnen rubber and noise a screechen like of tools. The shouts of these men. There noises all in a langwidge i dont speak. I couldent say what langwidge it is and there is no body here on the plat form to help but these foriners who can not under stand our langwidge though its my country. It is my country i was born here not there. Me and bud and sean and vincent. Francis to.

Dont get in a panic grace. Dont have an atack. Not here wear all these people can see you. Not here wear every one is a stranger you can not trust to help. But i can not help my selve either. I can not stop my selve from looken about desperate. I breath in through my nose and hold the air let it out slowly. Then again. Then again slowly and more. I can not help my selve.

My hands are not right. They arent right in them selves.

The clippey told you this was your stop he wouldent lie. His job is to help. It is like annette said. That is what they are payed for. They are payed to help not to lie and mis lead folk. To help.

So there i say to my selve. You are all right grace. You are in the right place all right. It has to be.

I am looken up at the sign on the plat form which i can not read even if i strain all day. I will never be able to read that sign. I will never know what it says. It says partick your right gracie. That is what it says. It must. But it isent any use to wander be cause you cant know for sure. Not you. Not that sign or any sign be cause they were all right every one is right you are to stupid to unders tand not just a foriners langwidge but even your own langwidge.

You can not speak
you can not read
you can not rite it.

Not even if you have your proper glasses can you read it. Not you grace. You will never be able to do that. You are going round and round in circles. Every one can see you to. Marie and bud and vincent and annette and even francis they can all see as well. Per haps even mr tarick sarwar could of told. Every one you know except for sean whose to young. Except he wont always be he will grow up and then he will see to. Even bobby that you trusted seen it.

This is not a good situashoun grace. Bobby sayed that then. This is not a good situashoun getten lost in your own neighbour hood.

Francis your daughter and vincent your son You were there own mother grace. They tried to lose you that day. That is what they think of you. That is what they think about what you have given up for them.

I can not believe it has been a whole year already. 1 whole yer and 22 days how many hours how many minutes more.

Well. I stand there and feel spots of rain here and there on my face and hair. The men on the scaff old are bateren away at there work and have took no notice of me down here just as well. It is just selve indulgence on my part as per ushial. It was me wanted to get away. So what if it isent partick station which it is it must be. Even if it isent the right station you only have to cross and go back and you will be home dry gracie. Except it is it must be. It is partick. It is your own neighbour hood. These people are your neighbours. They cant understand you but they are in your own neighbour hood. You are home and dry nearly. Well not home dry but back at partick wear you know.

You can cross over to the other side and go back.

There is no thing to it people do it all the time even you have done it be fore plenty.

This isent the stop after ex hibishoun centre. You can see that now silly. You can tell it isent any wear but partick. Ex hibishoun centre is under a bridge of some kind. A walk way or for traffic.

So this is still partick. It is just so long since you have come in this far that they are re constructen it. They are doing it up grace. Dont be afraid gracie. Remember you were looken not to be so fear full of every dashed thing well this is your first big step. A wee step for man kind but an effen big leap for you grace. For you gracie boats. So now you have to be true to your stupid name sail away in to the sunset even though it is clowedy as any thing plus you cant swim either.

You would drown in a shallow bath.

They are just doing builden work here and thats all it is. About time to it was in a teribel shoddy state. I bet the effen moven stairs are switched of to. Bud would put money on that. If bud was here he would make a joke out of it and see me all right down the steps. If bud was here. How ever you have left bud behind today gracie. You are here on your lone some so get on with it silly. One foot in front of an other.

You have got to get to the door first grace. Then through to the moven stairs which will be tricky if they arent switched of. There is some one holden the door for me so i go through and follow him its a man he says no bother when i say thanks. I let him go on to the moven steps first be four me and he stands moven on them. They are switched on and there it is again a tingle in my skin and hair when i step on too. I hold on to the hand rail which is wet from some one but i keep hold any way and it takes me down then theres the next bit getten of okay at the bottom. It is easy to slip or trip up lucky i have thought not to wear those holiday shoes espadrills. I have good solid semen shoes. Sturdy.

I wander if marie has called to find out wear i am. I ament looken forward to speaken to her explainen. Still she might have got your lugidge gracie.

It is rainen a bit out side the stashoun now. The cloweds have got really dark in the mean time. I take out my purse and count what money i have. It isent much thats for sertin but enough in case of an emergancy like i dont know what. To make a phone call to vincent i supose though would he help not likely. He would just moan. It is getten to the point wear we will have to pay and get our land line re conected. Though bud has got not much money to speak of though he tries his best. It isent like he gets payed to look after sean for me. He just does it any way.

I walk round to dumbarton road and go to the cross lights. There are a load of people about buses and cars every wear. Woolies is on the other side but i dont feel like goen in unless maybe the rain comes on heavy. O what the hell grace i say to my selve it is only water you can only get so wet dafty. I keep walken on woolies side of the street past the post office then i turn back and go in. There it is what im looken for. Post cards.

I take one out it with a picture of some thing or other on it. It is just a blur to me but that is okay. It will do okay. So long as it isent one of those rude ones but i dont think so. A lands cape i think. One of those scottish places we never seem to go to even though it is v nice. Bud has cycled down before he bet vincents bike. My son vincent was ragen about that but to be fair he never rode it. It was too wee for him he fairly shot up the last couple of years. He is as tall as well not so tall as bud but broader. He is a big lad vincent. Some of the time i can here him doen excersizes in his room in the mornen and at night to. He comes out all sweaty and puffed. If it isent that that hes doen then i think i am better of not knowen thank you very much.

How can some one change so much in so short a space of time i wander. When he was small he was so funny and smiley but now he hardly even speaks. He is totally in to the army he would join up he says. There are posters on the walls of his room of a chalinger tank. That is his ambishoun to drive a chalinger tank. To tell you the truth i ament sure he still has it up that poster. I ament inclined to look around his room even with glasses. It is a bomb site in there. It makes me shudder just to think of. It is funny how he is so clean and tidy with him selve but his room is so filthy. Plus i know for a fact that he hasent changed those sheets of his for over a month i dont think. Well. If he wants them washed he can dashed well do it him selve. I ament goen any wear near them.

I go over to the counter with the post card and use one of there pens on a bit of string an old chewed biro. It is on a long string some one must have gone down on there knees on the ground to chew it up. I take the chewed cap of this chewed biro it makes me sorry for who ever did it.

Except i cant think of what i can rite. I am no good with letters. I can not effen well rite any thing except a name and address.

So thats what i do.

I rite my name and adress on it in big letters then go to the counter and wait to pay for a stamp. Then i am goen to drop it into the post box and spend ages tryen to put it in the slot getten all embarased be cause of all the folk waiten their turn be hind me. I can feel my neck getten red.

So i dont put it in. I stuff it in the pocket of my coat.

I am so tired now i think about goen back home but decide to keep on any way. You have come this far gracie its only a bit further. Not far.

Out of the post office and turn left along dumbarton road.

You shoulent do this grace.

You should turn a round and go home.

 It isent any use to hope.

Hope is no good to you.

You have to live with out hope.

It will eat you up.

Dont let it grace.

Dont let it eat you.

But still you know you will go on hopen wont you. You can feel its already there in side you. You can feel it under your skin and in your belly and always moven. You are goen to go on any way. You are goen to grace. You are goen to francis. You are goen to your daughter wear she lived last. The place you have avoided out of bein afraid to be disapointid.

I come up stewartville street and go to the close door. It is an ex counsil bilden i know. There is a buzzer entry but the door is of its hindges and the close has a smell of bad cooken meat and bones. There is rubish on the stairs it looks like junk mail thrown about. I trip my foot on some thing heavy a book. There are a pile of them may be new yellow pages it is to dark to tell. I can see through to the back court that door is not there to. I can see the day light come in it would be shut and locked if it was there. That makes me think of some thing strange of the day bein shut and locked to. It makes me think that mixed with thinken of francis shut and locked and not wanten to open the door. I hold my breath it is so smelly. It is to flights up or it was. It has been over a year already though i have often walked past and looked but not come in. It was as if comen in was to break some thing open in side my selve some door that i would not of been abel to shut again after. And i needed to be abel to shut it after. I am not sure openen in is wise even now.

I dont want to touch any thing it seems filthy in here but i hang on to the banister any way. I hang on to it all the way up. When i get to the door i know i have to take an other breath and then my hands are shaky again. I can here sounds comen from inside this flat. I press the door buzzer but dont here if it rung so i do it again.

No thing i think. It isent worken. I take a deep breath again and then chap on the door. Except be four any one even comes to the door i know she will have moved on some wear else. I know in side my selve that she isent here. I am sure of it now.

I should go i want to. If she was still here you would of known be four to day. This is all just foolish ness on my part. Francis has gone grace you know that. She wont be here. I am sayen this to my selve quiet but a loud. Except i can still here the music comen from inside. There is some one in there. I can here them move about to. Some one comes towards the door i can here them step on floor boards no carpets clack clack clack. The person opens it and my hands shake.

It is a girl but not francis. I know be four she even speaks. i cant say how i just know. Maybe it is the way she stands or her perfume which smells v nice and expensive. Francis never wore perfume not that she dident want to. She wanted all the things she couldent have more so even than my selve. More so even than vincent.

Hello i say to her. You dont know me.

No the girl says slow in a nice voice. Can i help you she says.

I ament sure i says. My daughter lived here a while ago.

O the girl says.

I smell paint comen from in side of the flat. Paint and varnish too i think. They are decoraten.

Im grace i tell her. My daughter was francis.

Are you all right the girl asks. She comes closer.

I cant think what else to say.

Im afraid i dont know any francis. What is her sir name.

Do you live here i ask her to get away from that stupid name. She would know of francis if shed met her any way. There isent any doubt she would remember her.

Yes well no she says. Weve had the place for a while but it wasent fit to live in until recently. Weve only been in 3 or 4 weeks me and my partner.

I just nod.

Francis was here some time ago last time i saw her i say. I guess you wouldent of come across her.

I dont think so she says. Are you sure your all right. Do you want to come in and sit down for a minute.

I just stand there. I thought i was ready to do this. I ament ready at all. I look at the girl and say whats your name. It isent me thats speaken but some body else i dont know who. It is the sort of voice you can only let a stranger here though. You can only let some one you dont know at all here it. No body at home can here it not even bud. If you let them here it at home they would eat you up gracie you know that.

Emma the girl says.

I am sorry to of been a nuisance emma i say. I will go now and let you get on.

How old is francis the girl asks. Some one did come back once i think. My partner said some one was here. He said a girl came not long after we bought the place.

A girl i say. Did he say what she was like.

In what way.

I dont know what this question means i am thinken.

Do you mean what did she look like she asks me.

Yes i say did he say what she was like.

He dident. He said there was a girl tryen to get in one night he was in bed. I was a sleep. He opened the front door and there was a girl in the close tryen to get in the front door usen a wrong key. She ran away be fore he could get a decent look at her.

O i say. Francis.

This girl emma says no thing for a few seconds and we both stand there.

Then she says look why dont you come in and sit down for a minute. Just for a minute.

I dont know i am so grate full to this emma that i just let her lead me in though she is a stranger. In side i am un sure of what to think but i know it was francis who came that night. I know it for sure.

She takes me through the hall all dark floor boards and smells of varnish and i listen to my footsteps on them and think it isent as comfy as carpet.

Francis was here. Now you are hopen for all sorts of things that wont happen. You are so silly you should of learned your lesson after the last time but you never do do you. After last time francis relapsed into dependency you made your selve give up on her and now you are goen to go back on it.

It will eat you up it will eat you alive.

Grace i say to my selve.

Gracie gracie grace.

You were her own mother and she tried to lose you but its you who lost her. It is your own fault.

I can not describe it though. I just know that im afraid and i dont care all at the same time. Thats all.

I have hardly ever been in a house so taste full like this. No i have a few times but they were of wealthy old people so they had all old peoples things in them old peoples taste. So its true to say that ive never been in a house like this then. It isent a contra dicshoun. This emma calls it a flat but its a house to me even if it is ex counsil. It is so difirent from be four it dosent even compare. She says there tryen to give it the wow factor. Well. It has certainly wowed me and it isent even nearly finished yet. They have torn out all the old carpets and taken out a false ceilen in the bath room. They are on the proses of fitten a new kitchen but the liven room is the only thing that is nearly done.

Of course i have seen houses like this i know they are there. It is an ex counsil house like ours and the counsils. It is bigger now but it wasent before when francis was here. It was small then. Some how this emma has grown it. It is so big and bright and feels free as if you are not in a house at all but just in a hall of light. I can not decribe it. It is all wood and light and space and air. It is heavenly there is even a stand up piano in the corner. It is beautiful. It is not finished or even nearly but its beautiful. We sit drinken tea errol gray just ordinary despite what you might supose. I would of sworn she was one for elder flower and rasp berry or some other non sense but no im so glad its ordinary.

Are you feelen any better she asks.

I was okay i tell her. Just a bit tired from the walk.

This emma can tell that is non sense. She tilts her head and goes quiet. I will have to be care full what i say around her.

How come it is so roomy here it used to be cramped.

She laughs.

It is just how you use the dimenshouns you have got to work in she tells me. It is how you use light and space in particular.

O.

She laughs again. I am funny to her.

I am looken at some kind of pattern book beside me on the couch. There is lots of rolls of paper and cuttens and things of that nature to. I pick up one or two and hold them to the light to see them better. Theres patterns that are like brush strokes or brush strokes thats like a pattern.

My partner is an interior disiner she says.

I nod. So your an interior disiner then to.

She laughs again. Hes not really my business partner she says.

He is your boy friend i say. I stare to wear her eyes should be when i say this.

I guess you could call him that yes. Im a student.

I begin to feel sweat comen of my hands she is one of those people who will ask you if you have read this or read that and there is no right anser for me. No is no good and yes is no good. She is waiten for me to ask what she studys but i have experiens of this no way will she get it out of me.

I am doen reserch on canser cells up at the university.

It must be interesten i say. What kind of canser cells i ask. If that isent a stupid question.

It isent stupid at all. They are called colloidal cells. I know it sounds boren. It isent though its fasinaten. Kind of.

She sighs like she has sayed this to folk be four.

I should be worken to day but we really need this place up and runnen as soon as posibel. The sooner we can move out the better. I am helpen my partner with desine ideas for the other flat. The one we will actually live in.

You want to move out already but you have only just moved in.

This emma takes a sip of her tea.

No she says its just so we can get it on the market while prices are boyant.

You are buyen some wear else already i say. That is mad.

No she says again. We rent another place already. Were investen in property.

This emmas face is young now that im up close beside her on the settee. She is pretty this emma. She would be ages with francis except francis got a lot older in the last few years. In her head as well as else wear. I am older to i reckon. This girl the same age as my daughter is investen in property and i have never owned a house in my life that wasent the counsils to.

We rent halve our other place out to profeshionals. We want to sell this one and fatten that one up for the market first. It will be our next littel piggy.

I look at her and she laughs embarased.

This littel piggy went to market this littel piggy stayed home she says and then goes quite again.

I sip my tea and we sit for a while. She dosent seem to mind this quite ness or me in her house.

So was your daughter francis liven here alone.

I have not got a good answer for this. I ament sure. There were others here on and of. Several. There was a man or may be a few she went with. I dont tell this emma this though. She is still a stranger to me despite the tea.

She shared the place with some others i say. I dident know them really. We were not on talken terms really.

You and francis.

Me and francis and the folk she shared with either.

Do you have a picture of her you could leave with us grace she asks me. In case francis shows up.

I can not help but smile at this. She wont show up again you can bet on that i say to this emma stranger. This emma obviously dosent know our francis to well if she thinks she is stupid enough to turn up here again after her partner has caught her. Of course you arent bein fair gracie. This emma has been kind to you. Well. It isent her fault grace she is only tryen to help. Surely that is what they are payed for sciens students isent it. Sciens was invented to help man kind wasent it grace. Surely that is what they are payed for students with money.

Francis wont be back i tell her.

Emma says maybe your right. It wouldent be smart to come back if you got caught tryen to break in to some ones house.

Now you have let this stranger make a fool of you grace. You have let her take you in.

I think i better be goen i say. I have taken up enough of your time.

O she says. Im sorry. I dident mean any thing by it.

Well i say. Then i have no thing else to tell her. I button up my coat and go over to wear the door i came in was. The walls are all blank all white they tell you no thing then a dark rectangle the door all dark wood.

Please the girl says i dident mean to upset you. Sit down for a minute you havent finished your tea.

No i say its okay its not your fault i am just a bit done in. I should go.

She stands up and comes over. Listen she says there are some things the people here before left be hind. We were goen to throw them out.

Maybe she came back to get her things i say flat and cold.

Maybe she says. Your right she probably was. Dillon my partner must have scared her. She would of been tryen her key in a lock we changed.

I nod.

Do you want to have a look she asks. The things we put them in card board boxes in the other room. The babys room. Its suposed to be ready but well we have probably got time.

She is pregnant this emma. It dosent show i say.

3 months she says and puts her hand on her tummy.

I want to say congratulashouns to this girl emma but i can not. There is a bunched fist pushen its way out of my throat from my belly. I want to say you are so lucky but i can not. I want to ask do you know if its a boy or a girl but i can not.

She is waiten for me to speak. I can not. Just for a second or to.

Can i see the babys room i say.

She pauses. Then she says of course come through.

She lets me take her arm like a blind person and we go back along the hall. She smells of paint and varnish and hard soap. I like it it is afford able this smell.

She drags a card board box out into the middle of the bare floor. There is no thing in this babys room except boxes and junk and dust cloths on the floor. Emma and her partner have not made much progress i am thinken. Still they have got plenty of time i supose. The baby will arrive in august a few more months to go. Some forin name indian i think diva if its a girl magnus or ranald if its a boy. They dont want to know there goen to be happy with either. I wouldent be happy with any of those names but it is not my baby it isent my bisness. They are okay names i supose a bit mad.

Do you have any other kids she asks me.

Yes i say but dont elaborate.

She knows already not to bother me more about it.

Well if you want to see if theres any thing you want you can just take it she says. It will only get thrown out other wise. Then she says she will leave me in peace to look.

Shout me if you need any help she says. I am goen to be painten next door.

When she is away i sit down cross legged by the box.

Wear is francis i say to no one. Listen i know you arent there god but if you are then im sorry i dont believe in you. Like i told you before im atheist a non practisen prodistant.

Wear is my daughter i say. I am so tired now. The fist in my throat is smaller. Im all alone in here. I wont have to expose my selve in front of a stranger.

I turn the box on to its side and empty the con tents on to the floor. There isent any thing of value just junk. Old trainers and clothes and dirt. There is a lot of jumbled up laces a lot of wires and plugs and bits of old computers and phones. Some books. No thing of interest really. No thing of francises like me she dosent read much. I wander how that happened. I wanted her to be able to but some how she never picked up the ability. I rumage amongst all this stuff but there is no thing i reconise. There are things knotted up with the laces and shoes. Hairbrushes. I pick them out one by one and bring them up close to me so i can see better. They are just ordinary cheap plastic. I tease some of the hair out of the teeth of one of the brushes and try to see its colour but its no use. It is just hair it could belong to any one at all. I am off some wear in my head and i just sit on the floor un ravelen these laces and layen them in to pairs for no good reason. I tie each pair at the end in one single knot so they will be to gether.

Our father had to be helped in to and out of his shoes once. I didnent mind doen it for him there wasent any one else to do it. Marie was gone. Some times then i would ask him about our mother but he would never give me a straight answer. He dident want to be reminded i supose. He was bitter about her goen away leaven us all. He was bitter about marie goen away leaven us to.

Your older sister have you heard from her he would ask. He always called her that after she left. Your older sister. He woudent use her name. He wouldent use our mothers name either. Your a good girl graciegirl he would say. I supose we werent enough for either of them. Your mother and your older sister.

It was strange when she left marie my older sister. I remember her just gone one day when i woke as if she just disapeared. She was just not there any more. Not even the marks she left on the kitchen lino were there. They had all been cleaned away.

It was under stood that we were not to discuss it.

Wear did she go i asked my father. She left he sayed. Shes away.

Will she be back.

Thats enough gracie our father sayed.

I pick up one of the books it is a note book of some kind. I flick through the pages it is a diary or some kind of exercise book with riten in it. Some ones hand riten. It is some sort of hand riten like a childs. There are lots of pages of this riten like a childs. One who never grew up in to an adult. I keep turnen the pages and then there is a page with words ritten over and over practisen or some thing. I flick through more pages but there isent any more of them it is all just sentences. I can only read some of what it says either. I go back to the front of the book and stare at it. There are drawens and things on the in side cover. Boxes and mazes and rectangular shapes drawn in 3 dimensions. They are like rooms joined on to other rooms all of them boxes all of them small with no doors between. Then i see it right up at the top corner. The only word i can re cognise the only word i have been looken for in this whole book.

Francises.

She has ritten her name on this jotter this diary. Francises. It belongs to her.

The only word i showed her how to rite her own name.

This riten is hers.

I lay down on the floor. I am tired out all i want to do is shut my eyes for a minute. I pull my coat up around me put my hand between my knees.

I should be on port adventurer the canary isles with my sister. I should be with my lugidge there.

I close my eyes i can see my lugidge comen round the carousel i can see my selve callen maries name smilen. Marie her face happy laughen just like mine. I can see palm trees and white sand and a littel child playen there and blue blue sea a sail on the horizon a white sail. Your a good girl gracie.

I dont know how long im a sleep for how would i but its dark and i am tryen pull my selve free long stingen nettles rushes that wrap there arms a round me tryen to pull me under. I know they sting but i can not feel pain only a sufocaten feelen of sadness and exhaustion and shame. The only light is from through the door out in the hall way. For a second i dont know wear i am then i do. This stranger is standen over me bent down touchen my shoulder gentley.

Grace she says are you awake grace. Youve been asleep for a while.

O. O what time is it.

A flood of heat rushes to my fore head it is dark i have to get home. I am not keen on goen home in the dark that is for sure. I can not call vincent to speak to bud be sides they wouldent be able to do any thing to help. We have no car. I will have to get back to partick station on my own in the dark with all the people about in the way.

Its a quarter to five emma says. I thought you looked so ex austed i should let you sleep a while.

I sit up. She has put a blanket over me a cushion under my

head. I can not believe i was so tired i dident even wake up. Normally i am a light sleeper i dont ever sleep solidly through the night. It could be be cause of buds night rovens though. It is so hard to sleep with him wanderen about next to you. Even littel sean takes up the whole bed despite his size.

This would have been francises room emma says.

I rub my face its numb on one side and chilled on the other.

Maybe. I ament to sure she had a room as such. When i was here be fore there were a lot of folk comen and goen. It is more likely she just slept wear she could.

Emma nods and says no thing.

I get up and shiver and flex my fingers. They arent right. They are sore the joints. The cold i would think. It does bother me some times in winter.

I shouldent have slept i say. I have to get home in the dark now. Bud will be conserned.

Buds your boy friend.

My partner to tell you the truth.

Emma laughs. I know its such a weird thing to call some one whose close to you isent it. Listen why dont you wait. My boy friend my partner i mean will be back from work soon. You could stay for some food and then he can drive you back home.

I shake my head. No i have been enough of a pest.

Its no troubel he wont mind.

It isent fair of me i say. I dont want to put you out.

She throws her hair over her shoulder. Non sense she says. You arent in any state to be goen home on your own.

I dont know if i should be bothered by this im sure she means well. It must be totally obvious that your as blind as a bat gracie. Did you expect her not to notice some how silly. Do you want a lift home or not grace. Well. Of course you do. Still you have got to refuse one more time for the sake of polite ness havent you graciegirl.

Well i say it is not fair on your boy friend. He will be looken forward to getten his tea and putten his feet up plus he dosent know me.

She laughs again a laugh that enjoys it selve i think. I can not imagine what my laugh sounds like to other people. What it makes them think about me. To tell the truth i hardly ever do laugh much. Some times with bud. He is on ocasion funny.

Dont worry about him it will be fine. You can tell me what you think of my disine for the other flat while i get the dinner started.

Okay then i say.

She is so easy in her selve this emma. I would imagine every thing she does is done with in this same way. She is pretty from what i can tell. She isent beautiful i dont think like francis was be four. I can tell she is a bit plainer than that but her way is difirent from francis. Francis is closed up like a pocket knife. She is tight and steelen her selve. The way she speaks is as though she is cutten you with words. Even if she said i love you to some one not me she never has she would say it and it would pierce you. There is an ugliness there i dont know wear it came from me per haps.

Do you like to cook emma asks me.

To tell you the truth i ament very good at cooken i say. Bud is not bad.

I was just goen to throw a few things to gether if thats okay.

I nod. I have never thrown any thing to gether in my life. I have put things to gether on the same plate but they were quite separate.

She laughs the same enjoyen laugh of be fore. I smile to.

The kitchen is another beautiful room but it is not finished either. But it doesent matter to me. It is the same size roughly as our own kitchen but it again feels huge some how. Plus there are loads of silver shinen bits and pieces kitchen ware about and littel ornaments and pictures every wear just thrown down to it would seem. Up close there is her hand behind it this hap hazard ness. The things in this kitchen have been thrown with some considerashoun no doubt about it.

This emma begins to cut ingrediants on the choppen board.

O i am sorry would you like some thing to drink she asks.

A cup of tea would be nice if thats all right.

Just then there is a ringen of a mobile phone and emma goes searchen a bout for it in the other room. I here here clatter some thing over then low talk. Then there are some tones of exasperashion though i am tryen not to listen in. She is gone for a while i can here occasional whinen sounds as though she is pleaden. When i here these sounds the hair stands up on the back of my neck. It is so needy and plaintif it chills me to the bone. I go over to the pan and stir it for a while maken sure it dosent stick. Then emma comes back in she is composed and calm.

Is every thing all right i ask but she ignores my question. She comes over to the cooker and i step back out of her way. She is quite but forced in her manner. She stirs furiously at the pan then adds som water from the tap.

O this needs some thing dosent it.

I dident taste it.

Dident you she says as though i have stolen some thing from her.

No i just stirred it. Maybe it needs salt.

She shakes her head. A little wine i think. Yes. Would you like a glass to. I think i am goen to have one. Will you think me a bad person if i do grace.

I shake my head it is up to you i say.

It isent like one glass can hurt is it. I am only 3 months gone. That is okay isent it.

I nod. I think one glass is okay emma. What can i tell you i put away more than one glass when i was expecten.

Hmm she says. Well so long as you dont tell dillon. Not that you can he says he isent goen to be back till late.

O.

I am sorry grace it dosent look like you will be getten that lift after all. But look. If you want i can call you a taxi later.

I am worried about what bud will say. I am worried how he will re act when i get in. Except it is only just gone five in the evenen. He hasent got any right to be angry. How many times has he come home in all sorts of states and you havent complained about it gracie. How many times. You would have to admit it is a lot. So he can bee off cant he. He can go jump you have a glass of wine and take the taxi if it is ofered. You can send the money for it back to emma. Bud can look after littel sean for an other night cant he. Yes.

Okay. I will join you for a glass.

Great.

She opens a cup board above the cooker.

I havent got any white red will have to do she says.

That is fine i say. White wine gives me bad acid but red is fine.

O are you sure i think theres some cold beer of dillons in the fridge.

No red is fine.

I had to train my selve to drink wine she says and laughs. I hated it.

That is funny so did i.

Really she says. Thats so weird isent it. I thought if i drank red wine people boys would think i was bow hemian a bit wild. I thought i could cultivate a followen if i was seen to drink red wine and smoken. But i hated the taste. I had to top it up with coke to drink it. Now when im on my own i drink red wine with coke in it like they do in spain. Especially now little magnus or ranald or diva is on the way.

They put coke in it do they. The spanish.

They drink it with coke in out of buckets.

That is to mad.

No its nice. I think so any way.

Did you manage to cultivate a followen then i ask her.

No she says unfortunately. I dident cultivate any thing but hang overs. Im a cheap date. Three glasses and im any bodies.

I dident like the taste either. I drank it only be cause my father drank beer which i hate.

You were rebelen.

That would of been the last time then.

I wasent much of a rebel either. Goen to do sciens was my big state ment. But I liked to rite about the sciens more than i liked to experiment with it. But this is boren let me show you the disine im thinken of usen.

She runs her hands under the tap and dries them then fetches her book from the other room. She stands next to me the pages all marked with strips of white paper.

There she says. What do you think.

She brings the book up close to my eyes and we edge under the kitchen light.

I can see these lines again strokes and curves. Riten like disines or disines like riten in this other langwidge i dont know. I get a strange feelen looken at it i wonder is this emma tryen to make me look stupid. What am i meant to think. They are pretty these disines but i dont know any thing about disine or about sciens or about these patterns she is maken me look at. O come on gracie i think she has been kind so far why would she try to make a fool out of you.

It is very pretty what are you goen to do with it.

It isent me really. Im only helpen. My boy friend

Your partner i interrupt and she laughs.

Effen hell she says. Im doen it again. My partner she says. My partner is goen to use it as the theme for one of the rooms. Each of the rooms is suposed to have a different theme.

That is mad i say.

No no she says it will be sutel. We hope. This is probably goen to be for our contem plashion room. We wanted it to be based around some kind of tilen. This is the one we liked the best. It is from portugal.

She shows me a blue and white tile patern.

It is nice i say. It is definitely very contemplatif.

She puts the book down on the work top and goes in to a drawer. She footers about for a bit and then i here pop the cork comen out of a bottle. She pours out wine then hands me a glass. She is warm next to me.

Salute she says. Bottoms up.

Yes i say. Cheers.

This wine is nice i swirl it round the in side of my mouth and save our it be four swallowen it down. Even i can tell i its a good wine.

So i say what is this pattern here then i say leafen through the book. I like all the curves. And the straight lines.

I dont know she says. It looks arabic to me. To geometric for me. To scientific.

And this wine i say changen the subject. What is it.

French says. I dont know any thing about wine except i worked so hard to like it im not given up on it now.

I know i say. Every time i drink wine i think im some one else not my selve. I think i can be some one other than who i am an adventurous person. Some one not afraid to change there life. Francis was like that once upon a time.

This emma says my partner dillon will be home later he can tell you who he saw. Did you find any thing in the box of hers.

I found a note book with her name on it. Thats all. I doubt she would of been tryen to get in just for that.

I doubt it to emma says and then we are both quiet for a bit. We arent sayen what we both know. Well that is okay. I prefer to not say out loud just now.

Do you want to show me it she asks her back to me.

In some ways i would but i will not say that to her. I just tell her i will look at it later.

Are there any indicashouns of what she was up to or wear she was goen emma asks.

Not to much i say. It is just scribbels and doodels. Nothing really. I would not expect her to rite any thing very re vealen.

Oh come one she says. It must say some thing. Let me have a look i might be abel to help.

So there you are gracie. You are on the spot once again. There is nothing for it. I take a deep breath and fumbel the note book. Here i say and she turns to take it. Then she is leafen through it and ocashoinally she laughs. She is also rattlen through her wine at a fare clip which is a worry but who am i to tell her stop. No one gracie you are no one.

Is there any thing i ask her.

Dident you read this through she ask all serius.

No i just glanced at it. I dont have my good glasses i can not see to well espeshially the small print.

She snorts yes it is always the small print that gets you in to troubel isent it.

I take a sip of wine a slow sip.

Well she says. It does say some things. Do you want me to read. The riten is very dificult to make out. Does francis have an eye site problem to. This is if you dont mind me sayen a bit dyslexic. It is like she never really progressed beyond the basic level.

I flinch in side at this. It is a reflecshioun on you grace. You were a bad mother even though francis tried to lose you and well she pretty much suck seeded. You should of tried to push her harder. Except francis never responded well to pushen.

She was not great at riten i say shamed. I have never sayed this to any one but bud. He under stood dident he. Yes. I think so. Your boy friend your partner bud. He dosent respond to pushen either. But he has still stayed hasent he grace. He is still there which makes him what i dont know. It makes him good i supose. Bud is a good man despit every thing that folk in the drum say about him. His temper his tantrums his front.

Oh says emma. I dident mean to judge or pry.

What does it say i ask impashent and embarased. I want to here.

Well she says as though taken a back. There is an other glug of wine.

There is some thing here like a story or a memory may be. When i was seven it starts. Will i read it.

Yes.

When i was seven i had my own key it says. My mother went out at night to work and she gave me a key. She would try to kiss me and told me to lock the door and not let any one in. I would scream and cry and try to make her stay.

You re member this dont you grace. You had forgotten now you re member. You remember that key.

Emma says do you want me to go on. She ask quietly as though speaken to a pahsient in a hospital. The way the nurse spoke to our father me and maries when he was dyen in that bed. O grace. O gracie.

Go on i say. I need to here.

She clears her throat. The key hung on a knitted cord around my neck it was the front door key. I could get out and run away i used to think but there was no wear to go. So i just stayed at home waiten. I was scared of the door bell. I was scared of bein all by my selve. I was not allowed to open the door to any one.

This is quite hard to read emma says interupten the flow. The riten is so chil ish. No offense.

Of course it is child ish. It is ritten by a child. My child. She has stayed a child be cause of you grace. You left her all alone. So she left you all alone. She tried that day in the garscadden woods when you walked of and left them. Her and vincent. You left them and there were stingen nettles up there. They tried to hold you back there was a face in the nettles the face of a young child a baby a fetus. But you were drunk weren't you gracie. You were drunk the day in the woods your children left you. You were how many months gone. Bobby came by and saw the state of you. Get in the car grace. Come on get in have you hurt your selve. All that mess. All that blood. This is not a good seen gracie. This is not a good seen at all.

You can here francises voice a young child as she is speaken. You can re member how you had to lock that door on her. How you had to leave her all alone while you went out at night to get money. To work for money.

So i played by my selve all night until she came home emma says. My mother. I had a key of my own in case ther was an emergency but was not allowed to go out or anser the door to any one except in an emergensy. My mother dident explane what emergency she probably dident want to friten me. I suppose it was in case of a fire or a burgler. But i was fritened be cause i was left alone with the key hangen on a knitted cord a round my neck. I wanted to run away but there was no wear to go. So i stayed and played with crayons and paper and invented difirent storys with happy endens. Until my mother came home.

Emma stops. She dosent say any thing neither do i. I just feel my selve nodden my head with out knowen why.

There is some more emma says but it isent very coherent like a poem she says do you want to here it to. I can not really make it out there is to much scoren out and doodlen.

That is enough emma i say. I think that is enough for now. And right then i burst in to tears maken a mess of my selve in this lovely kitchen why do they have a lovely kitchen these people have got every thing they have got it all havent they. Nothing will ever go wrong for them. They can buy house after house and sell them and get richer and richer and nothing will ever go wrong. Is it okay to hate them these people. What would bud say. Well. You know the anser to that dont you gracie. He would say it is not only okay it is your duty. Your right.

O i am sorry emma says. I have upset you. She comes over and starts to offer a hankie or something pushen it in my face and i take it. Thank you i say. I am okay. I am all right.

Are you sure she is asken. Here have some wine it will calm you.

I take a sip sniffelen embarased. It is just upsetten i say. I was not a good mother.

Dont say that grace that is not true. She hands me back the jotter and i roll it tight into a tube in my hands.

You had to do some thing very hard be cause you had to. And this was long a go. Your daughter is just riten some thing down it dosent mean she holds you responsibel. We all have to do hard things some times.

But i was responsibel. I was responsibel. I was her mother. I am her mother.

Let me sit a minit i say. I will be okay if i can just sit a minit. Okay.

She goes back to the choppen board and starts cutten things. She tosses some thing in to a pan then presses a buton boomf i see the flame comen on a yellow bloom. There are wander full smells emanaiten from that pan.

Is that garlic i say though i know fine well it is garlic.

Yes she tells me. Garlic and a few chalots and some chillys and anchofys.

Wont you wait for dillon your partner be fore eaten.

Not on your life she says. He wont let me cook him any thing he thinks he is the shef. He rushes me out of the kitchen in case i medal with his cooken. He is so anal about it i cant enjoy cooken if hes in. He is so precise about every littel thing. He has to have every thing exactly as it should be be fore he will even begin. And he cooks with out even maken any mess to. Ive got no idea how he does it.

Well what you are maken smells good to me i say.

I think its goen to be a kind of salsa. Horse spageti.

I have never eaten that and i dont think i have ever been fond of anchofy but i am willen to try to day i tell her.

Great she says. Here let me top up your glass.

Are you goen to have an other to i ask her.

She shrugs. It cant do any harm to have one more can it she says. It isent like i do this every day. O do you think i shouldent.

It is up to you emma it is your body.

Yes. It is isent it. Well that is the matter settled then.

This emma wants to quiz me while we eat. I am some what resis tant but in a suttil way. The food is delishous. We are still in the kitchen on high stools theres no table. The food has got capers in it i dont know about you but ive decided i love capers. Not olives ive pushed them to the side of my plate. This is mad. It isent like ive never been to a restorant be four but its better. Be cause i never expected it to happen. I am here by surprise.

She is a bit drunk i can tell. She is tearen in to the wine and not used to it.

So grace she says not slurren but not completeley right either.

Tell me about your selve.

There isent much to tell i say. I here glug glug glug.

O thats not true she says. Your daughter francis for one.

I would rather not talk about francis i say.

She sits up. Her body is straight i can make out she is tighter just about. Not so relaxed.

Then tell me about your selve.

I havent any thing to say about my selve i say.

Rubbish. Every body has a story.

Well i dont know about that i tell her. We are not so interesten.

Even that for gods sake she says. You arent we.

Yes but theres bud and vincent and sean to. We are all to gether in it.

Every one but your daughter.

Francis will be in it when she comes back.

What if she never comes back then.

I am drunk. This is no good. I have slept here and eaten here and it is not a good seen. Wears bobby. He would of driven me home. Its a fiat panda he drives. I would of sayed no. Im with bud now. Bud is your friend bobby.

This emma is so close and seems to care about francis though she hasent ever met her. Even slightly drunk i think she cares. What for i can not say. I should leave and not let her drink more but the truth is i drank through three of my own pregnansys. So i can not tell any one else what to do with there live there body. She is all paint and varnish and hard soap. It is hard through this wine to make the real person out. Me to.

I am hopen she will come back soon emma.

Eff it she says. I dont even know you. That is bad isent it. I am sorry. I am feelen the wine a bit. Tell me about this francis of yours. This daughter.

There isent a lot to tell. You know the most important bit already.

Then tell me about your selve she says may be seein i am about to get upset again.

I have told you every thing i can think of.

Yes. Yes. Sorry to be rude but i dont think you have told me any thing.

Well what else do you want to know i say.

What about francis. What if she never comes back.

I have had to much wine for this discushoun. This is no good. I have slept here on this strangers floor her babys room her contemplashoun room with her stupid tiles from portugal. I have eaten here and drank wine and it is now not a good seen for me. Wear is bobby i wander. He would drive me home. Bobby i would of sayed no to. I was with bud.

I think you and me should have an other drink. We both need to cheer up. It is a friday night and i have been abandoned. And you are on the run grace arent you.

I look at her. I am not runnen i say. Be sides wear would i run to.

Good point she says. Wear would any of us run to. Wear would you run if you could.

I dont know i say. To my sister on port adventurer i supose.

Mmmhmm. I would run to portugal emma says getten up and goen to the fridge. Do you want wine or beer. There is beer and wine it is dillons. Do you want a beer.

No i tell her i can not drink beer.

Emma cracks the tin open.

I can not drink it either. She laughs tippen her can in to the glass she had her wine in. But i should may be have it in stead. Just now any way.

This stranger is drunk to and isent to happy just now i can tell. She is pretty and all paint and varnish and hard soap. It is hard though to make the real person out. You to gracie. You to. You dont let any one through do you. You never let any one in side.

Never. Except to night. This emma is likely abel to read you like a book now. Like a book you your selve can not even read. What gives her the right. Nothing. Nothing gives her the right to read you.

Bottoms up emma says and i raise whats left in my wine glass.

O francis i know you have been here. I have got proof. Why my son vincent looks up to her so much i can not say. It is like he idolised her. May be that is why he is the way he is now. May be it isent all your fault as a bad mother grace. You dident know how the first one came a long and you lost that one then the next and you werent sure how to do it and then the next one came a long and so you did it again and you dident know if you got it right the first time. Well. Now you know dont you. Yes. That is why you dont let sean get to close isent it. That is why he clings to bud. Francis left so there was only you vincents mother grace and you arent worth idolisen aparintly. He is at the age wear he dosent really have any use for you and who can blame him eh. Soon he will be away to. He will join up or do some thing else like that and then he will be gone. And one day francis will come back for sean to. It will just be you and bud on your lonesome ownsome.

You are there own mother grace but you lost them your selve that time at the garscadden woods wear they left you all alone. Only bobby would help you. Buds pal bobby.

Get in the car grace. This is not a good situashoun. Did you take a fall you are all grass stanes and muck and there is blood. You are all bloodey grace.

O marie on the canary isles port adventurer. Your father used to tell you of the volcanos there dident he. Yes thats right he did. You used to love to here him talk of them and other far away places. It is funny if he never went it sounded as though he had. He made you think he had been every wear of course he couldent of could he even the emerald aisle wear he was born and grew up. He dident even go back after he died. He is still out there in that cemetery in clydebank. Well. I supose it is better than lyen un known un claimed in the grass up in garscadden woods like so many be four.

Your father was to good to you gracie he should of made you harder. He should of forced you to leave him when he was sick. That was when you should of left like your sister marie. What is it that marie has that you dont graciegirl. What is it that makes her abel. You are abel to you just think your not. But what is it that makes her abel to leave and your own daughter francis and your son vincent saw in her but not you. It must be some thing you can not put your finger on.

Tell me francis. What is it. Well gracie. You know the anser to that one now dont you. Yes.

Tell me. You own mother.

That is just not goen to happen though is it grace. Even if francis was here she would not tell you any thing. She has never told you any thing she did not want to in her whole life except to say she dosent want to be like you. And no wander if you put a leesh a round her neck to keep her tethered.

What are you thinken grace emma asks me.

All these things i am thinken are mixed up to gether. There all the time. Even when i am not thinken on these things they are still there some how.

There is no way i can tell you what i am thinken emma i say to her.

Why not i wont judge you.

This is the difirins between me and her. That is it in a nut shell. This emma thinks i am afraid she will judge me. I am afraid a judge will judge me. She is one of the few people i have met i am not afraid will judge me be cause she has no thing to do with my live she dosent know any one or any thing about my live and after tonight i will never see her again. She can go back to bein rich and pilen up the houses.

I know i tell her. It isent that.

What then she asks me.

I shake my head. If this is the moment i am meant to make some sort of big confeshoun or some thing it is just not hapenen. I ament much of a one for confeshouns especially to strangers and as a non practisen prodissent why would i be. But then i am tellen her all about the air port my glasses. I have told it so often now i know the story of by heart. So here i am tellen it again by way of given this girl some thing she seems to want. It is a way of tellen her no thing. But i tell it like it happened to some one else like a funny story even though it isent all that funny. She dosent laugh out of polite ness i guess. She listens in stead. She nod and she knows i think. She under stands be cause she can read you like a book grace. Then she wants to know about bud. Why not i think you can tell her about bud.

What happened to his leg if you dont mind me asken. Was it an accident.

A friend of buds had a dog i tell emma be cause it can not do any harm for her to know. She is un conectid with my life in any way.

Bud had to pay a debt to this man and he came to our door to get it early one mornen. Of course bud knew he was comen for him but there wasent much he could do. He needed more time to get the money. When i opened the door the friend burst in and set the dog on him while he was still in his bed.

O says emma.

Bud walks with a stick now. The dog got hold of him and wouldent let go. It bit through some thing important.

Emma says then what happened.

I shrug. Bud payed the money that was owed. Next time

any way.

That would make sense she says.

No i tell her. It would of made sense for the money to have been payed be four this man set his dog on him. Bud can not seem to resist pushen people i think. He will always go to far in every thing. With me and vincent and sean and francis. He will always push. He will push vincent until he gets a reacshoun and is to close to sean for his own good. One day he will get hurt and it will be worse than any dog bite.

I dont under stand why you would say that. Why will he be hurt.

Be cause when francis comes back she will take sean and then that will be him lost to i say but it comes out harder than meant. Even i am surprised at the sound of my selve. What are you snappen for grace the sober me says. You do not have to be so short with this girl she has been kind to you so far. It isent her fault she has a better life than you. It isent her fault that you do not know any thing about tiles or portugal or the property market or any of those things she has been tellen you about. She has her life and you have yours that is just the way of it graciegirl. That is what bud would of sayed. Or your father would of sayed to.

You dont talk much about francis do you she says eventualy.

Her bark is worse than her bite i say. Though not by a big margen.

She laughs and squeezes my arm.

Hey she says. Hey why dont we fone your sister on canary isles. Wouldent you like to do that.

Yes but we can use my fone.

Are you sure it is late she might be a sleep.

Well we will wake her up then wont we i am sure she will not mind her sister waken her up.

No i say but i am not at all sure about that. When i was a

child marie would go mental if you woke her. I mean she would go really mental.

Great this emma says and i begin to get a bit panicy i dont know what marie will say at all. I am tipsy i will have to explane every thing and i have not spoken to her in so long. My sister marie could always see through me she could always get the truth out of me no matter what. For a while i used to steal things from our father money from his wallet. I wouldent even spend it i just horded it up. Marie took the blame so often she made me confess she wouldent tell on me. She knew i could see how it hurted her in our fathers eyes. But she would not tell on me. He would give her a thrashen there was five pounds in my wallet you took it you wee bitch come here. She was black and blue after he used his hands on her and i was screamen and cryen and sayen please dont please daddy. I was to afraid to own up. And it was the not owen up that got my sister marie the thrashen. It wasent the money it was not admiten it. Of course marie just stared at me. She just stared.

But you owe her grace you owe it to speak to her and tell her why you did not show up on the canary isles port adventurer and you are so sick of always fearen every thing arent you. Vincent and francis got a scare that time you lost them and they walked away and so did you grace dident you. They pretty much succeeded in scaren you that time and it served you right. You could not even read that sign on the path back from the woods could you gracie. No. Already you had walked of and left them be cause they wouldent come when you called. You went one way and they an other and it was you that got lost in the end wasent it. It was you collapsed in the nettles. It was your own fault you got lost wasent it. You remember the sky that day dont you. It was thick the grasses were high and how far was the roman wall. It had seemed when you looked back that the wood was creepen down the hill it was un fathom abel. Francis was in there wasent she. Vincent was in there to wasent he. May be they were hidden may be a head and the night comen on so fast the burr of crickets in the nettles a heavy sluggish heat to. You mis placed your babies dident you grace. Yes. Yes. You left them in the woods and that wall of the romans not far. You remember callen out to them dont you callen in a risen panic a fisted throat knotted. Francis vincent you were shouten again and again and walken down the hill those dark woods be hind they were evil you would call them evil if you believed in any god wouldent you grace. Yes you would of called them evil if you were any thing at all but a not practised protestant un believer.

And then bobby with the car. Get in grace. This is not a good situashion. Wanderen. Why are you wanderen on your own your lonesome ownsome. What is that mess on you.

Get in the car. Get in be side bobby. Please.

My children are a shamed of me bobby you said. You were near to openen up right there. That was what bobby sayed those were his words. You can open up if you want gracie. There is no thing you can not tell me.

It would all have been better for you if they hadent been born at all.

No grace that isent true. That isent true at all. They would have been better of if you had stayed lost they would have been better on there own.

Well you have no idea how you are getten home to night this emma has not menshouned a taxi for me once yet and she is drunk. You will need to remind her gracie.

You will have to get a lift home with bobby grace. Or gregor he gave you his card dident he. Yes. Bobby would be better he is not a stranger. You will have to call him to come and get you. He can tell his wife some thing like he is goen to get a pint of milk or some thing of that natchure. You can get in the car with bobby again cant you. Do it with him in his car like you did be four. In your own neighbourhood grace. You can not say you havent thought about it. You know you have. The way bobby always looks at you he remembers. He has never forgotten. Buds friend bobby his best friend you did it with. Yes but bobby was some body elses man some body elses husband. You never let that stop you did you. No. You went back for more. That bobby. You kept goen back for more. And maybe that gregor would be the same. You can tell he likes you to cant you grace. Cant you graciegirl. Yes. He is an atractif man to. He has got a job and is abel bodied. Some one like that to take you out of your selve grace. That is what you need. Some one like that to take you out and away. Not some broken down cripple.

The honest truth is that you have not even been close to many men. It isent like some folk in the drum would have had you believe. It isent that many not compared to the long run or some other people you could menshion. Some things you would give if you thought you could get some thing in return. But not part of your selve gracie. You kept that door closed except to a few. Not like bud says. Of course he dosent say these un kind things un less he has been drinken. He can be sweet to.

Okay i will dial emma says what is the number. She puts the bottel of wine on the table between us i hold on to it for dear live. She says give me the number please and i find my purse with the piece of paper in it. I have a lot of difirint numbers on difirint coloured pieces of paper just in case though i hardly ever call any one and am thinken about the toilit now. So i give emma the piece of paper with all the codes on it and we sit at the table and she gets her fone. So i have heard any way though i dont worry so much right now with all this wine dedenen me. Emma is giglen and pressen all the buttons on her phone.

O i am way to tipsy she says. This is an effen night mair. You must think i am such a bad person. She is leanen over stroken her stomack looken as though she might vomit at any second. It would be good if she could get through well not all good. If she couldent that would mean i could put of explainen every thing to marie my sister. If she is angry she will just do that thing with no actual words. She will put these pauses in. I will keep talken and diggen my selve a bigger hole. And she will just keep on pausen and i will feel my selve caught straight away and rigel and rigel with out her even sayen any thing. Then she will do that other thing wont she gracie. She will do that clicken with her tung against her teeth. O that was the sound that used to drive you mad wasent it gracie. You and your father maries clicken used to drive you mad. It was like an effen bat rader homen in he used to say. Stop that marie. Quit it with the clicken will you. Maries clicken will be like a rader homen in on any tall tales you might tell on the phone grace. So you had better watch it. It is maries own special lie detecten devise that click.

I cant get through emma says. There is a womans voice speaken spanish on the other end of the line.

I know i tell her though i dont really. They always do that. I dont know why they do not just have a speshil english anser phone voice for calls from scotland. They have got all this modern mashinery now.

Emma stabs away at the mobile with her finger. It is like she is wanten to punch a hole right through it like she is wanten to punch the anser phone womans voice.

Well she says. Now we wait.

She repetes out loud what this spanish anser mashine voice says and sighs. I have to say i am some what im prest. I dont know if what she is sayen is proper spanish or not but it sounds as though it could be. Next she is holden the phone up in the air as though she is bored of the womans voice talken away. I smile i am indulgen her. Waiten here for my sister marie on port adventurer the canary isles to speak has been some thing i havent done in a lot of years. It is true i doubted her. Was she even there or is it an other wild goose chase for yours truly. Tryen to pin her down has been a long struggle for you hasent it grace. It has been a long long struggle. Just getten the hole story from your own father was dificult wasent it. And even he dident want to say he was ashamed he sayed.

Wear did my sister marie go that time. I asked our father me and maries once. Wear did she go. You remember dont you. She went away. Some one came and took her dident they.

Ach he just sayed. You are mis taken graciegirl. Your memorys are mixed up. You were only a wee girl then how would you know. Your sister marie was fine.

No i sayed to him. I re member it was a long time be four i saw her again after that day.

He was ill and dyen in that bed his voice very far away by then. It was as though he was speaken to you through a mask from some other place. His eyes were holden on holden on so tightly. He wouldent let go. He wouldent.

Wear did she go dad wear did you put her.

Gracie. Gracie he sayed.

Hey it is ringen emma says. At last.

Of course it is ringen i say for no good reason other than to say some thing. May be to seem a person of the world i dont know.

Emma says hello and i sit up listenen. Hello she says this is emma a friend of your sister. I am callen for her. Yes yes she says.

Emma nods at me it is dark but i can feel her grinnen at me.

O i am sorry i dident mean to wake you she says. Yes. Sorry. It must be getten on there. No no you dont know me. I am a friend of. Yes. No.

I look at emma i mouth to her. Give me the phone i am sayen my stomack all fizzles. But she wants to speak longer. Why i wander. It sounds as though my sister marie on port adventurer the canary isles is given her the third degree. I should be panicken by now but in stead i feel strong i take a big swig of wine it is cold cold copper or iron it is given me strength i can feel it. I feel strong be cause now we are here. It feels as if it could only be now at last here like this some how. I am reachen over and tuggen at the phone but emma is still tryen to talk down it.

No sorry emma says and her voice has changed. Some thing is wrong. Some thing is not right about this. O wear are you now grace.

I dident mean to bother you at this time of night. No i can assure you i dident. No not at all. Not at all. Yes. I am sorry. Yes i understand. Yes i am sorry. Yes. I apolojise.

I am reachen for the phone give me the phone i say to her please give it to me.

She hands me the phone i am sorry grace she says. You better have a go she says. You might have better luck.

There isent any one on the end of this phone. Emma has hung up.

She is taken the bottle and drinken and then wipen her mouth with her sleeve. She shudders right down to her belly and back.

Sorry she says. Wrong number.

Well who was it you were talken to then.

I ament very sure. I couldent understand all of what they were sayen. I think i might have dialled the wrong forin country by mistake. Sorry she says. Then giggles but stops when i look at her.

I just nod. I nod and nod and nod un till i feel i will burst my stomack full of fizzles again. This whole situashon is a joke. That is just what you have come to expect isent it grace. Things turnen in to a joke a joke on you grace. So it is.

My sister marie out there on port adventurer the canary isles. Are they ahead of us or not i can not even re member. It surely can not even be that late there. Will she be a sleep or a wake out there i dont even know. It is to mad to think about.

Lets try again grace emma says.

I shake my head no it feels as though it might be bad luck to try again to night. It will jinx some thing i am sure.

And any way it is true i can not even imajine speaken to her or visiten her not really. I had my chance at the air port and i dident take it. In stead i would like to get drunk good and drunk and go ou side and shout at people in the street. That would be a good end to to day i think. Other people do it you see them about you see them in drumchapel and partick too. They shout at strangers they lose all there in hibishouns they are free so long as they have the curadge. They are scarey some times those people folk keep out of there way. There is some thing scarey about some one so free they dont mind shouten in the street at passersby at strangers. Bud puts on an act like that some times but it is selve defense. His eyes are always there not gone like those people. The ones that are free of any care even from them selve. It is a free dom to scarey for most. But i can envy them some times that free dom. If you have got no thing then what more can you lose no thing. Bud has pulled me back from that once. Now here you are all over again. Well. To night i dont care. I want to go shouten down the street at strangers. I will be charitable and treat them all the same. I will knock of a polis mans hat and run of. They will never take me a live.

O i should get home i say to emma. I have taken up so much of your time all ready. Your partner will think you are being badly influensed.

Emma dosent here she is sitten up right with her eyes shut her hands hangen down over her knees. She has got the mobile in one hand and the bottel in the other she is like a budda in the kitchen light.

Emma i say are you okay. Emma.

She slumps right over and groans her back bucken like a pony.

O she says when she is done. O. I think i better go lie down.

She has spewed all over the toes of her shoes.

Just stay wear you are for a minute i tell her. Keep your head be tween your knees until it passes. I pat her back and hold her hair out of the way as she goes bucken again her mouth openen black.

O o o o o o.

My you are in some state emma i say to her after. I take the wine bottel from her and sit with it sippen ocashionally. I am not botheren with my glass. Do you want to goto your room i ask her but she is not replyen. She just sits with her eyes shut and every now and then she leans over and heaves but no more comes out she is empty. The heaves will not stop though she has just got to ride them out.

O o o o o o

Do you want some water of any thing i ask her after a while. Emma i say. Do you want some water.

She mumbles some thing and holds on to my hand. Grace she is sayen i am so sorry. Her hand is cold and wet it is disgusten then she is slumpen on me. Emma i say looken in her hand bag for a hankie or some thing. And there is her purse in stead i take it and put it in my own coat pocket quick quick grace if you do not think about it just do it. There it is in my own coat pocket my jeans then i am drinken the rest of the wine down and i am fizzlen there is a hand reachen in side me a copper hand spreaden its finger and it feels good so good i would like to feel like this for ever. I hold on to emmas hand and say i will go and get some water emma just you sit there. Then i get up and help her through to the bedroom an other lovely room and put her hand bag with the purse back be side her bed. I slide her legs in under her duvet aand take her shoes of. I put the cover over her

I take her mobile phone to. I get up and walk a round there is no body here but me. Her hands are under her head like a child sleepen. Then i am leanen over her and i slide my hand under her head and lift so i can slip her own hand out. She moans but does not come to and i work the engage meant ring of her finger. I dont even bother when she looks at me grace she is sayen grace what are you then she closes her eyes again and i lay her back down. Her ring finger is trailen out of the bed so i lift that back up and place it at her side on the bed. The ring fits on me so snug it gleams when i hold my fist up to the lamp light.

I do i say to my selve. Yes dillon i will. Of course i will marry you. As soon as possible. Tonight. Tomorrow. Whenever.

I can here whistlen comen some wear out side a siren. I am leaven the flat. I can here my shoes click down steps then the wet street the lights runnen down hill orange and white the tenement buildens on either side dark. Cars come up and down the hill i am feelen light and the warm wet weather is carryen me down it would be nice to live here so close to every thing goen on pubs and shops and so on. You have always had to live out in the sticks though havent you grace. It was always an ambishion of yours to live here in the town the west end with all its bustel and noise. But it has just not been an opshoun. Even if you could of bought a flat you would have had to buy in knightswood or drumchapel be cause of people like emma and her partner her fiance dillon buyen up all the cheap flats and sellen them out of your range. Isent that right grace. Yes. The world is made for people like them who already have got every thing and just want more. No thing can stop them can it. No. It is always the way of it bud would of sayed poor bud he must be at work thinken of home he must be worryen. What about sean what about vincent. You have not even found francis like as if you would any way. What were you thinken you would discover grace. What were you hopen for. Just some scraps of paper and some reminders of things you thought were all fogoten. No body ever forget any thing though do they gracie. No. Every one remembers every thing you do or say all there eyes blinken open and shut at you.

I am walken down the hill back to the main road i feel light and heavy at the same time. I come to a pub near the bottom you can feel the warmth fug from it just standen near the door way it is the rio café. I have never been in there is a group on in there you can here records or music. May be a djay of some descripshoun i recog nice the record it is one of those old ska records so beloved of bud

wenever you wine or grine it goes

you shake it up rite on time

it is some djay playen ska records from the caribean margaret might like this even though she is from trinidad and tobago or some wear. She loves music she is always sayen about how much she loves music and it is true even bud and i both like these records. I am thinken how to get home though i should dial some one.

I take out the phone a name is vibraten and flashen it is ringen but you can not even here it in here it is to loud. I decide not to anser it. I just watch it. It jumps along sporadic ally in my hand. It rings out after a minute and goes dead again.

I look at the numbers they are to small to make out i look at the phone buttons they are also to small to make out. But my fingers remember.

Hello i say. Is that bobby. Hello. Yes. It is me grace. Can you help me out.

But it is no use to night bobby is in coherent. He is already to drunk to even speak never mind drive any wear. Gracie he keeps sayen gracie am so glad you called. Gracie am so glad. You have called me up gracie. I am so so glad.

Then i can here some thing and then shouten it sounds as though his wife is screamen at him then there is no one on the end of the line at all though i can here arguwen and things bashen about and a telly or steryo in the back ground to. But bobby dosent come back to the phone so i hang up.

Now i am out side and needen the toilit but i do not want to go in a pub and use theres they are always horibel and disgusten. You can not be properly private either at a public convenians for obvious reasons. So i am holden on for now but down this dark street i am half tempted just to knock on some ones door and ask to use there fasility. It is a call of natchure i will say. When i was a small girl our father me and maries went and chapped on some ones door for me to use there facility. No body minded then i wander if they would now. I am in my fifth decade it might seem odd.

We were out for a walk the three of us then. Marie my sister was still all right then. She had not disapeared of and been taken away.

That is what he sayed to her our father. He sayed what you are doen is horibel and disgusten marie. Put some cloths on you arent a child any more.

What is so wrong with the human body marie my sister wanted to know. What is wrong with it we should all be proud of it and it was then we saw all the red.

Wear did she go i asked him when. She was away then for a long time.

Ach gracie. Ach gracie he sayed.

O but it is to dark to see here gracie. I wander down the street people go by.

The light on this phone flashes again it is vibraten in my palm. Some one ringen. I know who. I know who that will be it will be her boy friend her partner her fiancé dillon. It stops again and i get down to the mane road dumbarton road. There are people and cars and the sound of tires on wet ground the sound of shouts and yells. Friday night music bud calls it. You can here it all over drumchapel any night of the week he says. Friday night music. But i ament in drumchapel just now i have to get back to drumchapel. It is getten on bud will be thinken of goen home to.

I stand by the kerb squinten and try hailen a taxi a black hack looken out for there orange light comen towards me. After not long one stops and i try to open the door and can not even find the handel. Does the driver come out and help me does he eff. Eventually i get in. I have still got the remains of this wine bottel in my hand there is a littel left. I tell the driver the address of the college and he turns the car a round. Bud should still be there. Though i am not really wanten to see him just now it is as far as this money will take me.

He drives fast this taxi driver he lurches a bout all over the road. I am bouncen up and down he is not a talker thank good ness. I fumble about for the belt but can not get it in to the lock so i just hang on to the strap by the window instead.

There is the buzzen vibraten phone again.

I let it ring.

Then i answer it.

Who is this a mans voice says.

You had better go and get your fiancé i say.

Who is that wear is emma.

Your fiancé is lyen dead drunk in bed be cause you arent there to look after her. You had better go and help her.

Wear is emma who are you.

Your emma is lyen dead drunk in there in her bed. She is probably harmen your child. So you better take your stupid selve over there and get her. She might choke on her sick or anything.

Who is this what are you talken about.

I hang up. Straight away it starts to ring again and i unwind the window a bit and toss it out.

Hey says the driver what are you playen at back there. You can not be chucken things out of a moven taxi. Jesus christ. Are you bananas or what. You can not just sling any old shite out of my car. What is wrong with a bin.

The taxi driver keeps driven through some lights but as soon as he is through he pulls the car over.

Right he says. That is it. Out you get.

I am getten out i say. I do not want an idyit like you to drive me. What is your number i will report you.

O will you. Report away and he rattles of a number at me. He is a bit older this man he has large framed glasses black and is balden. He is twisted back to shout at me through his spechil window.

Pay up and get out my car. Your bananas you are.

I dig out the money in my purse i have got 5 so i look in emmas purse she has probably got lots of money. There is a note but it feels thin and crumpley. 1 pound. All she has got is 1 pound in her purse. Even i had more money than her and she was rich. It is lucky this old driver has stopped be cause i could not of got home any way.

Here i say. That is all i have.

I put 6 pounds on to his tray and he takes it. I try the door handel. It is locked he has locked it from his side.

That is short he says. That is only 6 pound.

Let me out.

I will drive us round to the polis if you do not pay my fare. This is a pound short.

Let me out i say to him. Let me out let me out.

He is starten the car again he is goen to drive to the polis.

Have it your own way you mad effen cow. Polis it is.

I will report you i shout let me out let me out.

Fine report us then. You report me and i will have you arrested.

He is about to turn us a round i am panicken my stomack all leapen up and down.

Okay okay i say.

Seen some sense he says.

Yes i say. What is your name i ask him.

Eh. What difirins does that make pay me my fare or we are goen to the polis.

On the back of the front passindger seat there is a number and a picture of the driver with his name. He is called james warden.

James i say. I do not have any more money. I am sorry i threw that phone out of the window. I have had a very bad day to day my head is some what messed up. I have drunk to much wine and need to get home. I am also desperate for the toilet. I am absolutely bursten if truth be told. That is all the money i have got please can you just let me out here and i promise i will not report you or any thing.

He is looken at me not sayen any thing.

James i say after the silence gets to much i really need to find a ladies soon.

Dont you pish on my effen seats he says raisen his voice again. I am not clearen that sort of thing up again.

I am sorry james i say. Really i am i do not want any bother if i could leave you my adress or some thing i will pay you the difirins i promise.

He scratches his head and is waggen a finger at me.

That is a pound i am out missus. I am getten short changed here.

I havent got any more you could let me away. It is only a pound. Please i say to him. I need to get out here.

He is drummen his fingers a tune.

What is that tune i wander. It is a well known tune.

Still bursten eh he says. I can feel him looken at me in the mirror. He drums away drum drum. I know the tune it is on the tip of my tunge.

So what are we goen to do now i ask him.

I know it it is the charge of the light brigade.

He drops me of some wear i dont know then drives away still angry and usen color full landwidge be cause i wouldent do what he wanted. For a lousy pound. I am fixen my selve under a rail way bridge next to some wear houses next to the river i think. May be the red clyde siders worked and lived some wear along here there is no one about though. I step over my puddle i could not wait any longer. There is no one about though. This is the middle of nay wear as bud would say. Til i see the main road.

I just have to keep walken down this dark street.

I keep goen i ament sure how far it is to the mane road it is so dark here but i am not even afraid. I just want to get to the road and a head i see bright lights and feel this strange warmth in the air it is febuary but it feels more like april or may is here. It feels like the seasons have got mixed up. The air is wet with smirr and the taxis turn past me and away.

I am not far from buds college i hope and it is not far from costigan house either. The vocashiounal college. Still it is posibel they have locked up for the night already in wich case i will go to costigan. It is still not to late to catch him though i hope. I have been in there once it was some sort of computer course. Of course it is not a real college just some wear people with no jobs can waste there time. There is no thing of any use to learn un less you want to drive a fork lift truck. There is no thing for folk like your selve is there gracie. No. Hair dressen and driven trucks is about it. I walk up the road though it is quite dark the street lights shine orange. I dont know the streets on this side of the main road i never come here. I keep looken up at the street signs on the tenements when we get near Dumbarton road but i can hardly even see the words never mind read them. They might as well be in a forin langwidge. I turn left then right and end up in some sort of terrace with a bit o parkland between the blocks and some railens and walk right round it getten more and more upset. What do they say these street signs and would it help you to know wear you were any way grace you dummy. You numpty. Bang thump there goes gracie boats the dummy. The dunce. What do these letters say. A b c e d j k n m p o x z y. Capitals please. What is a capital is it a city. You dont know what a capital is. Capitals please. What is a capital is it a city. You dont know what a capital is. Yes i do. Paris france. What a thicky. What a doh ball. Streets and more streets and the orange street lamps lighting the way wear. Do you know grace. Is there some one to ask. An elder lay person with a dog may be. Some one who will not be a threat. A child. Of course they are the worst of all the most threatenen. Do you recall when you were 7 grace. Your own mother left about then dident she. Can you even re member her. Do you even re member leaven your daughter with the key on a knitted cord. It was plain brown wasent it. Well. You never were all that great at knitten so brown would be about right for you not haven any imaginashoun. There only ever seemed to be brown wool.

I wander round and round looken at the street signs for no good reason then i see it. The main road and i sigh. I wander up to it not sure not orientatid for a second or 2 then i know which way. That taxi driver just turned me out in to the street i could have been any wear at all he dident care if i got lost or any thing. Well. Why should he even care. He is a stranger and you can not trust your selve with a stranger. That is what we tell small children why is it difirint for adults. I keep walken along the road in the direcshoun i think the college is in. It is not far of the main road.

I cross the road at some traffic lights and keep goen there are a few people about waiten for a bus there is life and i feel safer even though i am not fond of people genrally speaken. They will do you a wrong turn if they can in my experiens.

I can see the lights of the builden. The vocashiounal college. I go up and see the glass doors are shinen with light from inside but no sign of any one so i just push them but they dont move. I look about for a buzzer or some thing like that but maybe they have shut for the night. O that would mean a long long walk in the dark back to drumchapel. Wouldent it gracie. Can you manage that far. Probably if you have to but it will take you hours. I begin to feel a bit sick at the prospect or may be it is be cause of what you have just done. The way you treated that girl who showed you hospitality. On my finger i turn the ring round and round in my other in side pocket i can feel the jotter the book with francises name in it an some other riten you could not make out. Maybe it is a diary of some kind or some of her other scribblens. Well. It will have to wait just now. Francis will have to wait. I feel about on the wall and find a buzzer and press it. After a minute or 2 a voice ansers. I reconise it straight away. Bud.

Bud it is me grace i say let me in.

Gracie he says. What the eff are you doen here i was about to shut up shop. There is only my selve here i have to close up. You can not just turn up when ever you feel like it you numpty.

I know i am sorry just let me in a minute. It is wet out here i am getten soaked.

Effen hell he says. All right. Come on in. You better not get us in to any bother here. I shouldn't even be letten any one in. Push the door now.

I push the door and it lets me in and i am standen in a big hall way but theres no sign of bud yet. Then there is a shout up here it says and i look up. I can make a head leanen out over an up stairs banister or balcony.

Come up the stairs gracie. Straight a head and to your left he shouts. And quick time to.

I follow his instrucshouns and find the stairs and cling on to the banister all the way up. I am a bit un steady as the drink is affecten me. O the drink. Bud will know straight away. I begin to feel ill at the prospect of confessin my sins though i am not even relidgious. There he is at the top holden on him selve. Of course he dosent have his stick to day.

Jesus effen chirst he says you are goen to get us in some hot water if you aren't careful gracie.

He comes over and tries to kiss me but i turn away. It is no use of course.

But some how he dosent realise.

What is the matter with you then. Wear have you been any way.

Nothing bud i am just awful tired. I went up to partick and i dident have enough for the fare home so i came here. How was it to day did you get on all right.

Bud seems stressed . He is scratchen his head and stretchen out his leg.

Ooft he says. It went all right consideren.

Consideren what i say.

Consideren my leg is effen killen me what do you think. It is pure murder so it is. I will have to get the old peg leg out no doubt about it. Theres no way i can stand about here all day on my feet with out it. I will end up a crippel.

I laugh. I thought you sayed you were a crippel already.

Aye well i may be a cripple but i dont fancy enden up in a weel chair to boot. There is a limit to how much crippleled ness a bloke can stand. And i will not be standen at all if i dont take my walken stick.

So you are about ready to go home are you i ask him.

I have to shut up the libary and take care of the petty cash. There was an other janny here earlier but i sayed he should just head home i would be okay. They are trusten me a fare bit so i dont want to blow it.

Bud bends down and rubs his knee. I think they will be okay about the stick he says. I should of taken your advise gracie. Your not just a pretty face after all are you. Come and check the place out.

It is only after my eyes have adjusted to the bright ness i can see all the posters every wear. Riten every wear. All difirint lettern and sizes. The place is awash with words.

Your goen to have to sign in and out to gracie. Every thing is on cctv in here it will show up if you dont.

Here i was thinken i was done with words for the day and now i am here in a builden full of them and about to go in to a libary. It is as if there is some one always taunten me. Maybe it is that god up there that dosent exist. He has got it in for you right enough gracie. Our father me and maries used to say that communism was the opiate of the marxests though i never knew what he meant then. He could be quite god fearen in his own way. I think that is why i am not neither is marie my sister. Bud of course is not relidgeious. He is as near to god as a nun getten effed on a crucifix he always says then laughs his head of at his own joke. He will say this when ever he gets an opportunity. It amuses him no end to repeat his own jokes forever. He is like our father me and maries in that regard.

Do we have to bud i say. I am done in. Show me an other time.

Bud gets tetshy. What is wrong with right now he says. It will only take 5 minutes. I have got to finish up any way so you might as well take a gander.

All right i say but then can we go home.

That is what i sayed isent it. Did you not here me. I sayed we will finish up and head home. I tell you what though i am gaggen for drink. And a rolly.

Bud takes me through to an other big room and clicks on the strip lights which blink and buzz.

It has got a lot of books on shelfs just like all libarys. No thing of any interest just books by the dozen.

Bud is footerin with a tin box i can here it must be the float.

Not bad is it. Not a bad we library at all. Go and have a wee look a round while i take care of this.

What would i want a look a round for. It is only books. No thing of interest. But i wander over any wear and just about break my leg trippen over some thing.

It is a metal bucket full of water.

Effs sake bud shouts more like effs saaaaaake. Can you not take a step in any direction with out goen arse over tit. You have spilled all that water. Aw no. He comes limpen over with some thing it is a mop. He starts moppen and cursen. I am about sick of bein cursed for one night. We have got a leaky sky light here it is supposed to be getten fixed. The books are all goen to get ruined if we are not care ful. It is a damp disgrace so it is.

Who is we. Bud is we and the vocashounal colledge all ready. After one day. He has sold out all of his prinsiples and become part of the establish ment in only one day. And all these books. Pick one up gracie. Go on have a look to your self and see what you are suposedly missen out on. So i do. I go over to a shelf while bud is scrubben the carpet and pick one up it has a blue cover or it might be grey. What does it say grace. No thing. It has got grafs and tables in it. Lots of riten very hard to see never mind read.

Hey put that back will you bud snaps at me. You have done enough damage. You are some girl grace. Some kid.

Bud it was you told me to have a look about. If it is any ones fault it is your own.

Ach well i never says to touch any thing though did i.

He is waven his mop in my general direcshoun. Bud i say stop that waven. You are getten splashes all over me.

Serves you right you numpty. What are you even doen here.

I am getten angry at this be haviour. There is no need to make such a carry on.

I told you why i am here i say. I was short of the fare.

So you thought muggins here could see you home. Well i have not got enough money for 2. You should have gone to costigan house. It is not like it is far from here.

Do you want me to leave is that it bud. You want me to go and leave you and your stupid library and your books about what ever they are about.

Gracie no i am not sayen that. Be sides there is boind to be some in teresten books here even for you. He laughs at this it is a joke on me. He knows i would never try to read one not in a million years. But some how i dont feel like laughen.

You could take some money from the float i say. You could pay it back to morrow.

Not a chance i will get sacked it is my first day and you want me to thieve from my employers. Not a chance.

It is only a couple of pound for the bus bud. It is from the float. No one is goen to notis from the float.

All this time i have been turnen the ring on my finger round and round tryen to work it of be four bud notises except it is no use. It is stuck fast.

What are we argewn for gracie. I am not taken money from the float and that is that effs sake.

We both go surly quite. I go back over to the desk with the float on it and bud goes back to his moppen.

I look at the float and can feel my selve bristle be cause i know bud is keepen an eye on me. It makes me angry that he does not trust me. His papers and cutters choice and lighter are on the desk to. I pick up the lighter and begin to spark the flint over and over letten the flame catch and then shutting it of again. I know he is watchne me and i take the blue book and begin leafen through it again pretended to be interested in the grafs and diagrams i can barely make out.

Bud is whistlen now he is still pretendin not to be interested but i know he is tuned in to what i am doen. He sings low to him selve with his cracked voice. It is lead belly he is singen one of his favourites in the pines. The one that tells of the black girl who has no wear to sleep. Normally bud picks this on his guitar or some times banjo and he can make it sound good but here he has no gitar but even so it sounds good and makes me want to go to him. But you will not will you grace. No. Why. Be cause you are stuborn be cause you are sick fed up with every thing be cause you are a bad mother a bad person. That is when i realise what i am doen and see the corner of the page curl yellow and brown the bloom of fire comen to wards me.

Grace holy eff what the eff are you doen. Bud comes rushen over but i just sit with the book in my hands. Bud knocks it from me and it lands shut on the ground with a smack which puts out the fire. Bud grabs my shoulders and his face is right up in my own he is a red angry tomato. He is shaken me by the shoulders what are you playen at have you had a drink or some thing are you tryen to get me canned on my first day i can smell drink of you what is goen on here grace what is your game what if you set the sprinklers of this is all goen to be caught on cctv you get the eff out of here right now grace you should take your selve away from here shouldent you yes you should go gracie go over to costgan house and get a lift or some thing this is not a good seen here is it no you have over stepped the mark this time havent you grace bud would not hit you would he how do you know how he is marchen you down the stair o is he goen to hit you grace do you even know o grace. O gracie.

I am on the street again the rain constant light but constant and i know it isent far from the addicshouns forums i am near to costigan house so i start walken in that direcshoun i will ask margaret or michelle my friend michell my colleag michell to let me in. I would like a wash to. A clean up. Not that i am dirty espeshilly but not that i am all that clean either. Just you know. It has been a long day. I feel dirty which is the same thing. There are ash marks on my face i am sure. Of course if any one knew about this they would hate me and think i am horibel and digusten to. But what did i do really. Only pay a debt. Bud dident pay a debt and he lost the use of a leg. My debt was a lot smaller and i am still walken away. May be francis felt like this when she was left with the key round her neck. Yes. Bud has shown you the door and this ring is still stuck tight in my hand in my pocket. Francises diary or jotter rolled tight in your other hand inside your coat pockets. You should of set it a light shouldn't you not that book of diagrams. What harm had it ever done to you that book. This other book is the dangerus one. You shouldent look in side gracie. You should leave it well alone. It might destroy you it has may be got that power who knows. Not that i am supersticshous or any thing but just. Just some things sayed or ritten do seem to have power. Bud would of sayed that. There is no power greater than that of the ritten word. Except new clear power ha ha. That is so funny bud i say to him on such ocashouns. You are hilarious. Humph he will just say just you wait. Just you wait and see if bud spence is wrong.

Near to the traffic lights again and across the road to costigan house the moshion detecters turnen the light on the lawn as i cross by the side path. White light maken all the shadows darker than ever. Who could be standen watchen in the shadows. Any one could.

I go up the step and look over at the car park wear i saw francis but she isent there of course. Of course. It was just foolish ness on my part again.

I am ringen the buzzer.

What did you tell your selve grace. What did you say. You had to live with out hope that was it wasent it. Hope would be the thing that did you in if you let it get a grip. Well. You are nearly saved. You nearly gave in to it but not quite. You can carry on.

No body is anseren but i can here noise in side the curtanes are open a crack in the dinen room there is light and music comen from there. Up at the window i can see margaret standen in the middle of the room her back to the window. She is conducten a singsong for the elder lay. They are singen some thing i am not familiar with they are waven there arms a bout. I go back to the door and ring the buzzer again a few times. Some one ansers not michelle though it is ceecee. Evenchually i can here keys rattlen behind the door.

Gracie what are you doen here i havent got you down on the books for a shift.

Ceecee is the gay blade that is how he introduses him selve to every one hello my names ceecee the gay blade. He says this to all the elder lay of costigan house and every one likes ceecee even all the old men that normally hate gay blades. Though bud sayed ceecee the gay blade is to butch to be a gay man. He has got the belly of a beer drinker and tattoos he has never so much as tasted a gee and tee bud says. He has got a birds name tattood on his four arms. One on each. On the left he has got the name sandra and on the other dee though you can hardly read them now they are so old and blurry. How would he have those names if he was the gay blade bud sayed. They are obviusely old girl friends names.

He must have had them ritten be four he knew he was the gay blade i told bud. He must still of been confused about his own secshual identity.

He is not the only one bud sayed.

You look like some thing the cat boaked up ceecee says. Come on in.

I go to sign the register not even caren.

What is on to night ceecee.

O there haven a wee singsong. Margarets idea. Cheer every one up after old eddy munros passen. You would not believe the atmos fear in this place. It is totally dead. Margarets getten them all to sing caribean songs.

I can here all there old frale voices in there singen and laughen.

They are doen all the harry belafonte numbers. You want to here them.

I can here them i tell him. It sounds like good fun.

Aye well it was needed. O the tears and tantrums and the spillen of soup. Old gets.

Angelina angelina they are singen. Pick up your concertina. And play a song for me for. For i am comen home from thee sea.

Is michelle in i ask ceecee. I am not really suposed to be here.

No she finished at 6 doll. She went home with a face like thunder to. Some thing has went on in my absinthe.

You have not herd all the gossip then.

No but i would not pay any atenshoun to it if i did. That michelle i have no trust in her at all. She would steal your grave as soon as look at you and there would be room for skinny so and so as well. I herd there was some thing goen on between you and her and margaret but you have got my vote doll. Margaret has sayed to me she thinks you are getten stitched up by some one who shall re mane name less i.e. for example michelle and that she will not stand by and let the afourmenshined go un challenged.

Thank you ceecee that means so much to me i tell him. But i really just want to use the fone just now i am skint and need a sub for a fare can you help me.

Jeez o says ceecee. Talk about a chancer. Yes of course you can use the effen phone you dafty. I am sure costigan house can stretch to the price of a black hack.

Normally it is only the full time carers who get taxi fares payed but on ocashoun they will sub some one like my selve. We go down to the kitchen along the dim hall that smells of disin fectant and fabreeze.

Ceecee puts the kettle on the hob and then produces a packet of chocolate hob nobs.

My secret stash he says. None of these eejits here are getten any. Except your good selve of course. Poor white trash like that michelle can bring there own biscuits.

She wouldent thank you for them i say to him. She would likely just stop up the sink with them after.

Ceecee laughs his head of at this and i can not help but join in to.

She just balloons and then shrinks back down again dosent she.

Just then there is a woop from the liven room and then a hurray. I can here margarets voice she is laughen some others to. Then they are all singen with her leaden the way.

Yellow bird they are singen now. Up high in banana tree. Yellow bird. You sit all alone like me.

Bud would love this i say to ceecee. He would get his gitar out and have them all singen and laughen.

So what is his nibs up to these days. Still looken for a job.

He has found one. Well temporary. May be longer.

I dont menshoun him goen to hit me. I dont menshoun the book that got burnt.

O thats good news is it not. How long was that he was signen on.

I couldent say. It was a long time any way. It has been tough i tell ceecee.

Tell me about it. I have done time on the broo my selve it is not easy. Your bud has such a winnen person ality to ceecee is sayen sarcastic ally. He should be hosten who wants to be a millyonare.

Ceecee and bud pretend to disdane each other but there is a respect to i think. They ask after each other any way. They would neither of them admit it though. They have both got there pride.

O wait a minute ceecee says. What is this. He has finally popped the question grace. O that is a lovely ring.

I dont say any thing i can not think of any thing wear did i get this ring or any thing just not any thing. I should of kept my hand in my pocket o grace you are so stupid arent you. It is just a fact.

I will not even en choir wear his nibs found the money for that o let me have a look. O that is really nice grace o congrachulashouns. He did not win it at a raffel did he.

I am cuppen one hand over an other these hands are not right in them selves they know they are getten looked at stared at wear can i put them. There is no wear grace ceecee has seen the ring now. Tell him some thing grace tell him any thing.

Yes i say. That is right ceecee he won it.

O is that him gamblen again. May be that is not such good news. I mean congrachulashouns and every thing but if he is gamblen again. I mean that is teribel.

I think it isent very valuable ceecee i say. He just won it in a rafflel down the community centre. He is up there getten his leg re habilitatit every other week. He joins in some times that is wear he won the money for a deposit on this.

Needs must eh ceecee says. It is really swanky though so it is.

Come on and we will let margaret see.

O no please i say dont bother her. She is busy and i am not even meant to be here. I just want to get a fare home.

Ceecee is not even listenen though he is up and draggen me by the hand through to the dinen room. This room is bright and warm all the elder lay are here in there seats they are be tween songs and they seem happy even that mr tarick sarwar who had a stroke. Margaret is talken to him asken if he is all right then turns a round when ceecee calls her.

I can see she is not well dis posed to me at costigan house right this minute. Her body clicks out of kilter some what as though she had drawn a breath in to fortify her selve for some new chalinge. Well. I am ready to. I am twisten the ring a bout my finger it will not come of. Ceecee is sayen to margaret guess what the good news is. Guess what. Margaret is sayen i dont know what. But guess guess ceecee says. O please margaret is sayen. I am not guessen ceecee. We are not children. Then he tells her and she looks at me no she says. Never. Is that so. O grace congrachulashouns. Let me see the ring. O that is lovely. That is beauty full.

It is not so expensive i say to her. Bud surprised me.

Of course he did. Just this after noon grace. I dont remember you menshounen getten married earlier. No. I really can not remember notisen any ring either.

Yes i tell her. He asked me after i left. He even got down on his good knee to ask.

And you sayed yes did you. Well. I. Never. Well. I. Never in. Deed. Uh huh.

Margaret is suspishous i can tell. It is in her voise but she can not say any thing. She dosent know any thing.

Well show her it ceecee says. I hold out my hand.

Margaret takes it and peers at the ring she smells clean and fresh like a sitrus fruit.

O beauty full she says. He has very fine taste your fiancé. Very fine indeed. O but you say it isent expen sive. Why not show mr tarick sarwar. He was a jeweller were you not mr tarick sarwar.

He looks up as though hearen his name called by a distant relatif. His eyes wander as though he is desiden wether to anser to this name. You have got no wear to go now grace have you. You have got no wear to run.

Margaret says what do you think mr tarick sarwar. Is it a good stone. It must be grace. Uh huh uh huh. A good stone indeed.

Margaret ceecee says. I dont think grace wants to have her engagement ring evaluated right this minute.

O no of course not margaret laughs. O i am so rude forgive me. That is okay margaret. It is no problem.

Just then mr tarick sarwar taps on some thing his book the black one. He is smilen. He taps again on the book. He is sayen some thing i can not under stand.

Rerererre reeereee

He wants you to read to him grace margaret says. That seems to make him happy. If you read to him.

And there i have an other hot flush i feel my face go bright red.

I know i know mr tarick sarwar she says. But grace can not read it for you. Can you grace. It is all written in muslamic or some thing isent it mr tarick sarwar. Grace does not read muslamic. Do you grace.

No i say. I am afraid i do not.

And i dont think there is any one else in here who does either margaret says.

Mr tarick sarwar looks confused looks between ceecee and margaret taps his book his eyes sad.

Fuch of he says and i know just how he feels.

He is holden his hand up he is sayen some thing. They are not comen out the words that he wants and margaret says take your time. He closes his eyes and sighs then opens them again. He reaches for me my hand. It is no use you have got to show him the ring gracie. You have got to. Yes. He looks at it puts my hand up close to his eyes.

I can not get it of i say to margaret and ceecee. It is stuck.

Mr tarick sarwar holds it there so long until my arm is tired he just stares and stares. Then suddenly he just lets go and sinks back in his chair.

Nobody says any thing. Every one is looken at mr tarick sarwar. Fuch of. Rubsh. Junk.

He is looken very digni fyed and proud sitten there in his chair like that his eyes closed his suit on his beard and hair grey and black neat and combed.

Tssss margaret says. Such a filthy mouth he has to.

I know ceecee says. Absolutely shocken filthy mouth.

Well margaret says how can he tell with out the eye peace. He can not can he. That is how they can see if a diamond is flawed or not isent it.

Of course it isent a diamond at all. It is just glass isent it. Wear would bud get the money for a real diamond that is just daft. Any way it is the thought be hind it isent it. It is the intent.

Ceecee nods. Yes it is the intent grace you are quite right. She is quite right isent she margaret.

Margaret is nodden uh huh uh huh she says. Quite right. Of course of course.

There was some one came looken for you grace ceecee tells me in the kitchen while i wait for my lift. A girl i think. A woman. She dident leave any name in fact she just disapeared as soon as any one menshined leaven a message. O i say to ceecee. What did she look like. Was she tall. Did she have a knitted cord a round her neck. Would bud have hit you grace. Would he have done that. May be.

Ceecee slurps his tea and munches on a hob nob biscuit. I couldent tell you he says it was michelle ansered the door to her. Did she not menshine it to you. That is teribel if she dident menshine it to you grace. She is only interestit in her selve that michelle. She is only out to get what she can for number one.

Was there no message then.

No i think this person scarpered at the menshine of it. She was there one minute and gone the next. She had some man with her some shifty looken type.

She did not even leave a name or any thing.

No. Not a thing. Aparently she was very nervy very jittery. Hard looken.

That would be francis i think to my selve. Not beauty full any more. Nervy. Shifty. Hard looken. The sort of girl who never leaves any trace of her selve. But her finger prints are on every thing arent they grace yes yes they are every wear. Was she ever a good girl do you think. Did she ever do what you wanted or expected. No even when she was small she was wilful and contrary. She was in a world of her own with her drawen and so on. Like your sister marie wasent she. Yes. She was very like marie. Marie when marie was a littel girl be four she went.

Do you remember when she stabd vincent grace. All you did was leave them in the kitchen to gether for ten minues and tell them neither of them to touch the sharp knives and of course she did. And poor vincent still has that scar on his thumb wear the butter fly stitches went on. How he sat there so still and white in the hospital waiten room. So good a boy then. He brought you shells even though there is no sea near by the garscadden woods. He still brought shells he dug them up. Empty sea shells with mother of pearl in side.

The sodjers left them he sayed laughen. Up on the hill there by the woods. Shells.

He sat there so white and still and in thought and not angry with francis. Of course he worshiped francis. She got him to say he had done it to him selve. Cut him selve. But i got the truth from her vincent did no thing. She stabd him with a kitchen knife and gave him a scar be tween his thumb and finger. A white scar now you can hardly see it now. But then he wouldent of told on her he was loyal even if he got in troubel him selve. The story she made up to. Like marie. Marie would make up storys to she would talk about things and after a while you real ised it was not true it was not real.

Such as tellen us that we were not even her real sister and father. Such as sayen our father had strangeld our mother and buryed her in the wood. When i was small i some times believed these storys to except they kept changen. I was afraid of our father for a time. I believed her i am a shamed to say. I was afraid he would strangel me in my sleep like he did our mother just like my sister marie sayed. Then of course i would find her in my room standen over me a sleep. Shhshh she would say. Shhshh go back to sleep.

This is all just a dream. This is all a just a dream. This is all just a dream.

One day you will wake up gracie one day. It will be over the dream you will have a woken. Except that is not even true for a non practisen pro distant.

The door buzzer goes in the kitchen and ceecee goes to the intercom.

That is gregor for you grace. He says he will get you in the car.

I finish my tea it is look warm now. My head ache is back i am soberer but it is just a normal head ache of tired ness and wine now not a my grain.

I will get you to the door you look all in.

Thanks ceecee i will be okay. Please if that girl comes back tell her i have left or am away some wear.

Like a holiday.

Yes. Tell her i am with my sister marie on the canary isles.

Done ceecee says.

I go down the hall they are still in the liven room those that have not all ready gone to up to sleep. Just a few elder lay remainen a wake. I wander if i would of been good at margarets job. I wander that a lot a bout jobs. If i could do them or if i would under stand what is needed. I wander what would be the best job for me and i have not got any idea. The few times i was in school i was some times asked and i had ideas then. They were childish though. I wanted to be a vet or a horse rider or a ice figure skater be cause they were all the things marie my sister liked. Now i think it is like our father sayed i would be a good carer. Well what is wrong with that gracie. Some body has got to care for all these elder lay. It may as well be you. You could not be a vet any way you are to bad at readen and riten. You are stuck tryen to read the small print and that is a fact. The more you squirm the stucker you get. You have fallen in between the cracks of this life havent you gracie in be tween the sentenses in the small print which you dident read. Plus you are not even fond of dogs.

You haven't got your desint glasses then he says are you sure this is the right number.

I nod. Yes i am sure.

We are driven along not sayen any thing for some reason. Gregor mutters some thing at the lights or an other car now and then but other than that he does not talk or ask me why i called him or what the troubel is. We just drive a long and i stare up out of the window at the street lights the dark shadows of people the red and orange and white flashes. It is a friday night there is the feelen any thing could happen in side me my stomack is all fizzles again. I keep my hands clasped over the ring it will not come of i need a bit of butter or some thing. That time marie told me to get out when we were on holiday i spent all night driven a round to. She was haven some sort of moment to her selve. She was haven some kind of fit of some thing and you had to leave dident you gracie. And you dident have a penny on you then either did you just a few travellers checks you couldent cash at that time of night. You sat all night in a hotel lobby waiten for a guest to leave so you could get a room there. At least you will not be home less to night.

Thanks gregor i say.

No problem he tells me. He dosent say any thing else.

I supose this not your ideal way to spend a friday night.

What. O no. It is fine. Friday nights are not what they used to be.

Do you not have buster with you to night.

No. Buster is watchen the house for me. He would of just got all excited at this time of the night and would not let me at peace for hours after. So i just left him standen sentry duty.

Is he a good guard dog then i ask him. He is fiddlen with the music stashouns on the radio no doubt looken for rock.

There we go he says and claps my hand i get a kind of jolt he has touched the ring. But he dosent seem to notice it or if he does he dosent say any thing. The music is rock music it is metalicas enter night exit light. Take my hand. Of to never never land.

O he is no use at all gregor says laughen. He would open the door to a burglar if he had the thumbs for it. His troubel is wanten to be pals with every one.

We are zoomen down the road the street lights blurren by like comets.

I spoke to your vincent he says after a minute. Him and his pals.

O i say i ament sure i want to here this.

He is nodden.

So how did it go i say.

Well vincent still wants to join up. His pals are not so sure but he is.

I feel my selve crumple away in to just a small mound in side.

I think you should just support him in it. It is his choice.

So that is it then. I am goen to lose my son vincent as well as my daughter francis. He is joinen the army and they will send him of some wear to be shot at by people whose langwidge he can not even speak. He dident get any qualificashouns in school. He can not so much as say a word in french or any thing. Apart from merd which is not likely to be of much use.

I supose you told him it was a good idea i say to gregor.

He is consentraten on the road. He is weelen the steeren weel about and my body lurches to the side and then back and then to the side and then back like i am getten cast a bout by waves in the sea side. O francis you thought i had forgot. Every time i left the house you must of thought i had forgot mustent you. Then of course you did dident you gracie. You did forget all about it in the long run. Well. Time to re member again. Time to re mind your selve.

Grace i did no such thing. You think i could tell that boy any thing. You are very much mis taken. He has made up his mind. He is closed to hearen any one elses ideas about the army. And i know how he feels it is the same as i felt when i joined up.

O that was years a go.

So what. I was in northen eireland and in bosnia. It wasent all just sitten a bout playen my selve. I am tellen you it is no difirint and you will not convinse vincent other wise. So you might as well give him your blessen.

We are in old drumchapel road now i think though it isent easy to say it has a feel of home the madhouse. Gregor and me sit in silence i do not want to break it it will be like breaken every thing. It will be like taken it and smashen it in to bits. The jotter in my coat pocket is a bomb waiten to go of. You have already lit the fuse haven't you grace. Havent you. Yes. You should not of read it. You should have burnt that book be four the other one.

We are driven by hecla square i can reconise it even in the dark even with bad glasses even with no glasses in the dark. I would know it with my eyes shut i think. Gregor turns the car to go up to our house ours and the counsils well for 5 years left any way. Then it will just be rubbel.

Wait i say to gregor wait a moment please.

We are in the middel of the road grace i can not wait.

Can we go some wear else please. I do not feel like goen home just yet.

Greger turns the car again back down the way we were comen then he turns right along the mane road.

Okay so we are not goen home yet he says. Wear then.

I can see the houses and lights moven slowly by i can here the car endjin the crunchen road we are not driven fast we are goen slow.

Garscadden woods i say. I can not see them through the dark wind screen and the wipers on slow but they are up there. Lets go to garscadden woods for a while. Please.

Gregor dosent look at me. Okay grace he says. Garscadden woods it is.

Garscadden woods wear your children francis and vincent tried to lose you when you walked away from them all through the grass the nettels.

I always called it the bluebell woods gregor says.

We are sitten in the car in a lay by over looken the town. The lights are visible not so much else not even our houses the high flats they are obscured. Knightswood wear your father yours and maries brought you up and then left you is obscured. He died in a nurses tuck. O grace. O gracie boats wear is he now your father. No wear you are a non beliefer. He beliefed but you dont. Belief is a kind of hope and you can not afford that. Being hope less is safer you can not be let down you can not be disapointid. You can not have your children break your heart.

Most people a round her do i say.

So how come you dont then grace.

I am not from a round here i tell him. This is just wear i have been for the last while.

Gregor puts the light on for a second and then of again reachen about for some tobacco and the smell of it makes me think of bud hoe he was getten ready to knock you down. He was close to it. May be he still will if you go home. We sit in the car and look out of the window so much blacker now after the light. The trees and grasses seethen in the breeze the light rain. The wind is warm to warm for febuary. Gregor has got the radio turned of now so we can here the woods out side. Enter night.

Bluebells is a nicer name than garscadden he says. I dont even know what garscadden means. Do you.

It is just an other word gregor. They all do the same damage in my opinion.

Hmm he says lighten his cigarette. Do you want to go out side.

I am okay in doors i say.

The woods hiss and shush out side there is no one else a bout on this hill side.

Bud will be worryen about you gregor says.

I shake my head. I doubt that some how. Not to night any way. Be sides he has dis apeared on me often enough. Can you make me a cigaret please.

I dident know you smoked.

It has been years but to night i would like to just have one. I have made some mis takes to day so i guess one more can not hurt.

He is nodden and takes out his tobacco to roll an other. Then he is handen me it and oferen a light. I take a draw and exhale it also feels good i am straight away light headed. After it passes i take an other puff.

I used to come her with francis and vincent i say to gregor. A long time a go. Well. We dident come often i was not much of a country person.

Gregor laughs you are callen this the country he says. This is not the country. This is the countrys back green.

I smile and look at him. Gregor did you know me be four i ask him.

Be four he says. Be four what.

From a round here in drumchapel. Did you ever know me.

Gregor blows out smoke. What are you getten at grace. How would i of known you.

I shake my head no reason i say. I just wandered if you had seen me about or heard about me be four.

Gregor laughs. O aye we all knew about you grace. All any body ever does is talk about that grace barker ha ha. You worried about your reputashoun grace.

Ha ha i say. Yes.

Well what ever it is your worried about i dont want to know. Our slate is clean so far as i am conserned. Is that okay with you.

I nod. That is fine with me i say and we both laugh quietly.

We sit there just silent for a while listenen to the sounds the trees are maken. It is a haunten sound the wind through the grass and nettels. I shiver. It is like some long forgoten thing creepen up on you.

You know grace if you do not suport vincent you will lose him gregor says after a while. You know that dont you.

Yes. I know. But if i suport him i will lose him any way. It is lose lose for me.

You are not losen him. You are just trusten him to come back again.

Gregor takes my hand and i wrigell it a way. I tug at the ring with my other hand but it still will not come of.

I am sorry he says. I dident mean to. I can still feel the warm of his fingers touch on the back of my hand for a second.

I un wind the window a bit and drop the cigaret out. That was disgusten i say and he laughs quietly.

Then we sit.

I can here him breathe.

And then i am leanen over and he is kissen me on the mouth. Or i am kissen him i ament sertin who started it. I am climben over the seat and he is tryen to back up in it to make room. My head is pressen in to the roof. He is tryen to get my top un butoned. Oops he says. Oof. Just. Wait. I say no no dont wait. Aiyah he says. I am stuck. So am i. Hup. Hoof. Put the seat back. Put it back a bit i tell him and then it collapses and we are laughen. This car is a pretty beat up old girl right enough i say. I told you she needed warmen up a bit gregor says we are gigglen lyen flat down me on top. Lucky you have left buster or he would be scwashed i say and gregor and me are gigglen. Ah he says o. Ooyah. Howf. We are twisten a bout tryen to sit up straight but i can not get any thing to grip a hold of. Then there is a hard crack crack cracken.

We both freeze stiff. Every thing is lit up we are a light.

I crane my neck up. There is some one rappen on the drivers window with some thing hard. There is some one shinen a torch in to our car.

Open the door some one is sayen. Open up in there.

Then the rappen.

Jesus christ gregor says he is scramblen to get up right to get him selve to gether.

We are in a fankel tryen to get up out of the seat. Gregor gets the door handel in the back open and drags him selve on all fours most un dignifyed the torch light followen him in to the dark. I am here my selve is it posible they have not noticed me. No grace it isent posible they know you are in here you might as well come out and give up. O grace you will have to confess. You left that girl you left your own children here to. The seen of your crimes. You are found out. Only bobby knows. Get in the car grace this is not a good seen. You are all muck and blood. Did you fall. No. Collapsen is difirint from fallen. Your skirt was green grass staned your legs and hips all nettle stings.

I manage to sit up in the back and have no intenshoun of moven. But then the torch is sayen you to please miss. You have to get out the car please.

Polis men. To of them a man and a woman. The air is fresh it smells of a to early spring. Our father me and maries died in the spring time. In that bed. O the sound of him. His eyes holden on longer than he should of. Clingen to you and not letten go. He still wont let you go will he grace. No. Not ever.

Gregor is shaden his eyes from the torch with his hand.

Effen hell he is sayen. What now.

What is your name sir the man polis says. I can not see his face for the light.

What are we suposed to have done gregor says.

The woman polis shines her torch at me at my cloths. I am tryen to tuck my selve in better to look more respect abel.

Sir. Your name please. And adress. Miss you to.

Gregor tells him.

Miss the polis man says. Your name.

So i tell him. I tell him the name francis my daughters name of no fixed address. I do not look at him or gregor. We are from here i say we are from drumchapel. What have we done ofisir and madam.

You realise you could be arestid for this sort of be haviour sir.

What be haviour gregor says. What are you talken a bout. We were just out for a drive.

This is a popular place for ramblen the woman polis says. She is round looken and not tall either. In fact she does not seem very like a polis at all she is so short and fat.

Do you realise you could get charged for carryen out acts like this she says.

Like what eh gregor says. We were just sitten.

That did not look like sitten to me the man polis says. That looked like lyen down.

So we were lyen down whose bisness is it.

You realise we could arest you for public indecency.

We were in the car gregor says.

It dosent matter. If you are out side your own home then it is in public. We would be within our rights to have you to up in court on an anty soshial be haviour order. Lude and libidinous acts.

I have my hands clasped i am tryen tryen tryen to get the ring of but it will not come. It will not come at all.

For what gregor says we were not doen any thing. It is pitch black up here there is no one a round even.

Are you sayen you were un aware that this is a popular site for doggers.

Gregor just stands there. He starts to say some thing but then dosent.

Doggers i ask the woman polis. We have not got a dog with us.

She does not say any thing. She just starts to report on us in to her walky talky radio.

Doggen gregor says. Just that word as if it is an entirely new word he has never heard be four that he has to try out with his tung to see if it works all right.

Doggen he says again. Are you aresten us for doggen.

What are you to make of this gracie. Doggen they are sayen about you. They are maken you out to be some sort of animal a dog a bitch in heat is that it. Is that it gracie you are no dog. No. You have never been that you would not just go with any one would you except bud you went with him. But you never made him pay. Well. He is payen now. He is payen for sticken with you. He would have been right to hit you. You wish he had dont you grace. There would have been some relief in that like those folk that cut them selves. A good punch in the eye would of felt good it would of done you good. Except he dident hit you is it be cause he is weak grace. Is that it. No. Your father some times used his hands on you and your sister marie it did not make him strong. He was weaker than any one you have ever seen at the end. He was unable even to move in that bed the way the nurse the carer tucked him in. A weak man in a straight jacket that was all he was.

O grace bud will find out if they arrest you he will leave you will have no one no one at all. If he hasent already left. Wear would he go. Bobbys. No his wife would not have him. If he had hit you may be he would stay. Vincent will go francis will take sean bud will go you will be all a lone. Sean will be come dependent like his mother if he makes it even that far. That is why you have kept him at arms length isent it. You could not bare to see some one else suffer that way. Except it is more self ish. You could not bare to witness it and suffer your selve.

They are shinen a torch at your shoes why gracie. What can your shoes tell them what can your cloths tell them. Only what you have been up to grace only the way you are behaven. This ring will not come of. It will not budge gracie. It will not effen move.

Gregor is losen his temper he is waven his arms a bout. We were not doggen he says you pair of stupit sees. We dident even know did we.

Head lights sweep up the path through the trees toward us and we all stop waiten a car then an other slowly cruse by there are faces in the window staren at us. They speed up and keep moven when there lights see the polis man and woman the white van parked near by. The polis woman shines her torch in there windows as they go by then we are in the dark it is dis orienten it is so black out here i can literilly see eff all.

You were expectin company the woman says.

Listen gregor is sayen. We arent doggers we have got no thing to do with that kind of thing man. I have never even contem plated such a thing. Gods honest truth ofisir i would not of ever been in volved in such a thing. Grace neither. Isent that right grace. You would never consider such a thing would you.

Grace the polis man says. I thought you sayed your name was francis.

I can here there walky talkys cracklen words broken and snaped comen out of them. Gregor is getten very agitatit. Well. Words are always broken and snaped for you aren't they grace. They are jaggy things that can pierce you like broken glass. They are damaging to you. They are barbed wire. Even the way they look is to sharp. There are cracks be tween them letters a b d h i fj k z x c k k y. All harmful to you all cagen you. Out or in. You dont even know which do you. No. They could be a way in but it is the way in to a maze for you isent that right grace. Yes.

There is no need to get worked up sir. We all just have to stay calm here.

What do you mean i am calm.

We are not goen to charge you this time. We are just goen to give you a coshen.

You are given me a coshen gregor says. His arms keep goen to his head and back to his hips he is pecken back and forth wear he stands he keeps barellen out his chest.

A coshen why not give us the full boona he says. Why not just effen kneecap us while you are at it. An effen coshen. For what. Yous think i have not had a coshen be four. I will give you the cosh.

Gregor i say. It is okay.

Calm down sir or i will arrest you.

Effen come on then. Effen arrest me see if i give an eff. Doggen for effs sake what do you think i am. You polis have got dirty effen minds so you have. No thing better to do than drive a bout harasen folk out for an effen drive. Just an effen drive in the country.

Sir calm right down. Now.

The woman is half turned away she is talken in to her walky talky. She keeps looken back then sayen things in to it.

Dirty effen basterts so you are. Your minds are effen sewers.

Right that is it you are under arrest. You have the right to he says. You have the right

the polis is graben gregors hands gregor is swearen but not fighten the ofisir is chargen him with lude ness and libid inisness. He is chargen him with disordeley behaviour threatenen or abusive ness to a polis ofisir. And then the woman ofisir is tryen to put cuffs on me to i have done no thing i shout leave me a lone leave me. She is talken in her walky talky she is tryen to cuff my hands tryen to get these cuffs on leave me leave me i am shouten and buck and rench free scratch at her face ow she is sayen the other polis is on top of me they are they are they are o grace o gracie

you are un done your

your jeans they are un done

comen of you your bum hangen out

get in the van francis barker get in i need the toilit you are screechen

it is you and not you i need to pee you are sayen

i am runnen away down the hill the polis lady shouts

some thing after me i can here her panten hard the crackel oof her walky talky. There is no wear to go it is pitch then i am cutten in through the wet grass my feet leaden me wear my eyes can not. I fall and get up and fall again and get up again. I am wet through soaken. I can feel grit and stones rubben jaggen against my skin my big toe is hurten. The torch beam is there next to me when i look back. Stop francis the woman shouts. There is no wear for you to go. Stop.

I keep goen though and then fall again rollen this time. Bump bump i go down the hill then come right ways up again. I can not see an effen thing in this black ness. My glasses have come of. They are lyen on the ground some wear i can feel the nettel stings o grace. My duff glasses my spares. Was it here. May be it was here it hapened. You lost your children after they walked of you came down in the nettels the grass you were drunk. How many months gone were you. 3 or 4 may be. But you can not re member can you. Only that you were drunk and bobby found you all blood and muck wanderen the streets of your own neighbour hood for all to see. You never did come back to look for it did you. No. You told no one. Except bobby. He knew with out asken. That is why he always looks at you that way isent it. You and him have got that secret be tween you. No one else. Not bud. Not marie your sister on canary aisles port adventurer. O your bag is still goen round that carousel probably with your good glasses. But you lost your children here dident you. You lost your child. May be francis under stood. May be that is why she hates you. It is not only be cause you locked her in the house to look after vincent a baby looken after a baby. O that is teribel grace you nearly bled to death out there in the grasses. If bobby had not of come along and took you to the hospital you would not even be here now. Well. That might have been for the best for all conserned. No one would be abel to see this hapen if you had just died then. O gracie find your glasses o god who isent up there help me for once you in invisibel bastert.

I am clawen about on the ground in amongst the wet grass and earth but it is no use. I can not find them but i keep clawen any way. Then i feel a hard edge it is them i think. It is half buried in the dirt and i pull at it.. My hands not notisen the stingen nettles. But it is not them. It is an old tin lid like one you would get soup in. It is an old tin lid i think. How about that gracie. You have found treasure trove up here. Surely it is worth a lot of money. You will be rich. Your father yours and maries would have been proud he liked to go treasure hunten wwith you when you were both young. Of on advenchures to find the lost city of el dorado. Of to find pieces of 8. Them as dies will be the lucky ones he would say in a pirate voise. He dident know wear he picked that up he sayed it just amused him to say it. So like every thing else he sayed it over and over till it was worn out and dryed out and you could have humg it on the branches of the tree out side the kitchen window with his red under pants. The skull and cross bones of the good ship barker that not right gracie boats. We are all in this to gether aren't we. Yes. Except we werent. First your mother left you never saw her again did you. Then marie was taken away until only you were left and you should have gone to. But you were caged by then werent you. You were stuck be tween the words he sayed to you his love which is an enemy.

X z h o p p h y s s q u 8 1 67

the torch beam is back again though picken over the ground. Francis the polis lady is shouten. Stop francis or whoever you are. Grace. What are you even doen down there you will break your leg or some thing. Come on give your selve up.

The torch beam lights up a black river. My fingers feel hardness stiff ground under neath. I stand up on the road and turn round and get the light full in my face. The polis lady is comen down after me. I hold up my wrist to her torch light get back i say. I am holden the roman tin lid up to my own wrist. The lady stops at the edge of the road. She is panten and seems quite un fit for an ofiser of the law. If i was an ofiser of the law i would of hoped to be in a better state than that. It was all down hill as well.

She has the beam on me. Look she says panten. Your not goen to do any thing with that.

Just you try me i say to her. I press the tin lid in to the skin of my rist. It definitely feels sharp enough. I will cut this open right here i tell her.

Just calm down she says. Dont do any thing stupid will you please.

Go away then. Leave me alone or i will cut my selve.

And the more i say it the more it seems like the right thing to do. Sayen the words a loud make it seem posibil like it will happen that i will do it. I begin to feel strong in side so strong like i have never felt be four. It is surjen up from in side some wear some low place i dont know wear.

There is the sweep of light on the road the polis van comen round the bend. You are caught graciegirl. No to ways about it. The van stops a few feet away the head lights on me the torch light on me and i turn to the other polis be hind the weel and thrust my wrist and roman soup tin lid at him. I try to jiggle my hips to get my jeans to stay up the button and fly are un done. I will do it i shout at the driver. I will cut my selve.

Again i feel so strong. It is posibel to get of the carousel it is posibel to change every thing isent it. All you have to do is cut. It must be how my sister marie felt when she did it. I wander what it will be like to feel all that blood come gushen out. Does it even gush maybe it just trickels. True it gushed that time in the nettels when bobby found you. Get in the car grace what are you doen. This is not a good seen. That time marie my sister spun on the linoleum i dident even notice the blood. Of course she was in the nude so i was distractid some what. So was our father. It was only after when we saw the blood poolen a bout her feet. Her body all red like that. Jesus christ our father sayed. It is the human body it is beauty full my sister marie sayed. We should not be a shamed of it it is natural. She was piroetten in her own blood. It is just a body a shell she was sayen. The light is in side.

Will you take those beams of me please i shout to the air. I keep the edge of the lid pressed to my rist.

The polis man in the van switches his lights of and i am left with orange blurs in my eyes. You as well i say to the polis lady and she switches of her torch. All of a sudden it is pitch i can see no thing except faden blotches. They will not be abel to see either we are all in the dark now.

Grace the lady says quietly. Grace if that is your name why dont you put that thing down. What your plannen dosent have to happen.

O does it not i say.

It really dosent. Think about it.

I can here the hiss and crackel of her radio the voices on it. The sound like they are speaken from a satelite up in space some wear. Huston we have a problem grace barker is goen to top her selve ha ha. Good riddance to bad rubidge.

Grace the polis lady is sayen her voice calm in the dark. You have a family dont you. We know you do. We know you have a son. Vincent isent that his name. Isent it.

I press the tin lid in to my rist till it hurts. But of course they can not see me now. They are as blind as bats to. So you could cut your selve to ribbons gracie and no body would see. So what is the point.

Your sons name is vincent and your grand son is sean.

But i just stand there. I just stand listenen to the trees sighen. It is calm and clear the air up here. This is the bluebell woods but i have always known it as the garscadden woods. It is nice. I should of come up more often when the children were small.

Would you want your son to have to live with knowen what his mother did to her selve grace. That isent a nice thing for any one to grow up carryen a round is it. You wouldent like your grand son sean to grow up with out his grand mother would you.

I wander if this july wether will turn in to febuary wether any time soon. Or the seasons will get all mixed up. I am thinken about what marie would do. What would bud do. What would your father yours and maries do. Not what vincent would do be cause that would end up in may hem.

Grace the polis lady says. Okay. What do you want to do now grace.

I drop the lid and it clatters on the pave ment.

I want to go home i say.

For a half a second we are all just caught in that moment and then the next thing is i am bein man or woman handeld and there are lights on and huffen and puffen and my hands are getten twisted be hind my back. I feel there plastic hand cuffs bite into the bones of my rist so i can not turn it properly. Then they are hucklen me of to wards there polis van. Wear is gregor i wander then i see him in the van to. He dosent even look at me. He says no thing at all.

Come on bobby sayed come on you can not just wander a bout like this in your own neighbour hood. Look at the state of you you are half naked. Come on it is cold. Get in gracie.

Leave me alone bobby i sayed. I want to walk.

You are goen in the wrong direcshoun then. Come one grace get in the car.

So i got in the car. Wear are you taken me bobby i sayed. This isent the way home. This is a difirint way. What about vincent what about francis.

They are fine grace. They are okay.

Here he syed clean your selve of with that and he gave me a rag of some sort from his glove compart ment.

So we were driven a round bobby and me passen the bottel passen the houses and the street lights and the hot night. It was hot enough to here crickets make there noise. That is not so usual is it bobby i sayed.

Grace.

What do you want bobby.

Grace. You dont have to ask that. Do you. You know what.

Yes. I know.

Grace.

What do i get though bobby. Are you goen to look after me. Even in the state i am in.

Of course gracie. You know it.

Do i. Do i really know that bobby. Are you goen to care for me.

Any thing grace any thing at all.

Any thing. Good. Give me some money then and you will get what you want.

O gracie. Come on.

Give me some money bobby.

How much then. How much is enough.

I dont know bobby. You tell me what i am worth.

One note then an other then an other. He kept pullen money out of his pockets from every pocket there was money comen out he was rich he was a millyonare green notes and blue coins spillen out shinen in the dark how much do you want gracie how much do you need gold coins pieces of 8 pilen up a round us my feet sinken under there weight. Them as dies will be the lucky ones. Pieces of 8 sqwawk sqwawk sqwawk sqwawk. Your bag turnen round on the carousel on port adventurer canary aisles. Topplen over with no one to see.

An other small space grace.

A blue mat that stinks.

Lyen on a low shelf of con crete.

A toilit with no seat.

A toilit with no toilit paper.

They have got your shoes they have got your belt.

They have got your ring.

They have you de scribed they have you filed and logged and categorisid. They have taken down all your particulars. They have got you down in the small print in there ledger books. They have even taken a way your shoe laces. You couldent walk un less you went bear foot.

So you can not just hang your selve either can you no ha ha. They have a light on all night. They have shouten along the hall all night. They have a doctor speak to you through a cat flap. They take your pulse and ask a bout medi cashoun. They ig nore it when you bang the door when you shout. Except you do not shout and ball do you grace. No. You do not bang on the door. You stay quite. You stay still. You go in to your selve and you stay there. You are not who you sayed you were. You are not that person. You pull the blanket over your head and shut your eyes but even then you can still see there faces all of them. Your daughter francis your son vincent your sister marie. There is bud and your father to smilen and there is littel sean playen out side our house ours and the counsils. He is holden some thing up in his wee fist. What have you got sean what have you got for granny you are asken him. He opens his hand it is a bee. He has got a fat golden bee in his hand it is not distresed. He is standen there squinten in the sun light looken up at you oferen you his bee and you putten out your palm.

Any chance of a can break in here boss this girl on the oposite bench is sayen. She has got yellow skin. That is all i can tell with no glasses. But every thing in here is yellow. This girl keeps getten up on the bench and tryen to see of down the hall way. She hangs on the bars and no one else is talken much.

I am droppen blood so i am she says. I am a bout ready to drop here. I am tellen you. I am about ready for the nurse. Any chance of seen the nurse boss. I am meant to be seen the nurse.

There is 3 of us left in this cell though there were 6. The others have been called up to court. The rest of us are just waiten. All we have to do is wait. We wait all day here in this tiney cell big enough for two benches facen each other a urinal at the wall end. There is 6 of us not talken much staren at the floor. Hours have past all ready i am tired my my grane is comen back. I am waiten for the world to start spiltten again. The my grane is on its way sure as any thing. The girl with the yellow skin calls her selve gormley but that is the only name i know in here. No one introduces them selves except gormley and an older woman who know each other from out side. The older woman is not well she has a bad hang over. Her name is some thing like sherry or cherry.

Any chance of seeing the nurse here gormley shouts. Effs sake man come on.

Come on boss. Come on to eff. Effen droppen blood in here. My head is chanken man.

A screw walks down the hall but ignores gormley. She is very thin it seems like she could keel over at any minute.

Stinks of pish in here dintit she says. Pure effed that urinal man. What have they got us in here with a mans urinal for any way. That is sexist. That is against our human rights. You smell that aye man pure effen reeks in here. So it does man. Makes your eyes water. What you in for any way. What they pick you up for she asks me.

Aye well she says. Secrets safe in here that not right ha ha. Secrets safe with us.

I shouldent even be in here man. I should be down the road kicken back just now know what i mean. Feet up. Telly. So i should. Rum and coke. Could do with one now my heads effen bananas my heads effen goen bananas man. I am effen chanken. No elushouns me none at all man. I am goen up the jail tonight. Effen remanded sure if i get bail its a bonus man know what i mean. Always an effen bonus walken. It will be walken as well. Walkin all the way home man no got a penny on me. An effen long walk as well.

The older woman comes to a minute and looks at gormley and sticks her fist in the air knightswood she says. Knightswood young team.

This older woman sherry or cherry is not young though. She is old enough to know better.

My own sweet home gormley says laughen and slappen her hands on the bars as hard as she can. The sounds echos a bout dully in here but there is so much din from along the hall with others bangen and shouten it dosent attract any atenshoun. It goes through my head like getten whacked with a knotted rope that has soaked in a basin of water for an hour.

I am in some nick gormley says. It will take me 2 hour 2 hour on these effen crazy legs of mine eh. It is no joke man. It is not funny at all.

She sticks her chin out at the girl be side me she is just young a bit older than my son vincent.

What are you laughen at you wee fanny.

The girl be sides me shrugs. No thing she says i wasent laughen.

Better not be. Do you see this wee fanny doll.

It is me she is talken to. I look at her. I blink.

In and out of care since she was 10 year old. I will effen give you care. I will effen take care of you fanny.

The girl be sides me laughs a loud at this but gormley has not noticed and is talken away calm just like be four. This gormley is mainly just all mouth i think. She is putten on a hard man act.

No elushouns me she says. 2 year the polis have been looken for me. I wasent even aware they wanted me. 2 years man effen joke so it is. Breach of bail condishins dident even know i breached them man. Effs sake. I wasent even aware. I never got the letter i had moved. I am effen droppen blood here she shouts down the hall. I am about ready to go mental there is no tampons in here. I am leaken i have a medical condishin man. I am ready to go bananas. I am down another notch on my belt already man.

O what is your secret the older woman says laughen is it better than atkins.

The girl be sides me laughs to she has her hands tucked up in side her jumper huggen her selve.

You are not even wearen a belt she says.

Aye i know i havent got it with me i can hardly keep my effen trousers up walken about with them round my ankles all day. Effen joke man so it is effen can not keep them up at all. I am skinny but i am not that effen skinny i am droppen weight in here i am droppen blood. I am a whole effen notch down from last night i am effen tellen you. Goen to get the nurse boss gormley shouts down the hall. I am meant to be seen a nurse in here. You want me to drop dead is that the effen plan. Effen joke so it is.

She goes quite for a minute then says to me your first time is it.

No i say. My first in a long time.

Effen good laugh isent it hours are good arent they. Effen office hours man.

Effen monday mornen man effen cells are rattlen with folk. Sitten there the whole weekend. Be effen hours before you see the procurator. What you in for any way.

I look up at the ceilen it is yellow too there is no natural light in here there are no windows.

There is a bunch of charges i say. Resisten arrest.

Gormley does not say any thing.

I would effen plea that the older woman says. So i would. First time no bother. I would plea that.

It isent my first time i say quitely. But no one is botheren.

I am getten remanded no doubt about it gormley is sayen. I have no illusions. 2 year man 2 year that goes back. Effen missed a court appearance. I wasent even aware man. I was effen cowped on effen strangers couches for 2 year man how was i goen to see an effen letter man. I turned up on the day i last heard man. Not my fault they changed it. I am getten remanded the night man no doubt. Breach of bail condishins effen outrageous man effen total joke i am getten sent up for missen an effen letter man.

It is not my responsibility man. It is not my job to keep track of my selve it is theres.

Boss any chance of a can break in here.

A screw goes by what is it she says.

Any idea of the time boss. You heard from my lawyer yet. The name is gormley aye. Any chance of a can break in here i am droppen blood.

Then an other screw comes over and says barker and i sit up barker that is me i say. Right he says and i here them there keys in the lock and i am up and walken.

Aw good luck man says gormley and claps the back of my shoulder see you after.

I am hand cuffed again this time only one hand to a screw. Normally we wouldent put the cuffs on but we are packed out today after the week end says the screw. We are haven to use extra rooms so i have got to cuff you. That is okay i tell her. I am almost used to it now. Is it any difirint for the men in there cells. She laughs no. It is just the same. I can here them the men all shouten and bangen down the corridors. I can here the women to doen the same thing.

We walk a long and she asks me to wait and un cuffs me. I stand in a brown and yellow coridor the dim ness and bright ness contrasten. There is a water fountan next to me silver in the wall and i lean over and take a drink. Then i stand. The screw comes back and cuffs me again and we walk a long an other coridor. Then we turn down an other and an other. There are rooms and door all the way. There are rooms a long the way with doors open solisiters talken to there clients. Some are shut grey steel. There are letters on the walls c a d g x h i. It is made of letters this cage grace. You can not read them these direcshouns but you rote the way here all the same dident you. Yes. It is a long walk be four they turn me in to one of these rooms.

It is just a woman at a desk. For some reason i thought it was goen to be a man. The screw un cuffs me and tells me to have a seat. The woman is about my age i think. May be younger or older. I dont know. She has got big glasses and a comforten voice like warm chocolit milk.

Miss barker she says. I am joyce mackey i will be representen you to the procurator fiscal un less you have any objecshins. There is my card.

She hands me a card but i can not see the riten on it. I put it in my trouser pocket.

So no objecshins.

I shake my head.

She is busy riten stuff down and dosent look up except to ask more questions. She is probably riten with a fountan pen. That is what you like to picture isent it grace. A solisiter riten with a fountan pen like you used to get in school when you were quite small and were a good pupil. Of course they werent any use for you were they as a left handed person. That just meant you got covered in ink goen from left to right. As you have been doen ever since isent that right grace. Yes. You have been goen left to right in a right to left world ha ha. You have got ink on your face.

So grace joyce says. There are a couple of charges here arent there. A couple of them quite serious. And you also have a record of previous convicshins dont you.

This is one of those times she looks up.

I nod and she looks down and starts riten once more.

Uh huh she says. You have got a number of previus convicshins here that i am conserned a bout.

She looks up. But the first thing i should tell you is i think the chances of a custodial sentence are increased by your failure to stay away from alcohol. Now you are back here again and it is only 3 weeks since you were reprimanded by the procurator.

I touch the desk it is cold metal there is no thing in this room that has any thing naturel in it at all is there gracie. No. Not a thing. Not a window no naturel light no wooden desk no thing like that at all. I wander if i can ask for a paracetamol but now dosent seem like the right moment. I just rub my temples in stead pressen my fingers in. It helps for a minute.

You have been on a promise of good be haviour to the court havent you. For the last year. i see that you honored this and were simply caushioned by the court. That was three weeks a go wasent it.

She is riten again but stops to look up at me. She is waiten for me to say some thing but i just nod.

She starts readen from a piece of paper.

Mm hmm she says and then looks up at me. Do you have any thing to say about that grace.

Like what.

Of course it isent any of my bisness but if there are circumstanses the procurater should be aware of it may help.

I should not of had a drink i tell her. It was stupid.

You agreed you would abstain from alcohol dident you. That was a contributen factor to your previus convicshoun wasent it. I apolojise your reprimand by the court.

I supose it was.

And here you are charged with solisiten once again.

I wasent solisiten i say. It was not that.

She looks up at me and says no it wasent only that was it. I have here theft given a false name and also polis assault. Quite a list miss barker.

I dident assault any polis ofiser. They went for gregor they were usen polis brutality.

She scratches her head and stares at me.

Be that as it may miss barker. You are charged with assaulten a polis ofiser. But i am informed by the prosecushoun that the polis are willen to a agree a reduced charge of disorderly conduct then we are left with theft and solisiten. They are willen to drop the matter of supplyen a false name.

I wasent solisiten i say. No matter what the polis say.

Then do you wish to plea to theft. You have a number of previus convicshouns for solisiten miss barker. You wish to argew that this incident is of a difirint nature. I have to say the polis say you your selve sayed this man gregor payed you for sex.

I did not say that to them it is a lie. We were just sitten in the car we werent even doen any thing.

But the polis say you admitted this to them. I have a state

ment here in which you say gregor ofered me a run if i would do him. I was broke so i sayed all right i would. That is when the polis arived. Are you sayen that this statement is a fabricashoun.

Is it a fabricashoun grace. Did you say those things. It is posibil isent it. Yes. You would of sayed any thing then wouldent you. Yes. You would of tried to blame poor gregor some how. Even if you did your selve harm in the process. Can you even remember what you were thinken of. Can you re call grace. You were drunk werent you. You were to drunk to know how to act or to know to do the desint thing.

I am not sure if i sayed those things. I can not remember to well i tell joyce.

So do you wish to dispute the state ment. I mean the ofisir has written down what she claims you told her.

No i say. No i do not wish to dispute it.

Okay then joyce says. She goes to riten some thing down and lets me sit and wait again.

She looks up again. There is also this matter of theft she says. I gather a valuable engagement ring was taken from the person of a young woman and later found in your poseshoun miss barker. This young lady does not wish to press charges for her own reasons how ever that is im materiel. The court will press this case regard less be cuase of what it views as the very serius ciscum stanses that sur round it.

She looks at me again but i dont say any thing. I wait. I have got good at waiten in the polis cell.

Do you understand miss barker. This young woman was found unconshous by her partner who says he spoke to a woman who ansered the young ladys phone and who described her locashoun wear he subsequently found her uncoshous and in a state of intoxicashion. Money had been stolen as well as a valuable engage ment ring. It should be noted that the young lady in question was pregnant and as such is probably lucky that her condishin seems not to have harmed her child. I am not sugesten you were the cause of her condishin grace. She is an adult with a will of her own. But that you were present before hand is likely to colour the precepshion of the procurator fiscal. And all this with out even consideren the matter of the ring and stolen money.

There was no money in her purse i say. Hardly any thing. I thought these people could afford it with there three flat and buyen up places all over the city. But she had no thing. So i took the ring as well. These people have got every thing they will always get every thing they want i thought why not grace. They can afford it.

Joyce just looks at me and nods and then goes to riten.

I dont know why i say all this. It just comes out and i can not stop it.

Well joyce says looken up again. I am not sure what to tell you now miss barker.

Did the taxi driver report me i ask her.

Taxi driver she says what taxi driver are you referen to.

There was a taxi driver i tell her. But it dosent matter.

If there is some other insident besides the ones described in the polis reports then i had better advise you to keep it to your selve miss barker. There isent any taxi driver menshined in here. I would keep it that way grace. It will be better for you that way.

Joyce the solisiter asks me how i want to plead and i tell her not guilty to every thing.

That isent a good idea grace she says. You may argew against polis witneses that have your sworn statement if you wish. You can also dispute that the ring came in to your posesion by some other means. But i would advise against it.

So what do you want me to plead i say to her. What has happened to gregor i ask. How is he.

How do you think he is grace. He is comen be four the procureter to day. Like your selve. He will likely be charged with resisten arrest. From what i know that will be it. He hasent got a record they will not pursue it further. He will be sleepen at home to night if that is what you are worryed a bout. You should think of your selve now grace. Really.

She looks up at me again. Well she says. Lets consider the opshions shall we.

After words a screw a difirent one comes and cuffs me again and leads me out and back along the corridor and waits while the locked doors are opened for me and i am hand cuffed to an other different screw and we go back a long an other corridor i am sure a difirint corridor maybe a short cut and soon we are back again. I have not seen any windows to out side a long the way. There is no out side in here. There is only in side and plenty of it goen on for miles.

They uncuff me and put me back in the cell with gormley and sherry or cherry and the young girl. Then they close the cell door. Gormley is sitten down then standen up on the bench still tryen to see a long the corridor. She is wanten her solisiter. Sherry or cherry is smilen at me and asken me to sit down next to her. The girl be side shifts up and makes a space for me.

Be effen a few more hours be four you see the procurator gormley says. I have still no even seen my solisiter. That is the trith intit. I know fine i will be goen up on remand to night but still. Solisiter hasent even spoken to me yet has he.

Sherry or cherry smiles and says take your purse when you do see him and they both laugh. The orange light in these corridors and cells hurts my head i have got a my graine comen on.

Boss any chance you have heard from my solisiter gormley says as a screw goes past. Sherry does not seem to well the way her head slumps. I touch her shoulder and she starts.

O she says. Still here eh.

We sit and every one goes quite.

You going to plea gormley asks me after a while. First offense in how many year. I would effen plea that. Then you will be off home.

I dont think thats goen to happen i tell her. Not to night any way.

O you comen up the road with me are you gormley says. Eff it at least you are goen up be cause of some thing you did. What about me. I am goen to get jailed be cause i missed an effen letter. Wear is the justice in that eh. Just you tell me wear is the justice in that.

A long time passes hours of dead time some one comes for the young girl someoen comes for sherry or cherry. Gormley is still waiten. She is droppen blood she says. She is losen weight every minute she stays in that cell. It is effen in humane she says.

How have they got us in a cell with a mans urinal in it she says. That is what they think of us. Wear is the nurse. I should of seen a nurse by now.

There is all of a sudden a lot of noise from a long the corridor the other cells. There is the sound of some one kicken or bangen hard against there cell door. There is shouten and then others joinen in. What is happenen gormley shouts to one of the screws who is headed down that way. She is not hurried she is just walken a long at an even pace. She ignores gormely who is back up on her bench tryen to crane her neck practically through the bars on the window. She is so skinny it seems possible she can get her head through.

Boss whats goen on she says to every screw that is passen. Boss.

One of them stops eventually. She is shaken her head.

What is happenen gomley asks her.

What is happenen the screw says i will tell you what is happenen. Some manky cow has shat in her plastic tea cup is what is happenen. The rest of them want out of the cell and i for one can not blame them. That is just manky. She says she couldent hold on till she got a toilet break. And of course who is it has to clean the cup out. Muggins here.

I totally sympathise gormley says. I have got a medical condishin my selve and when you have got to go you have got to go can break or no can break. I am supposed to of seen a nurse but have i seen any one have i eff. How a bout seen if my soliciter has showed up yet boss.

The screw says whats your name then.

Gormley teresa gormley she says. Mccann is my soliciter.

I will see what i can do after i wash up says the screw.

Any chance of a can break while we are at it boss. I am droppen blood here.

Just then an other screw comes to the cell door. Barker he says is that you. I stand up. He is openen the door and i go out again hey gormley says i am still waiten to see my solisiter here. Wear are you taken her i have been waiten here 5 hours already and i have not seen my solisiter or the effen nurse either. Effs sake boss i am droppen blood here. I have been here for effen hours be four her. Effs sake man.

The screw says aye aye and puts the cuffs on me again and walks me down the hall to wait by the water fountain again. I lean over and take an other drink. The scew comes back and leads me down a long corridor then i have to wait with him at a steel door or metal any way be four he ex changes me with an other screw a bored semen female who takes me up a flight of stairs. Then we wait at an other door. When it opens a small rinkley man with a mustache looks round at us then i am passed through to him in to a bright room the court. Could it have turned out an other way grace. Could you not have ritten a better enden for your story. No. This is the script you have to play it out now. There is no other way now. The rinkley man takes one of the cuffs of me and puts it on his own rist. He tells me to sit in a kind of galley seat and i am facen all the solisiters and the procurator in the middle at the back. I look over at the seats to the side and the public gallery there are no faces i can not see any one bud or any one if they are there. I here some one cough delibiritly it is bud his cough i reconise the weeze at the end of it from all his cutters choice. O he will here every thing grace. It will all come out. Who else is here i wander. Who else is seen you in this state gracie. May be francis may be that emma. All of them staren at you. Laughen may be. Is vincent here to i wander. What about littel sean. At least he will not remember. He is to small to remember this. But all the rest will. They will all talk about it. Even if you asked them not to they will still talk and every one in the drum will know all a bout you grace how you left that young girl lyen there drunk.

Some one says my name out loud. I look at the man with the mustache. Stand up he says stand up. So i do it.

Grace barker the person says the solisiter. He is to far away to read.

I nod.

Can you confirm for the records of the court that you are grace barker the person asks again.

Yes i say. Yes i am.

Thanks you miss barker please sit down.

So you do what you are told dont you gracie dont you. Yes.

This is all a dream isent it marie. Tell me it is. This is all just a dream and you are goen to a wake. It is all just a dream soon you are goen to a wake.

The prosecushion is tellen the court every thing you are supposed to of done gracie. Every one in this room can here they can all see you sitten here. That is all you can do now grace. Just sit and wait for the procurater to anounce she will see you hung ha ha.

So you sit nice and wait like a good girl. Good girl gracie boats. There there.

<u>1 year 6 months 15 days 12 hours 50 minutes and</u>

he licked your chips dident he Natalie is asken Debra. She is tellen Steffi about Debras date with her new boy friend she met on her day release. Debra shouldent be in here in my opinion. She has got some mental health issues or some thing but they have got her in here any way. She can not stop setten fire to things. Some times that includes her selve. There are scars all over her hands. She just likes fire she says.

What did you let him lick your chips for Steffi says. Debra is looken non plussed.

I just offered him one and he started licken the whole lot Debra says.

Natalie and Steffi crack them selves up laughen at this. They are winden poor Debra up again.

Aye Natalie says. He licked her chips on the bus so she gave him the bag.

Steffi thinks this is the funniest thing she has ever heard. O o she says. Stop. I am goen to pee my selve.

Aye Natalie says. She gave him her pie as well in case he licked that to. Dident you Debs.

Debra nods she has got a sheepish look her big brown bovine eyes blinken at them through her lashes she spent so long tongen.

Natalies main goal in life is to have a laugh she says. Steffi is the one that does the most laughen though. Natalie just looks vishous like she would latch her jaws around your throat if you show her any weakness. She is getten a new tattoo when she gets out she says. It is goen to be of a frog sitten on a cannabis leaf.

O. Stop. Steffie is sayen. Goen to stop Nat. Please. I am goen to wet my selve in a minute.

He could of licked my pie if he had wanted Natalie says.

O Steffi is sayen. O ha ha. Stop.

Marie my sister on Portaventura the Canary Isles must have got used to similar places to this one after she went away. She must of got used to locked rooms and corridors. Maybe she even got to rely on in them after a while. Of course we both wander about our mother marie and my selve. We will always wander about her. I am staren out of the window at the green grass across the fence and the road I know must be on the other side of it some wear. It is a nice day a good plain day our father used to say. A white loaf day. A luke warm day. What you want is a good plain day he used to tell us. Me and Marie my sister. Be four she was sent away. Be four she got the shock treat ment.

Those places must have had locks and secure rooms and wards to. They would have had nurses to guard the patience. High windows out of reach. And she was in and out of places like that for years. Yet she was not ashamed of it. She would tell every one. It was only our father who was ashamed. It was only my selve. How many years was she in and out of those places those institushouns. How many shock treat ments. It is hard to say. I never asked her. It dident seem like you could ask. But how long I wander now. How long was it be four she walked out and dident come back.

Your mis taken graciegirl our father told me. Your memory is mixed up.

No dad. It isent. Not any more. I spoke to Marie on the phone only last night. She told me wear they sent her away to. She told me how you could of got her out sooner but dident.

Gracie. She was not well. She was a danger. You dont remember but she was a danger. Not just to her selve.

Well. May be so dad. May be i am a danger to.

O not you gracie. You just cared more. That is why you stayed.

Some one comes up be hind me. Jac. Are you all right there she is sayen. Are you okay there grace. Yes I say. I am fine. O let me have a look will you it is really comen on isent it. It is really comen on good isent it grace.

What is comen on good I say.

Your riten is comen on so well isent it. Look at all this. Pages and pages. Still avoiden any thing but the present though arent you ha ha. Well. I supose it is a part of your style now isent it. Every thing does just seem to happen all at once some how dosent it. Even the past.

Well I have got to live in the present Jac. Haven a past in here just means a record.

Yes she says I supose that is right. You have been here 3 months havent you. So it will be 1 year 6 months and how many days now since you last saw your daughter o i forget.

I dont say any thing. I am not keen on her revealen things about me out loud.

Jac is so small like a littel bird thin and rosey cheeked a robin red brest may be. She looks the same age as my selve but older. She has had to fight to keep her job she says. Worken with women in side has been the cul minashoun of a dream for her. She has a heart con dishoun. She has had to fight to stay in a job be cause of this.

Thinken a head isent a crime Grace. Hopen for a better future is normal we should all not just hope but work hard to make a better future for our selves and our loved ones.

I know Jac. It is just i have felt secure in here for the last while. I have got used to it. I am not sure i am ready for life out in the real world just yet. I have got no job or any thing.

Listen i am sure you will find work. You have your liason co ordinater now to help you and your readen and riten opens up so many more avenues.

I hope you are right but I am not so sure about that.

Well fingers crossed she says.

We are sitten in the learnen lab. In the small room of the side of C Hall. C Hall for C class offenders like you Grace. You could have tried harder and worked your way up the alphabet couldent you. All the way up to A Hall for the nutcases and dangerus folk except your case is a lower order of case isent it. You are just a numpty but at least you arent in D or E Hall for the total numptys ha ha. There are a few others in side with me we come here once a week. Every one likes it other wise they just have to watch telly 20 hours a day. One of the screws sits at the back all the time but does not inter fere or bat an eye lid at some of the things that are sayed in here. She has seen it all. For once every one is quite even Debra who has stomack tenshin. It is just bad luck for those that have to share a cell with her. Her stomack is rottin.

Debra looks over at me with her expreshoun of dis comfort. Her hair is still wet from washen earlier it is hangen in strands.

Have you got the red pen she asks me.

I shake my head it is probably on the floor some wear.

Jac is leafen through my notebook which I am not so keen on to tell you the truth. I am not used to haven things written down like this it is not so easy to have people stare at them to read them. There is no privisy in a place like this. It is like the note book Francis wrote her name in. That was Francises book but this is mine. Graces book.

You should be proud Grace you really should.

Well I say. I am not so sure a bout that. Proud to land in here.

O come on she says. You are just kidden me arent you. It is really good what you have done. All this work. You are a natural she says. Think wear you were three months back. Now tell me this is not a big deal.

I supose so I say to her. But I still make so many mis takes all these rules I keep on breaken.

You mean grammer.

That as well.

What then. You know you can tell me grace. It will not go any farther.

I know this. I know I can tell Jac any thing I need. She has never let me down. She has stuck by me when others dident. She has got me this far.

Are you goen to rite a bout the court she is asken me. That would be interesten.

She is still huffen a way on her inhaler. She leafs through the paper she is dis orderen them all which makes me panic a bit. I have not got a numberen system for them i organise them difirintly.

I take them of her but gently and she says okay okay I know. Dont touch.

I am not sure Jac I say to her. It is not some thing I am sure I want any one to read about. I think I would like it to be private. It is my personal history it is my record. So it will be between my selve and the procurator fiscal for now.

And I totally under stand that she says. I totally under stand. I can see how you would prefer to keep some things to your selve. But it might be use full for other previous offenders caught in your posishoun. It could be of benefit to them.

May be I say. But I would like to keep it for my selve just now. Just for just now. There is no privacy in this place. You are getten watched the hole time. Is that okay.

Jac spreads her hands of course of course. But there are so many issues it raises you know. I have got so many questions a bout it I really do.

It is not finished yet Jac I tell her. May be I will put you in it.

Oops I am not so sure about that ha ha she says. I get a strong wiff of her perfume it smells nice but not so dear as Annettes.

Remember you are on a promise of good be haviour ha ha. No solisiten or theft or attempts on your life or any body elses remember. No drinken.

I remember I tell her.

Any way do you want me to come with you to day or any thing she says. She has gone a bit more serius now. Do you need me for any thing. Do you want me to be there when you meet your daughter. Francis isent it.

Yes. Francis and my grandson. Littel Sean.

You just missed your son then.

He is off in basic trainen. But he is goen to rite. In a letter. It will be a first him riten a letter and a first me readen one from him .

No Bud though. Bud was your boy friend wasent he.

Partner i tell her. I can not say right now Jac.

Well. Per haps he will come round eventually.

I am not so sure about that. He has taken a lot of grieve.

Because of Francis.

No because of me. If I hadent refused to give her money he would still have the use of his leg. He took her debt on and he payed for it. She always did know how to wind him round her littel finger. I was always jealous of there relashonship. I think i used to punish Bud for helpen her. I was getten back at her and at him be cause i was jealous.

May be he saved her life grace.

May be.

May be he did saved her life dident he gracie. May be he also saved your own life. That is posibel isent it. Yes. He rescued you from your selve. This isent any way to live grace he sayed. Goen with strangers. How long do you think you can keep that up. You are in your forties you have been lucky so far. You are still a live. How long do you think that luck is goen to last.

Bud is a good man grace. Who else would of stuck by you through times like that. Not many. No one but bud.

Jac gathers up the pens and paper it is nearly time to go. She straightens my hair for me it is sort of sisterly but it also makes me a littel bit uncomfort abel.

You suit those glasses she says. Lucky for you they found you here to send on your case eh.

The screw is getten up the rest of the group putten there work in a folder for him and Jac looks about to make sure every thing is all right. Debra comes up wanten a hug of Jac who will not let her it is against the rules.

But I am your wee pal Debra says. Is that not right Jac. Me and Grace are your pals arent we Grace.

That is not wrong I say to her. Jac laughs and says away with the pair of you.

Still she pats Debras arm and says of you go now see you next week. Keep up the good work.

Debra rolls her eyes at me. You are away then Grace.

I nod and she looks at me she is happy for me but she is not happy either. It isent her fault who could be happy there friend was leaven and they have got to stay.

You will be okay Debra I tell her.

She nods and smiles again. Folk are always leaven me she says. I am always the one getten left be hind.

Me to I say.

The hat trick wins it says Jac and then says any way lets get goen in here. Grace is needen to get on.

I wink at Debra and she winks back and mouths the word bye then goes back to the rest of the group who are all rammyen about the place and winden up the screw some thing terrible. It isent there fault after this there is an hour of lunch then thats it the end. Back to C Hall for the rest of the day to do eff all. It is no wander you can get excited by a visit from a learnen worker like Jac. She is pretty much the high light of not just the day but the whole week.

So you dont want me to come with you or need help with any thing today Grace?

I dont think so Jac. I am good just now. But if I do I will ask.

Jac looks at me. She smiles a tight smile and holds up her hands with crossed fingers then turns her atenshoun to the others.

Last night my sister Marie cried on the phone. She was asken about a dog she says we had as a child. Do you know what happened to Bonnie she was asken. I had to think a minute about what dog she was talken about. I have never been that fond of them even as pets.

You mean our Labrador Goldie I sayed to her.

No she sayed. How could you not remember Bonnie our beautiful Golden Retriever.

Her name wasent Bonnie it was Goldie I sayed you have got it wrong Marie. It was a Labarador called Goldie we had.

Well. Then Marie got upset and sayed of course she was called Bonnie how could I not remember that. So i just sayed o yes Bonnie. Of course Bonnie was lovely. Dident she run away I sayed. Isent that what happened to her. And Marie sayed yes she must of run away. And we started talken about this dog Bonnie as if we both remembered her the same dog. We talked about how cheerful she was and how she used to give you a paw. After a while it was like I could remember this same dog Bonnie too. It was like I could remember locken Francis in with young Vincent on there own when I went out too. It was like rememberen every thing all at once. It was so sad when she ran away wasent it Marie sayed. Yes I told her. Very sad. She loved Bonnie so much Marie sayed. She wasent kind enough to her when we had her she sayed. She wished she had been kinder to her. It broke her heart when Bonnie disapeared. I told her it broke mine too. At least you have got Francis and Vincent she sayed. You are so lucky grace. You are so lucky to have your family. They will be a comfort to you one day.

Start clearen up folks the screw shouts five minutes and I need you out of here.

And I was wanten to rite and tell Marie all about my children Francis and Vincent that she has not seen since they were young and how Francis is goen to stay away from dependency and be a mother and how I have been prayen Vincent will come back to us safely even though I am a not practisen Protestant but our father me and Maries would of approved of it still I pray anyway please please God bring him back safe to our home ours and the counsils and also some funny stories about my grandson littel Sean like when he got a pea stuck in his ear and when he had blue diarea from eaten a crayon and also mention how hard it will be on Bud missen him like he missed Francis like they are both his own children. All these stories you were getten ready to tell werent you gracie.

But then the screw shouts

Time ladies please lets wrap it up in here

and by then it is all you can do to just rush forwards as fast as you can to the end of this sentence you are on right now and hope that it will be enough grace.

Acknowledgements

thanks to the Scottish arts council for the cash etc…

Other folk: a number of people have had a hand in helping me write this book. Special thanks must go to: Alan Bissett for encouragement with the early drafts, Alison Miller for numerous discussions on the train and much else besides, Ewan Morrison for the spark, Lesley McDowell for helpful criticism, Dave Manderson for letting me write it, Helen Sedgwick for consistent support, thoughts, edits and wine over the entire course of writing it, Anna Ehrlemark for always being at the other end, and to Fifi, for putting up with it all.

A final nod of gratitude to all the gang at Practical Tai Chi Chuan International: Dan Docherty, Charlie Gorrie, Billy Leggate, Colin English, Lee Marsh, Rachel Harris et al, for showing me the way, and for occasional lumps and bumps.